Willa Cather

was probably born in Virginia in 1873, although her parents did not register the date, and it is probably incorrectly given on her tombstone. Because she is so famous for her Nebraska novels, many people assume she was born there, but Willa Cather was about nine years old when her family moved to a small Nebraska frontier town called Red Cloud that was populated by immigrant Swedes, Bohemians, Germans, Poles, Czechs, and Russians. The oldest of seven children, she was educated at home, studied Latin with a neighbor, and read the English classics in the evening. By the time she went to the University of Nebraska in 1891—where she began by wearing boy's clothes and cut her hair close to her head— she had decided to be a writer.

After graduation she worked for a Lincoln, Nebraska, newspaper, then moved to Pittsburgh and finally to New York City. The publication of her first collection of stories, THE TROLL GARDEN (1905), led to a position at *McClure's* magazine, a popular muckraking periodical that encouraged the writing of new young authors. After meeting the author Sarah Orne Jewett, she decided to quit journalism and devote herself full time to fiction. Her first novel, *Alexander's Bridge,* appeared in serial form in *McClure's* in 1912. But her place in American literature was established with her first Nebraska novel, *O Pioneers!,* published in 1913, which was followed by her most famous pioneer novel, *My Antonia,* in 1918. In 1922 she won the Pulitzer Prize for one of her lesser-known books, *One of Ours. Death Comes for the Archbishop* (1927), her masterpiece, and *Shadows on the Rock* (1931) also celebrated the pioneer spirit, but in the Southwest and French Canada. Her other novels include *The Song of the Lark* (1915), *The Professor's House* (1925), *My Mortal Enemy* (1926), and *Lucy Gayheart* (1935). Willa Cather died in 1947.

Bantam Classics
Ask your bookseller for classics by these other American writers:

Louisa May Alcott
L. Frank Baum
Willa Cather
Kate Chopin
James Fenimore Cooper
Stephen Crane
Theodore Dreiser
W.E.B. DuBois
Alexander Hamilton
Nathaniel Hawthorne
Henry James
John Jay
Hellen Keller
Jack London
James Madison
L.M. Montgomery
Edgar Allan Poe
Upton Sinclair
Harriet Beacher Stowe
Henry David Thoreau
Mark Twain
Edith Wharton
Walt Whitman

The Troll Garden and Selected Stories by Willa Cather

Introduction by Rita Mae Brown

BANTAM BOOKS

NEW YORK · TORONTO · LONDON · SYDNEY · AUCKLAND

THE TROLL GARDEN AND SELECTED STORIES
A Bantam Classic Book / November 1990

ISBN 0-553-21385-7

Published simultaneously in the United States and Canada

_____

*Bantam Books are published by Bantam Books, a division of
Bantam Doubleday Dell Publishing Group, Inc. Its trademark,
consisting of the words "Bantam Books" and the portrayal of a
rooster, is Registered in U.S. Patent and Trademark Office and in
other countries. Marca Registrada. Bantam Books, 666 Fifth Avenue,
New York, New York 10103.*

_____

PRINTED IN THE UNITED STATES OF AMERICA

OPM   0 9 8 7 6 5 4 3 2 1

Contents

Introduction

Literature, like clothing, succumbs to fashion, sometimes beautiful and sometimes ridiculous. Willa Cather, since her death in 1947, has been treated with a cordial neglect by the literary world. Only recently has her work again been picked up and read with delight and profit. She was retrieved by feminist scholars and critics eager to celebrate any woman of literary achievement. While Cather, in her maturity, developed themes of female independence, she belongs to no one but herself, and therefore she belongs to each of us.

This collection contains four early stories, the first, "On the Divide," having been published in January 1896 when Willa Cather was twenty-two, and *The Troll Garden*, a collection, published in 1905. The release of this edition will confirm her status as a major force in our nation's literary development as well as mark her work as that wondrous pleasure, a "good read."

When writing of the prairie—even at this early stage of her career—Cather writes with the reticence born of assurance. The bombast of glittering adjectives, the sweetness of Victorian sentiment, the parade of ego disguised as fiction are not for her. She wrote about real people, real crises, and she wisely kept herself in the background.

As you read through these stories you will discover how she falters when setting a story in the East. Her voice, still free from Victorian circumlocutions, becomes artificial, arch.

Her ability to evoke an emotion from physical detail was well developed in her twenties. In "On the Divide" she writes of the Nebraska plain covered with "white leprous patches of frozen earth."

She continually expanded her craft. In these stories, even the socially mocking ones like "Flavia and Her Artists," Cather pushes herself to go deeper into character, deeper into the constraints a community places upon character. She did not look for glib answers or for Sunday-supplement psychological explanations about why people behaved as they did. In fact, Cather explains very little. She shows you, which is what a novelist is supposed to do. A nonfiction writer explains.

Her people, stranded on the prairies they had crossed an ocean to inhabit, are pressed into a mute bewilderment by the demands of nature and their own natures. For the defeated, there is the draining sense of merely filling time. For those still willing to fight for their individuality, Cather grants them the grace of sadness and harmony. Nothing is easy in her stories. Knowledge is hard won. Death may be a blessing. Liquor, an elixir of the gods, grants a few hours of forgetfulness.

Her Midwesterners struggle within their fatigued insularity. Most are unrepentant provincials, angry when one among them gets away, as in "The Sculptor's Funeral." Others have gotten away from the old drudgery only to realize, too late, what they also lost, as in "The Garden Lodge."

Cather's Midwesterners live with a social vulnerability quite unknown to Southerners with their elaborate ceremonies of politeness and their glamorous poise. As Nils, the hero in "The Bohemian Girl," says, "This is a perfect ferret fight here; you live by biting and being bitten."

All small towns can be confining, the people seemingly narrow-minded and unadventurous. Cather's view of the prairie explains why she left it. This view was revised when she matured as a writer; Nebraska became infused with a golden glow, which often happens the further one travels from childhood. It couldn't have been too golden, for she never returned to live there; the sense of harshness must have remained in her mind, if not on the page.

Perhaps vast spaces invited silences, the harshness of the environment left no time for frivolity. Her Midwesterners, close to their Scandanavian heritage, retained their value of hard work even as they lost the sense of the higher civilization from whence they came. But then that higher civilization offered them or their parents little or they would not have journeyed to this country. The scent of rejection lies buried in many of her stories, a scent now lost on modern readers who are that much further in time from the Northern European odysseys.

She writes of people whose relentless chores ground the days into fine powder. People who drank darkness on the edge of the prairie. To this muffled anguish the author is detached but not indifferent.

What I most enjoy about Willa Cather is that she sticks close to three-dimensional reality. She is not free with abstract nouns. She does not muster a brigade of adjectives. She does not indulge in false emotion, unless writing of the East or of other artists. Her style is as practical as the practicality of her characters. Of course, she is one of them. The world they inhabit was once her world, too. This sharp authenticity remains undimmed through time. Consider this passage from "The Garden Lodge":

> Caroline's coolness, her capableness, her general success, especially exasperated people because they felt that, for the most part, she had made herself what she was; that she had cold-bloodedly set about complying with the demands of life and making her position comfortable and masterful. That was why, everyone said, she had married Howard Noble. Women who did not get through life so well as Caroline, who could not make such good terms either with fortune or their husbands, who did not find their health so unfailingly good, or hold their looks so well, or manage their children so easily, or give such distinction to all they did, were fond of stamping Caroline as a materialist, and called her hard.

As a description of social reality this passage is as accurate today as the day it was written. Not only did Willa Cather have the ability to create believable characters, she could also create the communities in which those characters lived. The individual reflected the community even when rebelling against it, and the community reflected the individual.

This subtle sense of interplay was developed to a deeper degree as she aged.

Her keen awareness of the interplay has naïvely been attributed to Cather's lesbianism. True, any artist from an "outside" group is often far more accurate in describing communities and community pressures than a person unquestionably living inside the community. However, all artists are outlanders in this respect. Complacent people do not become artists. Crediting Cather's lesbianism as the source of her power as an artist cheats her of her complexity. Nor are the heterosexual relationships in her short stories and later novels a secret code for lesbian relationships. At times she did invest a heterosexual relationship with the equality generally present in a lesbian relationship, as in *O Pioneers!* Nonetheless, her heterosexual relationships seem to this reader quite true to the male-female relationships of her time.

To try and psychologize Cather's work is to cheapen it. If Willa Cather had wished to become a psychologist she would have. She chose to become a writer. Therefore read her as a writer and judge her on literary merit.

And Cather, like every other fine writer, will continue to go in and out of fashion, but her voice will always ring true. There is not an ounce of deception or self-pity in that voice.

Surrounded as we are today by a torrent of chat—even our news is presented as chat on television—it is difficult for us to cull the truth from the trivia. Our task is not to pull truth from lies nearly as much as it is to find the truth amidst the trivia. We are overstimulated, overinformed, oversold, and overloaded.

Fewer and fewer Americans work in three-dimensional reality. Few farm. Few raise stock. Few fish. Few are doctors or veterinarians compared to the millions trapped in service-industry jobs or in repetitive tasks disconnected from a sense of accomplishment.

This disconnection from the cycle of the seasons, the birth and death of animals and crops upon which one is dependent for life, has created a bizarre unreality among us. Many Americans no longer realize that actions have consequences. Many Americans delude themselves into believing they can control their lives while others believe they have no control at all; they are victims of fate.

Thankfully, Cather suffered neither of these delusions. Thankfully, she wrote of people who lived or died by their labor and by the choices they made. Actions did have consequences. There was no safety net: no social security check, no food stamps, no television shows announcing your "co-dependency." There was no sense that government would provide you with the necessities of survival. There was also no sense that the government was obliged to provide you with those necessities. All moral equations began and ended with the self. You were responsible. If you planted your wheat and Nature raised up a hailstorm to smash it down again, you were surely not responsible for the hailstorm but you were responsible for feeding yourself somehow. And if you couldn't feed yourself, so be it.

Willa Cather knew of that great truth which may best be expressed by this old saw: It doesn't matter if the rock hits the jug or the jug hits the rock, the jug still gets it. That's reality.

That's Willa Cather.

RITA MAE BROWN

Selected Stories

On the Divide

Near Rattlesnake Creek, on the side of a little draw stood Canute's shanty. North, east, south, stretched the level Nebraska plain of long rust-red grass that undulated constantly in the wind. To the west the ground was broken and rough, and a narrow strip of timber wound along the turbid, muddy little stream that had scarcely ambition enough to crawl over its black bottom. If it had not been for the few stunted cottonwoods and elms that grew along its banks, Canute would have shot himself years ago. The Norwegians are a timber-loving people, and if there is even a turtle pond with a few plum bushes around it they seem irresistibly drawn toward it.

As to the shanty itself, Canute had built it without aid of any kind, for when he first squatted along the banks of Rattlesnake Creek there was not a human being within twenty miles. It was built of logs split in halves, the chinks stopped with mud and plaster. The roof was covered with earth and was supported by one gigantic beam curved in the shape of a round arch. It was almost impossible that any tree had ever grown in that shape. The Norwegians used to say that Canute had taken the log across his knee and bent it into the shape he wished. There were two rooms, or rather there was one room with a partition made of ash saplings interwoven and bound together like big straw basket work. In one corner there was a cook stove, rusted and broken. In the other a bed made of unplaned planks and poles. It was fully eight feet long, and upon it was a heap of dark bed clothing. There was a chair and a bench of colossal proportions. There was an ordinary kitchen cupboard with a few cracked dirty dishes in it, and beside it on a tall box a tin washbasin. Under the bed was a pile of pint flasks, some broken, some whole, all empty. On the wood box lay a pair of shoes of almost incredible dimensions. On the wall hung a saddle, a gun, and some ragged clothing, conspicuous among which was a suit of dark cloth, apparently new, with a paper collar carefully wrapped in a red silk handkerchief and pinned to the sleeve. Over the door hung a wolf and a badger skin, and on the door itself a brace of thirty or forty snake skins whose noisy tails rattled ominously every time it opened. The strangest things in the shanty were the wide window-sills. At first glance they looked as though they had been ruthlessly hacked and mutilated with a hatchet, but on closer inspection all the notches and holes in the wood took form and shape. There seemed to be a series of pictures. They were, in a rough way, artistic, but the figures were heavy and labored, as though they had been cut very slowly and with very awkward instruments. There were men plowing with little horned imps sitting on their shoulders and on their horses' heads. There were men praying with a skull hanging over their heads and little demons behind them mocking their attitudes. There were men fighting with big serpents, and skeletons dancing together. All about these pictures were blooming vines and foliage such as never grew in this world, and coiled among the branches of the vines there was always the scaly body of a serpent, and behind every flower there was a serpent's head. It was a veritable Dance of Death by one who had felt its sting. In the wood box lay some boards, and every inch of them was cut up in the same manner. Sometimes the work was very rude and careless, and looked as though the hand of the workman had trembled. It would sometimes have been hard to distinguish the men from their evil geniuses but for one fact, the men were always grave and were either toiling or praying, while the devils were always smiling and dancing. Several of these boards had been split for kindling and it was evident that the artist did not value his work highly.

It was the first day of winter on the Divide. Canute stumbled into his shanty carrying a basket of cobs, and after filling the stove, sat down on a stool and crouched his seven foot frame over the fire, staring drearily out of the window at the wide gray sky. He knew by heart every individual clump of bunch grass in the miles of red shaggy prairie that stretched before his cabin. He knew it in all the deceitful loveliness of its early summer, in all the bitter barrenness of its autumn. He had seen it smitten by all the plagues of Egypt. He had seen it parched by drought, and sogged by rain, beaten by hail, and swept by fire, and in the grasshopper years he had seen it eaten as bare and clean as bones that the vultures have left. After the great fires he had seen it stretch for miles and miles, black and smoking as the floor of hell.

He rose slowly and crossed the room, dragging his big feet heavily as though they were burdens to him. He looked out of the window into the hog corral and saw the pigs burying themselves in the straw before the shed. The leaden gray clouds were beginning to spill themselves, and the snow flakes were settling down over the white leprous patches of frozen earth where the hogs had gnawed even the sod away. He shuddered and began to walk, trampling heavily with his ungainly feet. He was the wreck of ten winters on the Divide and he knew what that meant. Men fear the winters of the Divide as a child fears night or as men in the North Seas fear the still dark cold of the polar twilight. His eyes fell upon his gun, and he took it down from the wall and looked it over. He sat down on the edge of his bed and held the barrel towards his face, letting his forehead rest upon it, and laid his finger on the trigger. He was perfectly calm, there was neither passion nor despair in his face, but the thoughtful look of a man who is considering. Presently he laid down the gun, and reaching into the cupboard, drew out a pint bottle of raw white alcohol. Lifting it to his lips, he drank greedily. He washed his face in the tin basin and combed his rough hair and shaggy blond beard. Then he stood in uncertainty before the suit of dark clothes that hung on the wall. For the fiftieth time he took them in his hands and tried to summon courage to put them on. He took the paper collar that was pinned to the sleeve of the coat and cautiously slipped it under his rough beard, looking with timid expectancy into the cracked, splashed glass that hung over the bench. With a short laugh he threw it down on the bed, and pulling on his old black hat, he went out, striking off across the level.

It was a physical necessity for him to get away from his cabin once in a while. He had been there for ten years, digging and plowing and sowing, and reaping what little the hail and the hot winds and the frosts left him to reap. Insanity and suicide are very common things on the Divide. They come on like an epidemic in the hot wind season. Those scorching dusty winds that blow up over the bluffs from Kansas seem to dry up the blood in men's veins as they do the sap in the corn leaves. Whenever the yellow scorch creeps down over the tender inside leaves about the ear, then the coroners prepare for active duty; for the oil of the country is burned out and it does not take long for the flame to eat up the wick. It causes no great sensation there when a Dane is found swinging to his own windmill tower, and most of the Poles after they have become too careless and discouraged to shave themselves keep their razors to cut their throats with.

It may be that the next generation on the Divide will be very happy, but the present one came too late in life. It is useless for men that have cut hemlocks among the mountains of Sweden for forty years to try to be happy in a country as flat and gray and naked as the sea. It is not easy for men that have spent their youth fishing in the Northern seas to be content with following a plow, and men that have served in the Austrian army hate hard work and coarse clothing on the loneliness of the plains, and long for marches and excitement and tavern company and pretty barmaids. After a man has passed his fortieth birthday it is not easy for him to change the habits and conditions of his life. Most men bring with them to the Divide only the dregs of the lives that they have squandered in other lands and among other peoples.

Canute Canuteson was as mad as any of them, but his madness did not take the form of suicide or religion but of alcohol. He had always taken liquor when he wanted it, as all Norwegians do, but after his first year of solitary life he settled down to it steadily. He exhausted whisky after a while, and went to alcohol, because its effects were speedier and surer. He was a big man and with a terrible amount of resistant force, and it took a great deal of alcohol even to move him. After nine years of drinking, the quantities he could take would seem fabulous to an ordinary drinking man. He never let it interfere with his work, he generally drank at night and on Sundays. Every night, as soon as his chores were done, he began to drink. While he was able to sit up he would play on his mouth harp or hack away at his window sills with his jackknife. When the liquor went to his head he would lie down on his bed and stare out of the window until he went to sleep. He drank alone and in solitude not for pleasure or good cheer, but to forget the awful loneliness and level of the Divide. Milton made a sad blunder when he put mountains in hell. Mountains postulate faith and aspiration. All mountain peoples are religious. It was the cities of the plains that, because of their utter lack of spirituality and the mad caprice of their vice, were cursed of God.

Alcohol is perfectly consistent in its effects upon man. Drunkenness is merely an exaggeration. A foolish man drunk becomes maudlin; a bloody man, vicious; a coarse man, vulgar. Canute was none of these, but he was morose and gloomy, and liquor took him through all the hells of Dante. As he lay on his giant's bed all the horrors of this world and every other were laid bare to his chilled senses. He was a man who knew no joy, a man who toiled in silence and bitterness. The skull and the serpent were always before him, the symbols of eternal futileness and of eternal hate.

When the first Norwegians near enough to be called neighbors came, Canute rejoiced, and planned to escape from his bosom vice. But he was not a social man by nature and had not the power of drawing out the social side of other people. His new neighbors rather feared him because of his great strength and size, his silence and his lowering brows. Perhaps, too, they knew that he was mad, mad from the eternal treachery of the plains, which every spring stretch green and rustle with the promises of Eden, showing long grassy lagoons full of clear water and cattle whose hoofs are stained with wild roses. Before autumn the lagoons are dried up, and the ground is burnt dry and hard until it blisters and cracks open.

So instead of becoming a friend and neighbor to the men that settled about him, Canute became a mystery and a terror. They told awful stories of his size and strength and of the alcohol he drank. They said that one night, when he went out to see to his horses just before he went to bed, his steps were unsteady and the rotten planks of the floor gave way and threw him behind the feet of a fiery young stallion. His foot was caught fast in the floor, and the nervous horse began kicking frantically. When Canute felt the blood trickling down into his eyes from a scalp wound in his head, he roused himself from his kingly indifference, and with the quiet stoical courage of a drunken man leaned forward and wound his arms about the horse's hind legs and held them against his breast with crushing embrace. All through the darkness and cold of the night he lay there, matching strength against strength. When little Jim Peterson went over the next morning at four o'clock to go with him to the Blue to cut wood, he found him so, and the horse was on its fore knees, trembling and whinnying with fear. This is the story the Norwegians tell of him, and if it is true it is no wonder that they feared and hated this Holder of the Heels of Horses.

One spring there moved to the next "eighty" a family that made a great change in Canute's life. Ole Yensen was too drunk most of the time to be afraid of any one, and his wife Mary was too garrulous to be afraid of any one who listened to her talk, and Lena, their pretty daughter, was not afraid of man nor devil. So it came about that Canute went over to take his alcohol with Ole oftener than he took it alone. After a while the report spread that he was going to marry Yensen's daughter, and the Norwegian girls began to tease Lena about the great bear she was going to keep house for. No one could quite see how the affair had come about, for Canute's tactics of courtship were somewhat peculiar. He apparently never spoke to her at all: he would sit for hours with Mary chattering on one side of him and Ole drinking on the other and watch Lena at her work. She teased him, and threw flour in his face and put vinegar in his coffee, but he took her rough jokes with silent wonder, never even smiling. He took her to church occasionally, but the most watchful and curious people never saw him speak to her. He would sit staring at her while she giggled and flirted with the other men.

Next spring Mary Lee went to town to work in a steam laundry. She came home every Sunday, and always ran across to Yensens to startle Lena with stories of ten cent theaters, firemen's dances, and all the other esthetic delights of metropolitan life. In a few weeks Lena's head was completely turned, and she gave her father no rest until he let her go to town to seek her fortune at the ironing board. From the time she came home on her first visit she began to treat Canute with contempt. She had bought a plush cloak and kid gloves, had her clothes made by the dress maker, and assumed airs and graces that made the other women of the neighborhood cordially detest her. She generally brought with her a young man from town who waxed his mustache and wore a red necktie, and she did not even introduce him to Canute.

The neighbors teased Canute a good deal until he knocked one of them down. He gave no sign of suffering from her neglect except that he drank more and avoided the other Norwegians more carefully than ever. He lay around in his den and no one knew what he felt or thought, but little Jim Peterson, who had seen him glowering at Lena in church one Sunday when she was there with the town man, said that he would not give an acre of his wheat for Lena's life or the town chap's either; and Jim's wheat was so wondrously worthless that the statement was an exceedingly strong one.

Canute had bought a new suit of clothes that looked as nearly like the town man's as possible. They had cost him half a millet crop; for tailors are not accustomed to fitting giants and they charge for it. He had hung those clothes in his shanty two months ago and had never put them on, partly from fear of ridicule, partly from discouragement, and partly because there was something in his own soul that revolted at the littleness of the device.

Lena was at home just at this time. Work was slack in the laundry and Mary had not been well, so Lena stayed at home, glad enough to get an opportunity to torment Canute once more.

She was washing in the side kitchen, singing loudly as

she worked. Mary was on her knees, blacking the stove and scolding violently about the young man who was coming out from town that night. The young man had committed the fatal error of laughing at Mary's ceaseless babble and had never been forgiven.

"He is no good, and you will come to a bad end by running with him! I do not see why a daughter of mine should act so. I do not see why the Lord should visit such a punishment upon me as to give me such a daughter. There are plenty of good men you can marry."

Lena tossed her head and answered curtly, "I don't happen to want to marry any man right away, and so long as Dick dresses nice and has plenty of money to spend, there is no harm in my going with him."

"Money to spend? Yes, and that is all he does with it I'll be bound. You think it very fine now, but you will change your tune when you have been married five years and see your children running naked and your cupboard empty. Did Anne Hermanson come to any good end by marrying a town man?"

"I don't know anything about Anne Hermanson, but I know any of the laundry girls would have Dick quick enough if they could get him."

"Yes, and a nice lot of store clothes huzzies you are too. Now there is Canuteson who has an 'eighty' proved up and fifty head of cattle and—"

"And hair that ain't been cut since he was a baby, and a big dirty beard, and he wears overalls on Sundays, and drinks like a pig. Besides he will keep. I can have all the fun I want, and when I am old and ugly like you he can have me and take care of me. The Lord knows there ain't nobody else going to marry him."

Canute drew his hand back from the latch as though it were red hot. He was not the kind of man to make a good eavesdropper, and he wished he had knocked sooner. He pulled himself together and struck the door like a battering ram. Mary jumped and opened it with a screech.

"God! Canute, how you scared us! I thought it was crazy Lou—he has been tearing around the neighborhood trying to convert folks. I am afraid as death of him. He ought to be sent off, I think. He is just as liable as not to kill us all, or burn the barn, or poison the dogs. He has been worrying even the poor minister to death, and he laid up with the rheumatism, too! Did you notice that he was too sick to preach last Sunday? But don't stand there in the cold, come in. Yensen isn't here, but he just went over to Sorenson's for the mail; he won't be gone long. Walk right in the other room and sit down."

Canute followed her, looking steadily in front of him and not noticing Lena as he passed her. But Lena's vanity would not allow him to pass unmolested. She took the wet sheet she was wringing out and cracked him across the face with it, and ran giggling to the other side of the room. The blow stung his cheeks and the soapy water flew in his eyes, and he involuntarily began rubbing them with his hands. Lena giggled with delight at his discomfiture, and the wrath in Canute's face grew blacker than ever. A big man humiliated is vastly more undignified than a little one. He forgot the sting of his face in the bitter consciousness that he had made a fool of himself. He stumbled blindly into the living room, knocking his head against the door jamb because he forgot to stoop. He dropped into a chair behind the stove, thrusting his big feet back helplessly on either side of him.

Ole was a long time in coming, and Canute sat there, still and silent, with his hands clenched on his knees, and the skin of his face seemed to have shriveled up into little wrinkles that trembled when he lowered his brows. His life had been one long lethargy of solitude and alcohol, but now he was awakening, and it was as when the dumb stagnant heat of summer breaks out into thunder.

When Ole came staggering in, heavy with liquor, Canute rose at once.

"Yensen," he said quietly, "I have come to see if you will let me marry your daughter today."

"Today!" gasped Ole.

"Yes, I will not wait until tomorrow. I am tired of living alone."

Ole braced his staggering knees against the bedstead, and stammered eloquently: "Do you think I will marry my daughter to a drunkard? a man who drinks raw alcohol? a man who sleeps with rattle snakes? Get out of my house or

I will kick you out for your impudence." And Ole began looking anxiously for his feet.

Canute answered not a word, but he put on his hat and went out into the kitchen. He went up to Lena and said without looking at her, "Get your things on and come with me!"

The tones of his voice startled her, and she said angrily, dropping the soap, "Are you drunk?"

"If you do not come with me, I will take you—you had better come," said Canute quietly.

She lifted a sheet to strike him, but he caught her arm roughly and wrenched the sheet from her. He turned to the wall and took down a hood and shawl that hung there, and began wrapping her up. Lena scratched and fought like a wild thing. Ole stood in the door, cursing, and Mary howled and screeched at the top of her voice. As for Canute, he lifted the girl in his arms and went out of the house. She kicked and struggled, but the helpless wailing of Mary and Ole soon died away in the distance, and her face was held down tightly on Canute's shoulder so that she could not see whither he was taking her. She was conscious only of the north wind whistling in her ears, and of rapid steady motion and of a great breast that heaved beneath her in quick, irregular breaths. The harder she struggled the tighter those iron arms that had held the heels of horses crushed about her, until she felt as if they would crush the breath from her, and lay still with fear. Canute was striding across the level fields at a pace at which man never went before, drawing the stinging north winds into his lungs in great gulps. He walked with his eyes half closed and looking straight in front of him, only lowering them when he bent his head to blow away the snow flakes that settled on her hair. So it was that Canute took her to his home, even as his bearded barbarian ancestors took the fair frivolous women of the South in their hairy arms and bore them down to their war ships. For ever and anon the soul becomes weary of the conventions that are not of it, and with a single stroke shatters the civilized lies with which it is unable to cope, and the strong arm reaches out and takes by force what it cannot win by cunning.

When Canute reached his shanty he placed the girl upon a chair, where she sat sobbing. He stayed only a few minutes. He filled the stove with wood and lit the lamp, drank a huge swallow of alcohol and put the bottle in his pocket. He paused a moment, staring heavily at the weeping girl, then he went off and locked the door and disappeared in the gathering gloom of the night.

Wrapped in flannels and soaked with turpentine, the little Norwegian preacher sat reading his Bible, when he heard a thundering knock at his door, and Canute entered, covered with snow and his beard frozen fast to his coat.

"Come in, Canute, you must be frozen," said the little man, shoving a chair towards his visitor.

Canute remained standing with his hat on and said quietly, "I want you to come over to my house tonight to marry me to Lena Yensen."

"Have you got a license, Canute?"

"No, I don't want a license. I want to be married."

"But I can't marry you without a license, man. It would not be legal."

A dangerous light came in the big Norwegian's eye. "I want you to come over to my house to marry me to Lena Yensen."

"No, I can't, it would kill an ox to go out in a storm like this, and my rheumatism is bad tonight."

"Then if you will not go I must take you," said Canute with a sigh.

He took down the preacher's bearskin coat and bade him put it on while he hitched up his buggy. He went out and closed the door softly after him. Presently he returned and found the frightened minister crouching before the fire with his coat lying beside him. Canute helped him put it on and gently wrapped his head in his big muffler. Then he picked him up and carried him out and placed him in his buggy. As he tucked the buffalo robes around him he said: "Your horse is old, he might flounder or lose his way in this storm. I will lead him."

The minister took the reins feebly in his hands and sat shivering with the cold. Sometimes when there was a lull in the wind, he could see the horse struggling through the snow with the man plodding steadily beside him. Again the blowing snow would hide them from him altogether. He had no idea where they were or what direction they were going. He felt as though he were being whirled away in the heart of the storm, and he said all the prayers he knew. But at last the long four miles were over, and Canute set him down in the snow while he unlocked the door. He saw the bride sitting by the fire with her eyes red and swollen as though she had been weeping. Canute placed a huge chair for him, and said roughly,—

"Warm yourself."

Lena began to cry and moan afresh, begging the minister to take her home. He looked helplessly at Canute. Canute said simply,

"If you are warm now, you can marry us."

"My daughter, do you take this step of your own free will?" asked the minister in a trembling voice.

"No, sir, I don't, and it is disgraceful he should force me into it! I won't marry him."

"Then, Canute, I cannot marry you," said the minister, standing as straight as his rheumatic limbs would let him.

"Are you ready to marry us now, sir?" said Canute, laying one iron hand on his stooped shoulder. The little preacher was a good man, but like most men of weak body he was a coward and had a horror of physical suffering, although he had known so much of it. So with many qualms of conscience he began to repeat the marriage service. Lena sat sullenly in her chair, staring at the fire. Canute stood beside her, listening with his head bent reverently and his hands folded on his breast. When the little man had prayed and said amen, Canute began bundling him up again.

"I will take you home, now," he said as he carried him out and placed him in his buggy, and started off with him through the fury of the storm, floundering among the snow drifts that brought even the giant himself to his knees.

After she was left alone, Lena soon ceased weeping. She was not of a particularly sensitive temperament, and had little pride beyond that of vanity. After the first bitter anger wore itself out, she felt nothing more than a healthy sense of humiliation and defeat. She had no inclination to run away, for she was married now, and in her eyes that was final and all rebellion was useless. She knew nothing about a license, but she knew that a preacher married folks. She consoled herself by thinking that she had always intended to marry Canute someday, anyway.

She grew tired of crying and looking into the fire, so she got up and began to look about her. She had heard queer tales about the inside of Canute's shanty, and her curiosity soon got the better of her rage. One of the first things she noticed was the new black suit of clothes hanging on the wall. She was dull, but it did not take a vain woman long to interpret anything so decidedly flattering, and she was pleased in spite of herself. As she looked through the cupboard, the general air of neglect and discomfort made her pity the man who lived there.

"Poor fellow, no wonder he wants to get married to get somebody to wash up his dishes. Batchin's pretty hard on a man."

It is easy to pity when once one's vanity has been tickled. She looked at the windowsill and gave a little shudder and wondered if the man were crazy. Then she sat down again and sat a long time wondering what her Dick and Ole would do.

"It is queer Dick didn't come right over after me. He surely came, for he would have left town before the storm began and he might just as well come right on as go back. If he'd hurried he would have gotten here before the preacher came. I suppose he was afraid to come, for he knew Canuteson could pound him to jelly, the coward!" Her eyes flashed angrily.

The weary hours wore on and Lena began to grow horribly lonesome. It was an uncanny night and this was an uncanny place to be in. She could hear the coyotes howling hungrily a little way from the cabin, and more terrible still were all the unknown noises of the storm. She remembered the tales they told of the big log overhead and she was afraid of those snaky things on the windowsills. She remembered the man who had been killed in the draw, and she wondered what she would do if she saw crazy Lou's white face glaring into the window. The rattling of the door became unbearable, she thought the latch must be loose and took the lamp to look at it. Then for the first time she saw the ugly brown snake skins whose death rattle sounded every time the wind jarred the door.

"Canute, Canute!" she screamed in terror.

Outside the door she heard a heavy sound as of a big dog getting up and shaking himself. The door opened and Canute stood before her, white as a snow drift.

"What is it?" he asked kindly.

"I am cold," she faltered.

He went out and got an armful of wood and a basket of cobs and filled the stove. Then he went out and lay in the snow before the door. Presently he heard her calling again.

"What is it?" he said, sitting up.

"I'm so lonesome, I'm afraid to stay in here all alone."

"I will go over and get your mother." And he got up.

"She won't come."

"I'll bring her," said Canute grimly.

"No, no. I don't want her, she will scold all the time."

"Well, I will bring your father."

She spoke again and it seemed as though her mouth was close up to the key-hole. She spoke lower than he had ever heard her speak before, so low that he had to put his ear up to the lock to hear her.

"I don't want him either, Canute,—I'd rather have you."

For a moment she heard no noise at all, then something like a groan. With a cry of fear she opened the door, and saw Canute stretched in the snow at her feet, his face in his hands, sobbing on the doorstep.

Eric Hermannson's Soul

It was a great night at the Lone Star schoolhouse—a night when the Spirit was present with power and when God was very near to man. So it seemed to Asa Skinner, servant of God and Free Gospeller. The schoolhouse was crowded with the saved and sanctified, robust men and women, trembling and quailing before the power of some mysterious psychic force. Here and there among this cowering, sweating multitude crouched some poor wretch who had felt the pangs of an awakened conscience, but had not yet experienced that complete divestment of reason, that frenzy born of a convulsion of the mind, which, in the parlance of the Free Gospellers, is termed "the Light." On the floor before the mourners' bench lay the unconscious figure of a man in whom outraged nature had sought her last resort. This "trance" state is the highest evidence of grace among the Free Gospellers, and indicates a close walking with God.

Before the desk stood Asa Skinner, shouting of the mercy and vengeance of God, and in his eyes shone a terrible earnestness, an almost prophetic flame. Asa was a converted train gambler who used to run between Omaha and Denver. He was a man made for the extremes of life; from the most debauched of men he had become the most ascetic. His was a bestial face, a face that bore the stamp of Nature's eternal injustice. The forehead was low, projecting over the eyes, and the sandy hair was plastered down over it and then brushed back at an abrupt right angle. The chin was heavy, the nostrils were low and wide, and the lower lip hung loosely except in his moments of spasmodic earnestness, when it shut like a steel trap. Yet about those coarse features there were deep,

15

rugged furrows, the scars of many a hand-to-hand struggle with the weakness of the flesh, and about that drooping lip were sharp, strenuous lines that had conquered it and taught it to pray. Over those seamed cheeks there was a certain pallor, a greyness caught from many a vigil. It was as though, after Nature had done her worst with that face, some fine chisel had gone over it, chastening and almost transfiguring it. Tonight, as his muscles twitched with emotion, and the perspiration dropped from his hair and chin, there was a certain convincing power in the man. For Asa Skinner was a man possessed of a belief, of that sentiment of the sublime before which all inequalities are leveled, that transport of conviction which seems superior to all laws of condition, under which debauchees have become martyrs; which made a tinker an artist and a camel-driver the founder of an empire. This was with Asa Skinner tonight, as he stood proclaiming the vengeance of God.

It might have occurred to an impartial observer that Asa Skinner's God was indeed a vengeful God if he could reserve vengeance for those of his creatures who were packed into the Lone Star schoolhouse that night. Poor exiles of all nations; men from the south and the north, peasants from almost every country of Europe, most of them from the mountainous, night-bound coast of Norway. Honest men for the most part, but men with whom the world had dealt hardly; the failures of all countries, men sobered by toil and saddened by exile, who had been driven to fight for the dominion of an untoward soil, to sow where others should gather, the advance guard of a mighty civilization to be.

Never had Asa Skinner spoken more earnestly than now. He felt that the Lord had this night a special work for him to do. Tonight Eric Hermannson, the wildest lad on all the Divide, sat in his audience with a fiddle on his knee, just as he had dropped in on his way to play for some dance. The violin is an object of particular abhorrence to the Free Gospellers. Their antagonism to the church organ is bitter enough, but the fiddle they regard as a very incarnation of evil desires, singing forever of

worldly pleasures and inseparably associated with all for-
bidden things.

Eric Hermannson had long been the object of the
prayers of the revivalists. His mother had felt the power of
the Spirit weeks ago, and special prayer-meetings had
been held at her house for her son. But Eric had only
gone his ways laughing, the ways of youth, which are short
enough at best, and none too flowery on the Divide. He
slipped away from the prayer-meetings to meet the Camp-
bell boys in Genereau's saloon, or hug the plump little
French girls at Chevalier's dances, and sometimes, of a
summer night, he even went across the dewy cornfields
and through the wild-plum thicket to play the fiddle for
Lena Hanson, whose name was a reproach through all the
Divide country, where the women are usually too plain
and too busy and too tired to depart from the ways of
virtue. On such occasions Lena, attired in a pink wrapper
and silk stockings and tiny pink slippers, would sing to
him, accompanying herself on a battered guitar. It gave
him a delicious sense of freedom and experience to be
with a woman who, no matter how, had lived in big cities
and knew the ways of town folk, who had never worked in
the fields and had kept her hands white and soft, her
throat fair and tender, who had heard great singers in
Denver and Salt Lake, and who knew the strange lan-
guage of flattery and idleness and mirth.

Yet, careless as he seemed, the frantic prayers of his
mother were not altogether without their effect upon Eric.
For days he had been fleeing before them as a criminal
from his pursuers, and over his pleasures had fallen the
shadow of something dark and terrible that dogged his
steps. The harder he danced, the louder he sang, the
more was he conscious that this phantom was gaining
upon him, that in time it would track him down. One
Sunday afternoon, late in the fall, when he had been
drinking beer with Lena Hanson and listening to a song
which made his cheeks burn, a rattlesnake had crawled
out of the side of the sod house and thrust its ugly head in
under the screen door. He was not afraid of snakes, but he
knew enough of Gospellism to feel the significance of the
reptile lying coiled there upon her doorstep. His lips were

.cold when he kissed Lena goodbye, and he went there no more.

The final barrier between Eric and his mother's faith was his violin, and to that he clung as a man sometimes will cling to his dearest sin, to the weakness more precious to him than all his strength. In the great world beauty comes to men in many guises, and art in a hundred forms, but for Eric there was only his violin. It stood, to him, for all the manifestations of art; it was his only bridge into the kingdom of the soul.

It was to Eric Hermannson that the evangelist directed his impassioned pleading that night.

"*Saul, Saul, why persecutest thou me?* Is there a Saul here tonight who has stopped his ears to that gentle pleading, who has thrust a spear into that bleeding side? Think of it, my brother; you are offered this wonderful love and you prefer the worm that dieth not and the fire which will not be quenched. What right have you to lose one of God's precious souls? *Saul, Saul, why persecutest thou me?*"

A great joy dawned in Asa Skinner's pale face, for he saw that Eric Hermannson was swaying to and fro in his seat. The minister fell upon his knees and threw his long arms up over his head.

"O my brothers! I feel it coming, the blessing we have prayed for. I tell you the Spirit is coming! Just a little more prayer, brothers, a little more zeal, and he will be here. I can feel his cooling wing upon my brow. Glory be to God forever and ever, amen!"

The whole congregation groaned under the pressure of this spiritual panic. Shouts and hallelujahs went up from every lip. Another figure fell prostrate upon the floor. From the mourners' bench rose a chant of terror and rapture:

> "Eating honey and drinking wine,
>   *Glory to the bleeding Lamb!*
> I am my Lord's and he is mine,
>   *Glory to the bleeding Lamb!*"

The hymn was sung in a dozen dialects and voiced all

the vague yearning of these hungry lives, of these people who had starved all the passions so long, only to fall victims to the barest of them all, fear.

A groan of ultimate anguish rose from Eric Hermannson's bowed head, and the sound was like the groan of a great tree when it falls in the forest.

The minister rose suddenly to his feet and threw back his head, crying in a loud voice:

"*Lazarus, come forth!* Eric Hermannson, you are lost, going down at sea. In the name of God, and Jesus Christ his Son, I throw you the life line. Take hold! Almighty God, my soul for his!" The minister threw his arms out and lifted his quivering face.

Eric Hermannson rose to his feet; his lips were set and the lightning was in his eyes. He took his violin by the neck and crushed it to splinters across his knee, and to Asa Skinner the sound was like the shackles of sin broken audibly asunder.

II

For more than two years Eric Hermannson kept the austere faith to which he had sworn himself, kept it until a girl from the East came to spend a week on the Nebraska Divide. She was a girl of other manners and conditions, and there were greater distances between her life and Eric's than all the miles which separated Rattlesnake Creek from New York City. Indeed, she had no business to be in the West at all; but ah! across what leagues of land and sea, by what improbable chances, do the unrelenting gods bring to us our fate!

It was in a year of financial depression that Wyllis Elliot came to Nebraska to buy cheap land and revisit the country where he had spent a year of his youth. When he had graduated from Harvard it was still customary for moneyed gentlemen to send their scapegrace sons to rough it on ranches in the wilds of Nebraska or Dakota, or to consign them to a living death in the sagebrush of the Black Hills. These young men did not always return to the ways of civilized life. But Wyllis Elliot had not married a half-breed, nor been shot in a cowpunchers' brawl, nor wrecked by bad whisky, nor appropriated by a smirched adventuress. He had been saved from these things by a girl, his sister, who had been very near to his life ever since the days when they read fairy tales together and dreamed the dreams that never come true. On this, his first visit to his father's ranch since he left it six years before, he brought her with him. She had been laid up half the winter from a sprain received while skating, and had had too much time for reflection during those months. She was restless and filled with a desire to see something of the wild country of which her brother had told her so much. She was to be married the next winter, and Wyllis understood her when she begged him to take her with him on this long, aimless jaunt across the continent, to taste the last of their freedom together. It comes to all women of her type—that desire to taste the unknown which allures and terrifies, to run one's whole soul's length out to the wind—just once.

It had been an eventful journey. Wyllis somehow understood that strain of gypsy blood in his sister, and he knew where to take her. They had slept in sod houses on the Platte River, made the acquaintance of the personnel of a third-rate opera company on the train to Deadwood, dined in a camp of railroad constructors at the world's end beyond New Castle, gone through the Black Hills on horseback, fished for trout in Dome Lake, watched a dance at Cripple Creek, where the lost souls who hide in the hills gathered for their besotted revelry. And now, last of all, before the return to thraldom, there was this little shack, anchored on the windy crest of the Divide, a little black dot against the flaming sunsets, a scented sea of cornland bathed in opalescent air and blinding sunlight.

Margaret Elliot was one of those women of whom there are so many in this day, when old order, passing, giveth place to new; beautiful, talented, critical, unsatisfied, tired of the world at twenty-four. For the moment the life and people of the Divide interested her. She was there but a week; perhaps had she stayed longer, that inexorable ennui which travels faster even than the Vestibule Limited would have overtaken her. The week she tarried there was the week that Eric Hermannson was helping Jerry Lockhart thresh; a week earlier or a week later, and there would have been no story to write.

It was on Thursday and they were to leave on Saturday. Wyllis and his sister were sitting on the wide piazza of the ranchhouse, staring out into the afternoon sunlight and protesting against the gusts of hot wind that blew up from the sandy riverbottom twenty miles to the southward.

The young man pulled his cap lower over his eyes and remarked:

"This wind is the real thing; you don't strike it anywhere else. You remember we had a touch of it in Algiers and I told you it came from Kansas. It's the keynote of this country."

Wyllis touched her hand that lay on the hammock and continued gently:

"I hope it's paid you, Sis. Roughing it's dangerous business; it takes the taste out of things."

She shut her fingers firmly over the brown hand that was so like her own.

"Paid? Why, Wyllis, I haven't been so happy since we were children and were going to discover the ruins of Troy together some day. Do you know, I believe I could just stay on here forever and let the world go on its own gait. It seems as though the tension and strain we used to talk of last winter were gone for good, as though one could never give one's strength out to such petty things any more."

Wyllis brushed the ashes of his pipe away from the silk handkerchief that was knotted about his neck and stared moodily off at the skyline.

"No, you're mistaken. This would bore you after a while. You can't shake the fever of the other life. I've tried it. There was a time when the gay fellows of Rome could trot down into the Thebaid and burrow into the sandhills and get rid of it. But it's all too complex now. You see we've made our dissipations so dainty and respectable that they've gone further in than the flesh, and taken hold of the ego proper. You couldn't rest, even here. The war cry would follow you."

"You don't waste words, Wyllis, but you never miss fire. I talk more than you do, without saying half so much. You must have learned the art of silence from these taciturn Norwegians. I think I like silent men."

"Naturally," said Wyllis, "since you have decided to marry the most brilliant talker you know."

Both were silent for a time, listening to the sighing of the hot wind through the parched morning-glory vines. Margaret spoke first.

"Tell me, Wyllis, were many of the Norwegians you used to know as interesting as Eric Hermannson?"

"Who, Siegfried? Well, no. He used to be the flower of the Norwegian youth in my day, and he's rather an exception, even now. He has retrograded, though. The bonds of the soil have tightened on him, I fancy."

"Siegfried? Come, that's rather good, Wyllis. He looks like a dragon-slayer. What is it that makes him so different from the others? I can talk to him; he seems quite like a human being."

"Well," said Wyllis, meditatively, "I don't read Bourget as much as my cultured sister, and I'm not so well up in analysis, but I fancy it's because one keeps cherishing a perfectly unwarranted suspicion that under that big, hulking anatomy of his, he may conceal a soul somewhere. *Nicht wahr?*"

"Something like that," said Margaret, thoughtfully, "except that it's more than a suspicion, and it isn't groundless. He has one, and he makes it known, somehow, without speaking."

"I always have my doubts about loquacious souls," Wyllis remarked, with the unbelieving smile that had grown habitual with him.

Margaret went on, not heeding the interruption. "I knew it from the first, when he told me about the suicide of his cousin, the Bernstein boy. That kind of blunt pathos can't be summoned at will in anybody. The earlier novelists rose to it, sometimes, unconsciously. But last night when I sang for him I was doubly sure. Oh, I haven't told you about that yet! Better light your pipe again. You see, he stumbled in on me in the dark when I was pumping away at that old parlour organ to please Mrs. Lockhart.

It's her household fetish and I've forgotten how many pounds of butter she made and sold to buy it. Well, Eric stumbled in, and in some inarticulate manner made me understand that he wanted me to sing for him. I sang just the old things, of course. It's queer to sing familiar things here at the world's end. It makes one think how the hearts of men have carried them around the world, into the wastes of Iceland and the jungles of Africa and the islands of the Pacific. I think if one lived here long enough one would quite forget how to be trivial, and would read only the great books that we never get time to read in the world, and would remember only the great music, and the things that are really worth while would stand out clearly against that horizon over there. And of course I played the intermezzo from *Cavalleria Rusticana* for him; it goes rather better on an organ than most things do. He shuffled his feet and twisted his big hands up into knots and blurted out that he didn't know there was any music like that in the world. Why, there were tears in his voice, Wyllis! Yes, like Rossetti, I *heard* his tears. Then it dawned upon me that it was probably the first good music he had ever heard in all his life. Think of it, to care for music as he does and never to hear it, never to know that it exists on earth! To long for it as we long for other perfect experiences that never come. I can't tell you what music means to that man. I never saw any one so susceptible to it. It gave him speech, he became alive. When I had finished the intermezzo, he began telling me about a little crippled brother who died and whom he loved and used to carry everywhere in his arms. He did not wait for encouragement. He took up the story and told it slowly, as if to himself, just sort of rose up and told his own woe to answer Mascagni's. It overcame me."

"Poor devil," said Wyllis, looking at her with mysterious eyes, "and so you've given him a new woe. Now he'll go on wanting Grieg and Schubert the rest of his days and never getting them. That's a girl's philanthropy for you!"

Jerry Lockhart came out of the house screwing his chin over the unusual luxury of a stiff white collar, which his wife insisted upon as a necessary article of toilet while

Miss Elliot was at the house. Jerry sat down on the step and smiled his broad, red smile at Margaret.

"Well, I've got the music for your dance, Miss Elliot. Olaf Oleson will bring his accordion and Mollie will play the organ, when she isn't lookin' after the grub, and a little chap from Frenchtown will bring his fiddle—though the French don't mix with the Norwegians much."

"Delightful! Mr. Lockhart, that dance will be the feature of our trip, and it's so nice of you to get it up for us. We'll see the Norwegians in character at last," cried Margaret, cordially.

"See here, Lockhart, I'll settle with you for backing her in this scheme," said Wyllis, sitting up and knocking the ashes out of his pipe. "She's done crazy things enough on this trip, but to talk of dancing all night with a gang of half-mad Norwegians and taking the carriage at four to catch the six o'clock train out of Riverton—well, it's tommy-rot, that's what it is!"

"Wyllis, I leave it to your sovereign power of reason to decide whether it isn't easier to stay up all night than to get up at three in the morning. To get up at three, think what that means! No, sir, I prefer to keep my vigil and then get into a sleeper."

"But what do you want with the Norwegians? I thought you were tired of dancing."

"So I am, with some people. But I want to see a Norwegian dance, and I intend to. Come, Wyllis, you know how seldom it is that one really wants to do anything nowadays. I wonder when I have really wanted to go to a party before. It will be something to remember next month at Newport, when we have to and don't want to. Remember your own theory that contrast is about the only thing that makes life endurable. This is my party and Mr. Lockhart's; your whole duty tomorrow night will consist in being nice to the Norwegian girls. I'll warrant you were adept enough at it once. And you'd better be very nice indeed, for if there are many such young Valkyries as Eric's sister among them, they would simply tie you up in a knot if they suspected you were guying them."

Wyllis groaned and sank back into the hammock to consider his fate, while his sister went on.

"And the guests, Mr. Lockhart, did they accept?"

Lockhart took out his knife and began sharpening it on the sole of his plowshoe.

"Well, I guess we'll have a couple dozen. You see it's pretty hard to get a crowd together here any more. Most of 'em have gone over to the Free Gospellers, and they'd rather put their feet in the fire than shake 'em to a fiddle."

Margaret made a gesture of impatience. "Those Free Gospellers have just cast an evil spell over this country, haven't they?"

"Well," said Lockhart, cautiously, "I don't just like to pass judgment on any Christian sect, but if you're to know the chosen by their works, the Gospellers can't make a very proud showin', an' that's a fact. They're responsible for a few suicides, and they've sent a good-sized delegation to the state insane asylum, an' I don't see as they've made the rest of us much better than we were before. I had a little herdboy last spring, as square a little Dane as I want to work for me, but after the Gospellers got hold of him and sanctified him, the little beggar used to get down on his knees out on the prairie and pray by the hour and let the cattle get into the corn, an' I had to fire him. That's about the way it goes. Now there's Eric; that chap used to be a hustler and the spryest dancer in all this section—called all the dances. Now he's got no ambition and he's glum as a preacher. I don't suppose we can even get him to come in tomorrow night."

"Eric? Why, he must dance, we can't let him off," said Margaret, quickly. "Why, I intend to dance with him myself!"

"I'm afraid he won't dance. I asked him this morning if he'd help us out and he said, 'I don't dance now, any more,'" said Lockhart, imitating the laboured English of the Norwegian.

"'The Miller of Hofbau, the Miller of Hofbau, O my Princess!'" chirped Wyllis, cheerfully, from his hammock.

The red on his sister's cheek deepened a little, and she laughed mischievously. "We'll see about that, sir. I'll not admit that I am beaten until I have asked him myself."

Every night Eric rode over to St. Anne, a little village in the heart of the French settlement, for the mail. As the

road lay through the most attractive part of the Divide
country, on several occasions Margaret Elliot and her
brother had accompanied him. Tonight Wyllis had business with Lockhart, and Margaret rode with Eric, mounted
on a frisky little mustang that Mrs. Lockhart had broken to
the sidesaddle. Margaret regarded her escort very much
as she did the servant who always accompanied her on
long rides at home, and the ride to the village was a silent
one. She was occupied with thoughts of another world,
and Eric was wrestling with more thoughts than had ever
been crowded into his head before. He rode with his eyes
riveted on that slight figure before him, as though he
wished to absorb it through the optic nerves and hold it in
his brain forever. He understood the situation perfectly.
His brain worked slowly, but he had a keen sense of the
values of things. This girl represented an entirely new
species of humanity to him, but he knew where to place
her. The prophets of old, when an angel first appeared
unto them, never doubted its high origin.

Eric was patient under the adverse conditions of his
life, but he was not servile. The Norse blood in him had
not entirely lost its self-reliance. He came of a proud
fisher line, men who were not afraid of anything but the
ice and the devil, and he had prospects before him when
his father went down off the North Cape in the long Arctic
night, and his mother, seized by a violent horror of seafar-
ing life, had followed her brother to America. Eric was
eighteen then, handsome as young Siegfried, a giant in
stature, with a skin singularly pure and delicate, like a
Swede's; hair as yellow as the locks of Tennyson's amorous
Prince, and eyes of a fierce, burning blue, whose flash was
most dangerous to women. He had in those days a certain
pride of bearing, a certain confidence of approach, that
usually accompanies physical perfection. It was even said
of him then that he was in love with life, and inclined to
levity, a vice most unusual on the Divide. But the sad
history of those Norwegian exiles, transplanted in an arid
soil and under a scorching sun, had repeated itself in his
case. Toil and isolation had sobered him, and he grew
more and more like the clods among which he laboured. It
was as though some red-hot instrument had touched for a

moment those delicate fibers of the brain which respond to acute pain or pleasure, in which lies the power of exquisite sensation, and had seared them quite away. It is a painful thing to watch the light die out of the eyes of those Norsemen, leaving an expression of impenetrable sadness, quite passive, quite hopeless, a shadow that is never lifted. With some this change comes almost at once, in the first bitterness of homesickness, with others it comes more slowly, according to the time it takes each man's heart to die.

Oh, those poor Northmen of the Divide! They are dead many a year before they are put to rest in the little graveyard on the windy hill where exiles of all nations grow akin.

The peculiar species of hypochondria to which the exiles of his people sooner or later succumb had not developed in Eric until that night at the Lone Star schoolhouse, when he had broken his violin across his knee. After that, the gloom of his people settled down upon him, and the gospel of maceration began its work. *"If thine eye offend thee, pluck it out,"* et cetera. The pagan smile that once hovered about his lips was gone, and he was one with sorrow. Religion heals a hundred hearts for one that it embitters, but when it destroys, its work is quick and deadly, and where the agony of the cross has been, joy will not come again. This man understood things literally: one must live without pleasure to die without fear; to save the soul, it was necessary to starve the soul.

The sun hung low above the cornfields when Margaret and her cavalier left St. Anne. South of the town there is a stretch of road that runs for some three miles through the French settlement, where the prairie is as level as the surface of a lake. There the fields of flax and wheat and rye are bordered by precise rows of slender, tapering Lombard poplars. It was a yellow world that Margaret Elliot saw under the wide light of the setting sun.

The girl gathered up her reins and called back to Eric, "It will be safe to run the horses here, won't it?"

"Yes, I think so, now," he answered, touching his spur to his pony's flank. They were off like the wind. It is an old saying in the West that newcomers always ride a horse or two to death before they get broken in to the country. They are tempted by the great open spaces and try to outride the horizon, to get to the end of something. Margaret galloped over the level road, and Eric, from behind, saw her long veil fluttering in the wind. It had fluttered just so in his dreams last night and the night before. With a sudden inspiration of courage he overtook her and rode beside her, looking intently at her half-averted face. Before, he had only stolen occasional glances at it, seen it in blinding flashes, always with more or less embarrassment, but now he determined to let every line of it sink into his memory. Men of the world would have said that it was an unusual face, nervous, finely cut, with clear, elegant lines that betokened ancestry. Men of letters would have called it a historic face, and would have conjectured at what old passions, long asleep, what old sorrows forgotten time out of mind, doing battle together in ages gone, had curved those delicate nostrils, left their unconscious memory in those eyes. But Eric read no meaning in these details. To him this beauty was something more than colour and line; it was a flash of white light, in which one cannot distinguish colour because all colours are there. To him it was a complete revelation, an embodiment of those dreams of impossible loveliness that linger by a young man's pillow on midsummer nights; yet, because it held something more than the attraction of health and youth and shapeliness, it troubled him, and in its presence he felt as the Goths before the white marbles in the Roman Capitol, not knowing whether they were men or gods. At times he felt like uncovering his head before it, again the fury seized him to break and despoil, to find the clay in this spirit-thing and stamp upon it. Away from her, he longed to strike out with his arms, and take and hold; it maddened him that this woman whom he could break in his hands should be so much stronger than he. But near her, he never questioned this strength; he admitted its potentiality as he admitted the miracles of the Bible; it enervated and conquered him. Tonight, when he rode so close to her that he could have touched her, he knew that he might as well reach out his hand to take a star.

Margaret stirred uneasily under his gaze and turned questioningly in her saddle.

"This wind puts me a little out of breath when we ride fast," she said.

Eric turned his eyes away.

"I want to ask you if I go to New York to work, if I maybe hear music like you sang last night? I been a purty good hand to work," he asked, timidly.

Margaret looked at him with surprise, and then, as she studied the outline of his face, pityingly.

"Well, you might—but you'd lose a good deal else. I shouldn't like you to go to New York—and be poor, you'd be out of atmosphere, some way," she said, slowly. Inwardly she was thinking: *There he would be altogether sordid, impossible—a machine who would carry one's trunks upstairs, perhaps. Here he is every inch a man, rather picturesque; why is it?* "No," she added aloud, "I shouldn't like that."

"Then I not go," said Eric, decidedly.

Margaret turned her face to hide a smile. She was a trifle amused and a trifle annoyed. Suddenly she spoke again.

"But I'll tell you what I do want you to do, Eric. I want you to dance with us tomorrow night and teach me some of the Norwegian dances; they say you know them all. Won't you?"

Eric straightened himself in his saddle and his eyes flashed as they had done in the Lone Star schoolhouse when he broke his violin across his knee.

"Yes, I will," he said, quietly, and he believed that he delivered his soul to hell as he said it.

They had reached the rougher country now, where the road wound through a narrow cut in one of the bluffs along the creek, when a beat of hoofs ahead and the sharp neighing of horses made the ponies start and Eric rose in his stirrups. Then down the gulch in front of them and over the steep clay banks thundered a herd of wild ponies, nimble as monkeys and wild as rabbits, such as horse-traders drive east from the plains of Montana to sell in the farming country. Margaret's pony made a shrill sound, a neigh that was almost a scream, and started up the clay bank to meet them, all the wild blood of the range breaking out in an instant. Margaret called to Eric just as he threw himself out of the saddle and caught her pony's bit. But the wiry little animal had gone mad and was kicking and biting like a devil. Her wild brothers of the range were all about her, neighing, and pawing the earth, and striking her with their forefeet and snapping at her flanks. It was the old liberty of the range that the little beast fought for.

"Drop the reins and hold tight, tight!" Eric called, throwing all his weight upon the bit, struggling under those frantic forefeet that now beat at his breast, and now kicked at the wild mustangs that surged and tossed about him. He succeeded in wrenching the pony's head toward him and crowding her withers against the clay bank, so that she could not roll.

"Hold tight, tight!" he shouted again, launching a kick at a snorting animal that reared back against Margaret's saddle. If she should lose her courage and fall now, under those hoofs— He struck out again and again, kicking right and left with all his might. Already the negligent drivers had galloped into the cut, and their long quirts were whistling over the heads of the herd. As suddenly as it had come, the struggling, frantic wave of wild life swept up out of the gulch and on across the open prairie, and with a long despairing whinny of farewell the pony dropped her head and stood trembling in her sweat, shaking the foam and blood from her bit.

Eric stepped close to Margaret's side and laid his hand on her saddle. "You are not hurt?" he asked, hoarsely. As he raised his face in the soft starlight she saw that it was white and drawn and that his lips were working nervously.

"No, no, not at all. But you, you are suffering; they struck you!" she cried in sharp alarm.

He stepped back and drew his hand across his brow.

"No, it is not that," he spoke rapidly now, with his hands clenched at his side. "But if they had hurt you, I would beat their brains out with my hands. I would kill

them all. I was never afraid before. You are the only
beautiful thing that has ever come close to me. You came
like an angel out of the sky. You are like the music you
sing, you are like the stars and the snow on the mountains
where I played when I was a little boy. You are like all
that I wanted once and never had, you are all that they
have killed in me. I die for you tonight, tomorrow, for all
eternity. I am not a coward; I was afraid because I love
you more than Christ who died for me, more than I am
afraid of hell, or hope for heaven. I was never afraid
before. If you had fallen—oh, my God!" He threw his
arms out blindly and dropped his head upon the pony's
mane, leaning limply against the animal like a man struck
by some sickness. His shoulders rose and fell perceptibly
with his laboured breathing. The horse stood cowed with
exhaustion and fear. Presently Margaret laid her hand on
Eric's head and said gently:

"You are better now, shall we go on? Can you get
your horse?"

"No, he has gone with the herd. I will lead yours, she
is not safe. I will not frighten you again." His voice was
still husky, but it was steady now. He took hold of the bit
and tramped home in silence.

When they reached the house, Eric stood stolidly by
the pony's head until Wyllis came to lift his sister from the
saddle.

"The horses were badly frightened, Wyllis. I think I
was pretty thoroughly scared myself," she said as she took
her brother's arm and went slowly up the hill toward the
house. "No, I'm not hurt, thanks to Eric. You must thank
him for taking such good care of me. He's a mighty fine
fellow. I'll tell you all about it in the morning, dear. I was
pretty well shaken up and I'm going right to bed now.
Good night."

When she reached the low room in which she slept,
she sank upon the bed in her riding dress, face downward.

"Oh, I pity him! I pity him!" she murmured, with a
long sigh of exhaustion. She must have slept a little. When
she rose again, she took from her dress a letter that had
been waiting for her at the village post-office. It was closely

written in a long, angular hand, covering a dozen pages of foreign note-paper, and began:

> My Dearest Margaret: If I should attempt to say *how like a winter hath thine absence been*, I should incur the risk of being tedious. Really, it takes the sparkle out of everything. Having nothing better to do, and not caring to go anywhere in particular without you, I remained in the city until Jack Courtwell noted my general despondency and brought me down here to his place on the sound to manage some open-air theatricals he is getting up. *As You Like It* is of course the piece selected. Miss Harrison plays Rosalind. I wish you had been here to take the part. Miss Harrison reads her lines well, but she is either a maiden-all-forlorn or a tomboy; insists on reading into the part all sorts of deeper meanings and highly coloured suggestions wholly out of harmony with the pastoral setting. Like most of the professionals, she exaggerates the emotional element and quite fails to do justice to Rosalind's facile wit and really brilliant mental qualities. Gerard will do Orlando, but rumor says he is *épris* of your sometime friend, Miss Meredith, and his memory is treacherous and his interest fitful.
>
> My new pictures arrived last week on the *Gascogne*. The Puvis de Chavannes is even more beautiful than I thought it in Paris. A pale dream-maiden sits by a pale dream-cow and a stream of anemic water flows at her feet. The Constant, you will remember, I got because you admired it. It is here in all its florid splendour, the whole dominated by a glowing sensuosity. The drapery of the female figure is as wonderful as you said; the fabric all barbaric pearl and gold, painted with an easy, effortless voluptuousness, and that white, gleaming line of African coast in the background recalls memories of you very precious to me. But it is useless to deny that Constant irritates me. Though I cannot prove the charge against him, his brilliancy always makes me suspect him of cheapness.

Here Margaret stopped and glanced at the remaining pages of this strange love-letter. They seemed to be filled chiefly with discussions of pictures and books, and with a slow smile she laid them by.

She rose and began undressing. Before she lay down she went to open the window. With her hand on the sill, she hesitated, feeling suddenly as though some danger were lurking outside, some inordinate desire waiting to spring upon her in the darkness. She stood there for a long time, gazing at the infinite sweep of the sky.

"Oh, it is all so little, so little there," she murmured. "When everything else is so dwarfed, why should one expect love to be great? Why should one try to read highly coloured suggestions into a life like that? If only I could find one thing in it all that mattered greatly, one thing that would warm me when I am alone! Will life never give me that one great moment?"

As she raised the window, she heard a sound in the plum bushes outside. It was only the house-dog roused from his sleep, but Margaret started violently and trembled so that she caught the foot of the bed for support. Again she felt herself pursued by some overwhelming longing, some desperate necessity for herself, like the outstretching of helpless, unseen arms in the darkness, and the air seemed heavy with sighs of yearning. She fled to her bed with the words, "I love you more than Christ who died for me!" ringing in her ears.

III

About midnight the dance at Lockhart's was at its height. Even the old men who had come to "look on" caught the spirit of revelry and stamped the floor with the vigor of old Silenus. Eric took the violin from the Frenchmen, and Minna Oleson sat at the organ, and the music grew more and more characteristic—rude, half mournful music, made up of the folksongs of the North, that the villagers sing through the long night in hamlets by the sea, when they are thinking of the sun, and the spring, and the fishermen so long away. To Margaret some of it sounded like Grieg's

Peer Gynt music. She found something irresistibly infectious in the mirth of these people who were so seldom merry, and she felt almost one of them. Something seemed struggling for freedom in them tonight, something of the joyous childhood of the nations which exile had not killed. The girls were all boisterous with delight. Pleasure came to them but rarely, and when it came, they caught at it wildly and crushed its fluttering wings in their strong brown fingers. They had a hard life enough, most of them. Torrid summers and freezing winters, labour and drudgery and ignorance, were the portion of their girlhood; a short wooing, a hasty, loveless marriage, unlimited maternity, thankless sons, premature age and ugliness, were the dower of their womanhood. But what matter? Tonight there was hot liquor in the glass and hot blood in the heart; tonight they danced.

Tonight Eric Hermannson had renewed his youth. He was no longer the big, silent Norwegian who had sat at Margaret's feet and looked hopelessly into her eyes. Tonight he was a man, with a man's rights and a man's power. Tonight he was Siegfried indeed. His hair was yellow as the heavy wheat in the ripe of summer, and his eyes flashed like the blue water between the ice packs in the north seas. He was not afraid of Margaret tonight, and when he danced with her he held her firmly. She was tired and dragged on his arm a little, but the strength of the man was like an all-pervading fluid, stealing through her veins, awakening under her heart some nameless, unsuspected existence that had slumbered there all these years and that went out through her throbbing fingertips to his that answered. She wondered if the hoydenish blood of some lawless ancestor, long asleep, were calling out in her tonight, some drop of a hotter fluid that the centuries had failed to cool, and why, if this curse were in her, it had not spoken before. But was it a curse, this awakening, this wealth before undiscovered, this music set free? For the first time in her life her heart held something stronger than herself, was not this worthwhile? Then she ceased to wonder. She lost sight of the lights and the faces and the music was drowned by the beating of her own arteries. She saw only the blue eyes that flashed above her, felt only the warmth of that throbbing hand which held hers and which the blood of his heart fed. Dimly, as in a dream, she saw the drooping shoulders, high white forehead and tight, cynical mouth of the man she was to marry in December. For an hour she had been crowding back the memory of that face with all her strength.

"Let us stop, this is enough," she whispered. His only answer was to tighten the arm behind her. She sighed and let that masterful strength bear her where it would. She forgot that this man was little more than a savage, that they would part at dawn. The blood has no memories, no reflections, no regrets for the past, no consideration of the future.

"Let us go out where it is cooler," she said when the music stopped; thinking, *I am growing faint here, I shall be all right in the open air.* They stepped out into the cool, blue air of the night.

Since the older folk had begun dancing, the young Norwegians had been slipping out in couples to climb the windmill tower into the cooler atmosphere, as is their custom.

"You like to go up?" asked Eric, close to her ear.

She turned and looked at him with suppressed amusement. "How high is it?"

"Forty feet, about. I not let you fall." There was a note of irresistible pleading in his voice, and she felt that he tremendously wished her to go. Well, why not? This was a night of the unusual, when she was not herself at all, but was living an unreality. Tomorrow, yes, in a few hours, there would be the Vestibule Limited and the world.

"Well, if you'll take good care of me. I used to be able to climb, when I was a little girl."

Once at the top and seated on the platform, they were silent. Margaret wondered if she would not hunger for that scene all her life, through all the routine of the days to come. Above them stretched the great Western sky, serenely blue, even in the night, with its big, burning stars, never so cold and dead and far away as in denser atmospheres. The moon would not be up for twenty minutes yet, and all about the horizon, that wide horizon, which seemed to reach around the world, lingered a pale white light, as of a universal dawn. The weary wind brought up to them the heavy odours of the cornfields. The music of the dance sounded faintly from below. Eric leaned on his elbow beside her, his legs swinging down on the ladder. His great shoulders looked more than ever like those of the stone Doryphorus, who stands in his perfect, reposeful strength in the Louvre, and had often made her wonder if such men died forever with the youth of Greece.

"How sweet the corn smells at night," said Margaret nervously.

"Yes, like the flowers that grow in paradise, I think."

She was somewhat startled by this reply, and more startled when this taciturn man spoke again.

"You go away tomorrow?"

"Yes, we have stayed longer than we thought to now."

"You not come back any more?"

"No, I expect not. You see, it is a long trip halfway across the continent."

"You soon forget about this country, I guess." It seemed to him now a little thing to lose his soul for this woman, but that she should utterly forget this night into which he threw all his life and all his eternity, that was a bitter thought.

"No, Eric, I will not forget. You have all been too kind to me for that. And you won't be sorry you danced this one night, will you?"

"I never be sorry. I have not been so happy before. I not be so happy again, ever. You will be happy many nights yet, I only this one. I will dream sometimes, maybe."

The mighty resignation of his tone alarmed and touched her. It was as when some great animal composes itself for death, as when a great ship goes down at sea.

She sighed, but did not answer him. He drew a little closer and looked into her eyes.

"You are not always happy, too?" he asked.

"No, not always, Eric; not very often, I think."

"You have a trouble?"

"Yes, but I cannot put it into words. Perhaps if I could do that, I could cure it."

He clasped his hands together over his heart, as

children do when they pray, and said falteringly, "If I own all the world, I give him you."

Margaret felt a sudden moisture in her eyes, and laid her hand on his.

"Thank you, Eric; I believe you would. But perhaps even then I should not be happy. Perhaps I have too much of it already."

She did not take her hand away from him; she did not dare. She sat still and waited for the traditions in which she had always believed to speak and save her. But they were dumb. She belonged to an ultra-refined civilization which tries to cheat nature with elegant sophistries. Cheat nature? Bah! One generation may do it, perhaps two, but the third— Can we ever rise above nature or sink below her? Did she not turn on Jerusalem as upon Sodom, upon St. Anthony in his desert as upon Nero in his seraglio? Does she not always cry in brutal triumph: "I am here still, at the bottom of things, warming the roots of life; you cannot starve me nor tame me nor thwart me; I made the world, I rule it, and I am its destiny."

This woman, on a windmill tower at the world's end with a giant barbarian, heard that cry tonight, and she was afraid! Ah! the terror and the delight of that moment when first we fear ourselves! Until then we have not lived.

"Come, Eric, let us go down; the moon is up and the music has begun again," she said.

He rose silently and stepped down upon the ladder, putting his arm about her to help her. That arm could have thrown Thor's hammer out in the cornfields yonder, yet it scarcely touched her, and his hand trembled as it had done in the dance. His face was level with hers now and the moonlight fell sharply upon it. All her life she had searched the faces of men for the look that lay in his eyes. She knew that that look had never shone for her before, would never shine for her on earth again, that such love comes to one only in dreams or in impossible places like this, unattainable always. This was Love's self, in a moment it would die. Stung by the agonized appeal that emanated from the man's whole being, she leaned forward and laid her lips on his. Once, twice and again she heard the deep respirations rattle in his throat while she held them there, and the riotous force under her head became an engulfing weakness. He drew her up to him until he felt all the resistance go out of her body, until every nerve relaxed and yielded. When she drew her face back from his, it was white with fear.

"Let us go down, oh, my God! let us go down!" she muttered. And the drunken stars up yonder seemed reeling to some appointed doom as she clung to the rounds of the ladder. All that she was to know of love she had left upon his lips.

"The devil is loose again," whispered Olaf Oleson, as he saw Eric dancing a moment later, his eyes blazing.

But Eric was thinking with an almost savage exultation of the time when he should pay for this. Ah, there would be no quailing then! If ever a soul went fearlessly, proudly down to the gates infernal, his should go. For a moment he fancied he was there already, treading down the tempest of flame, hugging the fiery hurricane to his breast. He wondered whether in ages gone, all the countless years of sinning in which men had sold and lost and flung their souls away, any man had ever so cheated Satan, had ever bartered his soul for so great a price.

It seemed but a little while till dawn.

The carriage was brought to the door and Wyllis Elliot and his sister said goodbye. She could not meet Eric's eyes as she gave him her hand, but as he stood by the horse's head, just as the carriage moved off, she gave him one swift glance that said, "I will not forget." In a moment the carriage was gone.

Eric changed his coat and plunged his head into the water tank and went to the barn to hook up his team. As he led his horses to the door, a shadow fell across his path, and he saw Skinner rising in his stirrups. His rugged face was pale and worn with looking after his wayward flock, with dragging men into the way of salvation.

"Good morning, Eric. There was a dance here last night?" he asked, sternly.

"A dance? Oh, yes, a dance," replied Eric, cheerfully.

"Certainly you did not dance, Eric?"

"Yes, I danced. I danced all the time."

The minister's shoulders drooped, and an expression

of profound discouragement settled over his haggard face. There was almost anguish in the yearning he felt for this soul.

"Eric, I didn't look for this from you. I thought God had set his mark on you if he ever had on any man. And it is for things like this that you set your soul back a thousand years from God. O foolish and perverse generation!"

Eric drew himself up to his full height and looked off to where the new day was gilding the corn-tassels and flooding the uplands with light. As his nostrils drew in the breath of the dew and the morning, something from the only poetry he had ever read flashed across his mind, and he murmured, half to himself, with dreamy exultation:

"'And a day shall be as a thousand years, and a thousand years as a day.'"

The Enchanted Bluff

We had our swim before sundown, and while we were cooking our supper the oblique rays of light made a dazzling glare on the white sand about us. The translucent red ball itself sank behind the brown stretches of cornfield as we sat down to eat, and the warm layer of air that had rested over the water and our clean sand bar grew fresher and smelled of the rank ironweed and sunflowers growing on the flatter shore. The river was brown and sluggish, like any other of the half-dozen streams that water the Nebraska corn lands. On one shore was an irregular line of bald clay bluffs where a few scrub oaks with thick trunks and flat, twisted tops threw light shadows on the long grass. The westen shore was low and level, with cornfields that stretched to the skyline, and all along the water's edge were little sandy coves and beaches where slim cottonwoods and willow saplings flickered.

The turbulence of the river in springtime discouraged milling, and, beyond keeping the old red bridge in repair, the busy farmers did not concern themselves with the stream; so the Sandtown boys were left in undisputed possession. In the autumn we hunted quail through the miles of stubble and fodder land along the flat shore, and, after the winter skating season was over and the ice had gone out, the spring freshets and flooded bottoms gave us our great excitement of the year. The channel was never the same for two successive seasons. Every spring the swollen stream undermined a bluff to the east, or bit out a few acres of cornfield to the west and whirled the soil away to deposit it in spumy mud banks somewhere else. When the water fell low in midsummer, new sand bars were thus exposed to dry and whiten in the August sun. Sometimes these were banked so firmly that the fury of the next freshet failed to unseat them; the little willow seedlings emerged triumphantly from the yellow froth, broke into spring leaf, shot up into summer growth, and with their mesh of roots bound together the moist sand beneath them against the batterings of another April. Here and there a cottonwood soon glittered among them, quivering in the low current of air that, even on breathless days when the dust hung like smoke above the wagon road, trembled along the face of the water.

It was on such an island, in the third summer of its yellow green, that we built our watch fire; not in the thicket of dancing willow wands, but on the level terrace of fine sand which had been added that spring; a little new bit of world, beautifully ridged with ripple marks, and strewn with the tiny skeletons of turtles and fish, all as white and dry as if they had been expertly cured. We had been careful not to mar the freshness of the place, although we often swam to it on summer evenings and lay on the sand to rest.

This was our last watch fire of the year, and there were reasons why I should remember it better than any of the others. Next week the other boys were to file back to their old places in the Sandtown High School, but I was to go up to the Divide to teach my first country school in the Norwegian district. I was already homesick at the thought of quitting the boys with whom I had always played; of leaving the river, and going up into a windy plain that was all windmills and cornfields and big pastures; where there was nothing wilful or unmanageable in the landscape, no new islands, and no chance of unfamiliar birds—such as often followed the watercourses.

Other boys came and went and used the river for fishing or skating, but we six were sworn to the spirit of the stream, and we were friends mainly because of the river. There were the two Hassler boys, Fritz and Otto, sons of the little German tailor. They were the youngest of us; ragged boys of ten and twelve, with sunburned hair, weather-stained faces, and pale blue eyes. Otto, the elder, was the best mathematician in school, and clever at his books, but he always dropped out in the spring term as if the river could not get on without him. He and Fritz caught the fat, horned catfish and sold them about the town, and they lived so much in the water that they were as brown and sandy as the river itself.

There was Percy Pound, a fat, freckled boy with chubby cheeks, who took half a dozen boys' story-papers and was always being kept in for reading detective stories behind his desk. There was Tip Smith, destined by his freckles and red hair to be the buffoon in all our games, though he walked like a timid little old man and had a funny, cracked laugh. Tip worked hard in his father's grocery store every afternoon, and swept it out before school in the morning. Even his recreations were laborious. He collected cigarette cards and tin tobacco-tags indefatigably, and would sit for hours humped up over a snarling little scroll-saw which he kept in his attic. His dearest possessions were some little pill bottles that purported to contain grains of wheat from the Holy Land, water from the Jordan and the Dead Sea, and earth from the Mount of Olives. His father had bought these dull things from a Baptist missionary who peddled them, and Tip seemed to derive great satisfaction from their remote origin.

The tall boy was Arthur Adams. He had fine hazel eyes that were almost too reflective and sympathetic for a boy, and such a pleasant voice that we all loved to hear him read aloud. Even when he had to read poetry aloud at school, no one ever thought of laughing. To be sure, he was not at school very much of the time. He was seventeen and should have finished the High School the year before, but he was always off somewhere with his gun. Arthur's mother was dead, and his father, who was feverishly absorbed in promoting schemes, wanted to send the boy away to school and get him off his hands; but Arthur always begged off for another year and promised to study. I remember him as a tall, brown boy with an intelligent face, always lounging among a lot of us little fellows, laughing at us oftener than with us, but such a soft, satisfied laugh that we felt rather flattered when we provoked it. In after-years people said that Arthur had been given to evil ways as a lad, and it is true that we often saw him with the gambler's sons and with old Spanish Fanny's boy, but if he learned anything ugly in their company he never betrayed it to us. We would have followed Arthur anywhere, and I am bound to say that he led us into no worse places than the cattail marshes and the stubble fields. These, then, were the boys who camped with me that summer night upon the sand bar.

After we finished our supper we beat the willow thicket for driftwood. By the time we had collected enough, night had fallen, and the pungent, weedy smell from the shore increased with the coolness. We threw ourselves down about the fire and made another futile effort to show Percy Pound the Little Dipper. We had tried it often before, but he could never be got past the big one.

"You see those three big stars just below the handle, with the bright one in the middle?" said Otto Hassler; "that's Orion's belt, and the bright one is the clasp." I crawled behind Otto's shoulder and sighted up his arm to the star that seemed perched upon the tip of his steady forefinger. The Hassler boys did seine-fishing at night, and they knew a good many stars.

Percy gave up the Little Dipper and lay back on the sand, his hands clasped under his head. "I can see the North Star," he announced, contentedly, pointing toward it with his big toe. "Anyone might get lost and need to know that."

We all looked up at it.

"How do you suppose Columbus felt when his compass didn't point north any more?" Tip asked.

Otto shook his head. "My father says that there was another North Star once, and that maybe this one won't last always. I wonder what would happen to us down here if anything went wrong with it?"

Arthur chuckled. "I wouldn't worry, Ott. Nothing's apt to happen to it in your time. Look at the Milky Way! There must be lots of good dead Indians."

We lay back and looked, meditating, at the dark cover of the world. The gurgle of the water had become heavier. We had often noticed a mutinous, complaining note in it at night, quite different from its cheerful daytime chuckle, and seeming like the voice of a much deeper and more powerful stream. Our water had always these two moods: the one of sunny complaisance, the other of inconsolable, passionate regret.

"Queer how the stars are all in sort of diagrams," remarked Otto. "You could do most any proposition in geometry with 'em. They always look as if they meant something. Some folks say everybody's fortune is all written out in the stars, don't they?"

"They believe so in the old country," Fritz affirmed.

But Arthur only laughed at him. "You're thinking of Napoleon, Fritzey. He had a star that went out when he began to lose battles. I guess the stars don't keep any close tally on Sandtown folks."

We were speculating on how many times we could count a hundred before the evening star went down behind the cornfields, when someone cried, "There comes the moon, and it's as big as a cart wheel!"

We all jumped up to greet it as it swam over the bluffs behind us. It came up like a galleon in full sail; an enormous, barbaric thing, red as an angry heathen god.

"When the moon came up red like that, the Aztecs used to sacrifice their prisoners on the temple top," Percy announced.

"Go on, Perce. You got that out of *Golden Days.* Do you believe that, Arthur?" I appealed.

Arthur answered, quite seriously: "Like as not. The moon was one of their gods. When my father was in Mexico City he saw the stone where they used to sacrifice their prisoners."

As we dropped down by the fire again some one asked whether the Mound-Builders were older than the Aztecs. When we once got upon the Mound-Builders we never willingly got away from them, and we were still conjecturing when we heard a loud splash in the water.

"Must have been a big cat jumping," said Fritz. "They do sometimes. They must see bugs in the dark. Look what a track the moon makes!"

There was a long, silvery streak on the water, and where the current fretted over a big log it boiled up like gold pieces.

"Suppose there ever *was* any gold hid away in this old river?" Fritz asked. He lay like a little brown Indian, close to the fire, his chin on his hand and his bare feet in the air. His brother laughed at him, but Arthur took his suggestion seriously.

"Some of the Spaniards thought there was gold up here somewhere. Seven cities chuck full of gold, they had it, and Coronado and his men came up to hunt it. The Spaniards were all over this country once."

Percy looked interested. "Was that before the Mormons went through?"

We all laughed at this.

"Long enough before. Before the Pilgrim Fathers, Perce. Maybe they came along this very river. They always followed the watercourses."

"I wonder where this river really does begin?" Tip mused. That was an old and a favorite mystery which the map did not clearly explain. On the map the little black line stopped somewhere in western Kansas; but since rivers generally rose in mountains, it was only reasonable to suppose that ours came from the Rockies. Its destination, we knew, was the Missouri, and the Hassler boys always maintained that we could embark at Sandtown in floodtime, follow our noses, and eventually arrive at New Orleans. Now they took up their old argument. "If us boys had grit enough to try it, it wouldn't take no time to get to Kansas City and St. Joe."

We began to talk about the places we wanted to go to. The Hassler boys wanted to see the stockyards in Kansas City, and Percy wanted to see a big store in Chicago. Arthur was interlocutor and did not betray himself.

"Now it's your turn, Tip."

Tip rolled over on his elbow and poked the fire, and

his eyes looked shyly out of his queer, tight little face. "My place is awful far away. My Uncle Bill told me about it."

Tip's Uncle Bill was a wanderer, bitten with mining fever, who had drifted into Sandtown with a broken arm, and when it was well had drifted out again.

"Where is it?"

"Aw, it's down in New Mexico somewheres. There aren't no railroads or anything. You have to go on mules, and you run out of water before you get there and have to drink canned tomatoes."

"Well, go on, kid. What's it like when you do get there?"

Tip sat up and excitedly began his story.

"There's a big red rock there that goes right up out of the sand for about nine hundred feet. The country's flat all around it, and this here rock goes up all by itself, like a monument. They call it the Enchanted Bluff down there, because no white man has ever been on top of it. The sides are smooth rock, and straight up, like a wall. The Indians say that hundreds of years ago, before the Spaniards came, there was a village away up there in the air. The tribe that lived there had some sort of steps, made out of wood and bark, hung down over the face of the bluff, and the braves went down to hunt and carried water up in big jars swung on their backs. They kept a big supply of water and dried meat up there, and never went down except to hunt. They were a peaceful tribe that made cloth and pottery, and they went up there to get out of the wars. You see, they could pick off any war party that tried to get up their little steps. The Indians say they were a handsome people, and they had some sort of queer religion. Uncle Bill thinks they were Cliff-Dwellers who had got into trouble and left home. They weren't fighters, anyhow.

"One time the braves were down hunting and an awful storm came up—a kind of waterspout—and when they got back to their rock they found their little staircase had been all broken to pieces, and only a few steps were left hanging away up in the air. While they were camped at the foot of the rock, wondering what to do, a war party from the north came along and massacred 'em to a man, with all the old folks and women looking on from the rock. Then the war party went on south and left the village to get down the best way they could. Of course they never got down. They starved to death up there, and when the war party came back on their way north, they could hear the children crying from the edge of the bluff where they had crawled out, but they didn't see a sign of a grown Indian, and nobody has ever been up there since."

We exclaimed at this dolorous legend and sat up.

"There couldn't have been many people up there," Percy demurred. "How big is the top, Tip?"

"Oh, pretty big. Big enough so that the rock doesn't look nearly as tall as it is. The top's bigger than the base. The bluff is sort of worn away for several hundred feet up. That's one reason it's so hard to climb."

I asked how the Indians got up, in the first place.

"Nobody knows how they got up or when. A hunting party came along once and saw that there was a town up there, and that was all."

Otto rubbed his chin and looked thoughtful. "Of course there must be some way to get up there. Couldn't people get a rope over someway and pull a ladder up?"

Tip's little eyes were shining with excitement. "I know a way. Me and Uncle Bill talked it over. There's a kind of rocket that would take a rope over—lifesavers use 'em—and then you could hoist a rope ladder and peg it down at the bottom and make it tight with guy ropes on the other side. I'm going to climb that there bluff, and I've got it all planned out."

Fritz asked what he expected to find when he got up there.

"Bones, maybe, or the ruins of their town, or pottery, or some of their idols. There might be 'most anything up there. Anyhow, I want to see."

"Sure nobody else has been up there, Tip?" Arthur asked.

"Dead sure. Hardly anybody ever goes down there. Some hunters tried to cut steps in the rock once, but they didn't get higher than a man can reach. The Bluff's all red granite, and Uncle Bill thinks it's a boulder the glaciers left. It's a queer place, anyhow. Nothing but cactus and desert for hundreds of miles, and yet right under the Bluff there's good water and plenty of grass. That's why the bison used to go down there."

Suddenly we heard a scream above our fire, and jumped up to see a dark, slim bird floating southward far above us—a whooping crane, we knew by her cry and her long neck. We ran to the edge of the island, hoping we might see her alight, but she wavered southward along the rivercourse until we lost her. The Hassler boys declared that by the look of the heavens it must be after midnight, so we threw more wood on our fire, put on our jackets, and curled down in the warm sand. Several of us pretended to doze, but I fancy we were really thinking about Tip's Bluff and the extinct people. Over in the wood the ring doves were calling mournfully to one another, and once we heard a dog bark, far away. "Somebody getting into old Tommy's melon patch," Fritz murmured sleepily, but nobody answered him. By and by Percy spoke out of the shadows.

"Say, Tip, when you go down there will you take me with you?"

"Maybe."

"Suppose one of us beats you down there, Tip?"

"Whoever gets to the Bluff first has got to promise to tell the rest of us exactly what he finds," remarked one of the Hassler boys, and to this we all readily assented.

Somewhat reassured, I dropped off to sleep. I must have dreamed about a race for the Bluff, for I awoke in a kind of fear that other people were getting ahead of me and that I was losing my chance. I sat up in my damp clothes and looked at the other boys, who lay tumbled in uneasy attitudes about the dead fire. It was still dark, but the sky was blue with the last wonderful azure of night. The stars glistened like crystal globes, and trembled as if they shone through a depth of clear water. Even as I watched, they began to pale and the sky brightened. Day came suddenly, almost instantaneously. I turned for another look at the blue night, and it was gone. Everywhere the birds began to call, and all manner of little insects began to chirp and hop about in the willows. A breeze sprang up from the west and brought the heavy smell of ripened corn. The boys rolled over and shook themselves. We stripped and plunged into the river just as the sun came up over the windy bluffs.

When I came home to Sandtown at Christmas time, we skated out to our island and talked over the whole project of the Enchanted Bluff, renewing our resolution to find it.

Although that was twenty years ago, none of us have ever climbed the Enchanted Bluff. Percy Pound is a stockbroker in Kansas City and will go nowhere that his red touring car cannot carry him. Otto Hassler went on the railroad and lost his foot braking; after which he and Fritz succeeded their father as the town tailors.

Arthur sat about the sleepy little town all his life—he died before he was twenty-five. The last time I saw him, when I was home on one of my college vacations, he was sitting in a steamer chair under a cottonwood tree in the little yard behind one of the two Sandtown saloons. He was very untidy and his hand was not steady, but when he rose, unabashed, to greet me, his eyes were as clear and warm as ever. When I had talked with him for an hour and heard him laugh again, I wondered how it was that when Nature had taken such pains with a man, from his hands to the arch of his long foot, she had ever lost him in Sandtown. He joked about Tip Smith's Bluff, and declared he was going down there just as soon as the weather got cooler; he thought the Grand Canyon might be worth while, too.

I was perfectly sure when I left him that he would never get beyond the high plank fence and the comfortable shade of the cottonwood. And, indeed, it was under that very tree that he died one summer morning.

Tip Smith still talks about going to New Mexico. He married a slatternly, unthrifty country girl, has been much tied to a perambulator, and has grown stooped and grey from irregular meals and broken sleep. But the worst of his difficulties are now over, and he has, as he says, come into easy water. When I was last in Sandtown I walked home with him late one moonlight night, after he had balanced his cash and shut up his store. We took the long way around and sat down on the schoolhouse steps, and between us we quite revived the romance of the lone red rock and the extinct people. Tip insists that he still means to go down there, but he thinks now he will wait until his boy Bert is old enough to go with him. Bert has been let into the story, and thinks of nothing but the Enchanted Bluff.

The Bohemian Girl

The transcontinental express swung along the wind-
ings of the Sand River Valley, and in the rear seat of the
observation car a young man sat greatly at his ease, not in
the least discomfited by the fierce sunlight which beat in
upon his brown face and neck and strong back. There was
a look of relaxation and of great passivity about his broad
shoulders, which seemed almost too heavy until he stood
up and squared them. He wore a pale flannel shirt and a
blue silk necktie with loose ends. His trousers were wide
and belted at the waist, and his short sack coat hung open.
His heavy shoes had seen good service. His reddish-brown
hair, like his clothes, had a foreign cut. He had deep-set,
dark blue eyes under heavy reddish eyebrows. His face
was kept clean only by close shaving, and even the sharp-
est razor left a glint of yellow in the smooth brown of his
skin. His teeth and the palms of his hands were very
white. His head, which looked hard and stubborn, lay
indolently in the green cushion of the wicker chair, and as
he looked out at the ripe summer country a teasing, not
unkindly smile played over his lips. Once, as he basked
thus comfortably, a quick light flashed in his eyes, curiously dilating the pupils, and his mouth became a hard,
straight line, gradually relaxing into its former smile of
rather kindly mockery. He told himself, apparently, that
there was no point in getting excited; and he seemed a
master hand at taking his ease when he could. Neither the
sharp whistle of the locomotive nor the brakeman's call
disturbed him. It was not until after the train had stopped
that he rose, put on a Panama hat, took from the rack a
small valise and a flute case, and stepped deliberately to
the station platform. The baggage was already unloaded,

51

and the stranger presented a check for a battered sole-leather steamer trunk.

"Can you keep it here for a day or two?" he asked the agent. "I may send for it, and I may not."

"Depends on whether you like the country, I suppose?" demanded the agent in a challenging tone.

"Just so."

The agent shrugged his shoulders, looked scornfully at the small trunk, which was marked "N.E.," and handed out a claim check without further comment. The stranger watched him as he caught one end of the trunk and dragged it into the express room. The agent's manner seemed to remind him of something amusing. "Doesn't seem to be a very big place," he remarked, looking about.

"It's big enough for us," snapped the agent, as he banged the trunk into a corner.

That remark, apparently, was what Nils Ericson had wanted. He chuckled quietly as he took a leather strap from his pocket and swung his valise around his shoulder. Then he settled his Panama securely on his head, turned up his trousers, tucked the flute case under his arm, and started off across the fields. He gave the town, as he would have said, a wide berth, and cut through a great fenced pasture, emerging, when he rolled under the barbed wire at the farther corner, upon a white dusty road which ran straight up from the river valley to the high prairies, where the ripe wheat stood yellow and the tin roofs and weathercocks were twinkling in the fierce sunlight. By the time Nils had done three miles, the sun was sinking and the farm wagons on their way home from town came rattling by, covering him with dust and making him sneeze. When one of the farmers pulled up and offered to give him a lift, he clambered in willingly. The driver was a thin, grizzled old man with a long lean neck and a foolish sort of beard, like a goat's. "How fur ye goin'?" he asked, as he clucked to his horses and started off.

"Do you go by the Ericson place?"

"Which Ericson?" The old man drew in his reins as if he expected to stop again.

"Preacher Ericson's."

"Oh, the Old Lady Ericson's!" He turned and looked at Nils. "La, me! If you're goin' out there you might 'a' rid out in the automobile. That's a pity, now. The Old Lady Ericson was in town with her auto. You might 'a' heard it snortin' anywhere about the post-office er the butcher shop."

"Has she a motor?" asked the stranger absently.

" 'Deed an' she has! She runs into town every night about this time for her mail and meat for supper. Some folks say she's afraid her auto won't get exercise enough, but I say that's jealousy."

"Aren't there any other motors about here?"

"Oh, yes! we have fourteen in all. But nobody else gets around like the Old Lady Ericson. She's out, rain er shine, over the whole county, chargin' into town and out amongst her farms, an' up to her sons' places. Sure you ain't goin' to the wrong place?" He craned his neck and looked at Nils' flute case with eager curiosity. "The old woman ain't got any piany that I knows on. Olaf, he has a grand. His wife's musical; took lessons in Chicago."

"I'm going up there tomorrow," said Nils imperturbably. He saw that the driver took him for a piano tuner.

"Oh, I see!" The old man screwed up his eyes mysteriously. He was a little dashed by the stranger's non-communicativeness, but he soon broke out again.

"I'm one o' Miss Ericson's tenants. Look after one of her places. I did own the place myself once, but I lost it a while back, in the bad years just after the World's Fair. Just as well, too, I say. Lets you out o' payin' taxes. The Ericsons do own most of the county now. I remember the old preacher's fav'rite text used to be, 'To them that hath shall be given.' They've spread something wonderful—run over this here country like bindweed. But I ain't one that begretches it to 'em. Folks is entitled to what they kin git; and they're hustlers. Olaf, he's in the Legislature now, and a likely man fur Congress. Listen, if that ain't the old woman comin' now. Want I should stop her?"

Nils shook his head. He heard the deep chug-chug of a motor vibrating steadily in the clear twilight behind them. The pale lights of the car swam over the hill, and the old man slapped his reins and turned clear out of the road, ducking his head at the first of three angry snorts from behind. The motor was running at a hot, even speed, and passed without turning an inch from its course. The driver was a stalwart woman who sat at ease in the front seat and drove her car bareheaded. She left a cloud of dust and a trail of gasoline behind her. Her tenant threw back his head and sneezed.

"Whew! I sometimes say I'd as lief be *before* Mrs. Ericson as behind her. She does beat all! Nearly seventy, and never lets another soul touch that car. Puts it into commission herself every morning, and keeps it tuned up by the hitch-bar all day. I never stop work for a drink o' water that I don't hear her a-churnin' up the road. I reckon her darter-in-laws never sets down easy nowadays. Never know when she'll pop in. Mis' Otto, she says to me: 'We're so afraid that thing'll blow up and do Ma some injury yet, she's so turrible venturesome.' Says I: 'I wouldn't stew, Mis' Otto; the old lady'll drive that car to the funeral of every darter-in-law she's got.' That was after the old woman had jumped a turrible bad culvert."

The stranger heard vaguely what the old man was saying. Just now he was experiencing something very much like homesickness, and he was wondering what had brought it about. The mention of a name or two, perhaps; the rattle of a wagon along a dusty road; the rank, resinous smell of sunflowers and ironweed, which the night damp brought up from the draws and low places; perhaps, more than all, the dancing lights of the motor that had plunged by. He squared his shoulders with a comfortable sense of strength.

The wagon, as it jolted westward, climbed a pretty steady up-grade. The country, receding from the rough river valley, swelled more and more gently, as if it had been smoothed out by the wind. On one of the last of the rugged ridges, at the end of a branch road, stood a grim square house with a tin roof and double porches. Behind the house stretched a row of broken, wind-racked poplars, and down the hill slope to the left straggled the sheds and stables. The old man stopped his horses where the Ericsons' road branched across a dry sand creek that wound about the foot of the hill.

"That's the old lady's place. Want I should drive in?"
"No, thank you. I'll roll out here. Much obliged to you. Good night."

His passenger stepped down over the front wheel, and the old man drove on reluctantly, looking back as if he would like to see how the stranger would be received.

As Nils was crossing the dry creek he heard the restive tramp of a horse coming toward him down the hill. Instantly he flashed out of the road and stood behind a thicket of wild plum bushes that grew in the sandy bed. Peering through the dusk, he saw a light horse, under tight rein, descending the hill at a sharp walk. The rider was a slender woman—barely visible against the dark hillside—wearing an old-fashioned derby hat and a long riding skirt. She sat lightly in the saddle, with her chin high, and seemed to be looking into the distance. As she passed the plum thicket her horse snuffed the air and shied. She struck him, pulling him in sharply, with an angry exclamation, "*Blázne!*" in Bohemian. Once in the main road, she let him out into a lope, and they soon emerged upon the crest of high land, where they moved along the skyline, silhouetted against the band of faint colour that lingered in the west. This horse and rider, with their free, rhythmical gallop, were the only moving things to be seen on the face of the flat country. They seemed, in the last sad light of evening, not to be there accidentally, but as an inevitable detail of the landscape.

Nils watched them until they had shrunk to a mere moving speck against the sky, then he crossed the sand creek and climbed the hill. When he reached the gate the front of the house was dark, but a light was shining from the side windows. The pigs were squealing in the hog corral, and Nils could see a tall boy, who carried two big wooden buckets, moving about among them. Halfway between the barn and the house, the windmill wheezed lazily. Following the path that ran around to the back porch, Nils stopped to look through the screen door into the lamplit kitchen. The kitchen was the largest room in the house; Nils remembered that his older brothers used to give dances there when he was a boy. Beside the stove stood a little girl with two light yellow braids and a broad,

flushed face, peering anxiously into a frying pan. In the
dining-room beyond, a large, broad-shouldered woman
was moving about the table. She walked with an active,
springy step. Her face was heavy and florid, almost without wrinkles, and her hair was black at seventy. Nils felt
proud of her as he watched her deliberate activity; never a
momentary hesitation, or a movement that did not tell.
He waited until she came out into the kitchen and, brushing the child aside, took her place at the stove. Then he
tapped on the screen door and entered.

"It's nobody but Nils, Mother. I expect you weren't
looking for me."

Mrs. Ericson turned away from the stove and stood
staring at him. "Bring the lamp, Hilda, and let me look."

Nils laughed and unslung his valise. "What's the matter, Mother? Don't you know me?"

Mrs. Ericson put down the lamp. "You must be Nils.
You don't look very different, anyway."

"Nor you, Mother. You hold your own. Don't you
wear glasses yet?"

"Only to read by. Where's your trunk, Nils?"

"Oh, I left that in town. I thought it might not be
convenient for you to have company so near threshing-time."

"Don't be foolish, Nils." Mrs. Ericson turned back to
the stove. "I don't thresh now. I hitched the wheat land
onto the next farm and have a tenant. Hilda, take some
hot water up to the company room, and go call little Eric."

The tow-haired child, who had been standing in mute
amazement, took up the tea-kettle and withdrew, giving
Nils a long, admiring look from the door of the kitchen
stairs.

"Who's the youngster?" Nils asked, dropping down
on the bench behind the kitchen stove.

"One of your Cousin Henrik's."

"How long has Cousin Henrik been dead?"

"Six years. There are two boys. One stays with Peter
and one with Anders. Olaf is their guardeen."

There was a clatter of pails on the porch, and a tall,
lanky boy peered wonderingly in through the screen door.
He had a fair, gentle face and big grey eyes, and wisps of
soft yellow hair hung down under his cap. Nils sprang up

and pulled him into the kitchen, hugging him and slapping him on the shoulders. "Well, if it isn't my kid! Look at the size of him! Don't you know me, Eric?"

The boy reddened under his sunburn and freckles, and hung his head. "I guess it's Nils," he said shyly.

"You're a good guesser," laughed Nils giving the lad's hand a swing. To himself he was thinking: "That's why the little girl looked so friendly. He's taught her to like me. He was only six when I went away, and he's remembered for twelve years."

Eric stood fumbling with his cap and smiling. "You look just like I thought you would," he ventured.

"Go wash your hands, Eric," called Mrs. Ericson. "I've got cob corn for supper, Nils. You used to like it. I guess you don't get much of that in the old country. Here's Hilda; she'll take you up to your room. You'll want to get the dust off you before you eat."

Mrs. Ericson went into the dining-room to lay another plate, and the little girl came up and nodded to Nils as if to let him know that his room was ready. He put out his hand and she took it, with a startled glance up at his face. Little Eric dropped his towel, threw an arm about Nils and one about Hilda, gave them a clumsy squeeze, and then stumbled out to the porch.

During supper Nils heard exactly how much land each of his eight grown brothers farmed, how their crops were coming on, and how much livestock they were feeding. His mother watched him narrowly as she talked. "You've got better looking, Nils," she remarked abruptly, whereupon he grinned and the children giggled. Eric, although he was eighteen and as tall as Nils, was always accounted a child, being the last of so many sons. His face seemed childlike, too, Nils thought, and he had the open, wandering eyes of a little boy. All the others had been men at his age.

After supper Nils went out to the front porch and sat down on the step to smoke a pipe. Mrs. Ericson drew a rocking-chair up near him and began to knit busily. It was one of the few Old World customs she had kept up, for she could not bear to sit with idle hands.

"Where's little Eric, Mother?"

"He's helping Hilda with the dishes. He does it of his own will; I don't like a boy to be too handy about the house."

"He seems like a nice kid."

"He's very obedient."

Nils smiled a little in the dark. It was just as well to shift the line of conversation. "What are you knitting there, Mother?"

"Baby stockings. The boys keep me busy." Mrs. Ericson chuckled and clicked her needles.

"How many grandchildren have you?"

"Only thirty-one now. Olaf lost his three. They were sickly, like their mother."

"I supposed he had a second crop by this time!"

"His second wife has no children. She's too proud. She tears about on horseback all the time. But she'll get caught up with, yet. She sets herself very high, though nobody knows what for. They were low enough Bohemians she came of. I never thought much of Bohemians; always drinking."

Nils puffed away at his pipe in silence, and Mrs. Ericson knitted on. In a few moments she added grimly: "She was down here tonight, just before you came. She'd like to quarrel with me and come between me and Olaf, but I don't give her the chance. I suppose you'll be bringing a wife home some day."

"I don't know. I've never thought much about it."

"Well, perhaps it's best as it is," suggested Mrs. Ericson hopefully. "You'd never be contented tied down to the land. There was roving blood in your father's family, and it's come out in you. I expect your own way of life suits you best." Mrs. Ericson had dropped into a blandly agreeable tone which Nils well remembered. It seemed to amuse him a good deal and his white teeth flashed behind his pipe. His mother's strategies had always diverted him, even when he was a boy—they were so flimsy and patent, so illy proportioned to her vigor and force. "They've been waiting to see which way I'd jump," he reflected. He felt that Mrs. Ericson was pondering his case deeply as she sat clicking her needles.

"I don't suppose you've ever got used to steady work,"

she went on presently. "Men ain't apt to if they roam around too long. It's a pity you didn't come back the year after the World's Fair. Your father picked up a good bit of land cheap then, in the hard times, and I expect maybe he'd have give you a farm. It's too bad you put off comin' back so long, for I always thought he meant to do something by you."

Nils laughed and shook the ashes out of his pipe. "I'd have missed a lot if I had come back then. But I'm sorry I didn't get back to see father."

"Well, I suppose we have to miss things at one end or the other. Perhaps you are as well satisfied with your own doings, now, as you'd have been with a farm," said Mrs. Ericson reassuringly.

"Land's a good thing to have," Nils commented, as he lit another match and sheltered it with his hand.

His mother looked sharply at his face until the match burned out. "Only when you stay on it!" she hastened to say.

Eric came round the house by the path just then, and Nils rose, with a yawn. "Mother, if you don't mind, Eric and I will take a little tramp before bedtime. It will make me sleep."

"Very well; only don't stay long. I'll sit up and wait for you. I like to lock up myself."

Nils put his hand on Eric's shoulder, and the two tramped down the hill and across the sand creek into the dusty highroad beyond. Neither spoke. They swung along at an even gait, Nils puffing at his pipe. There was no moon, and the white road and the wide fields lay faint in the starlight. Over everything was darkness and thick silence, and the smell of dust and sunflowers. The brothers followed the road for a mile or more without finding a place to sit down. Finally, Nils perched on a stile over the wire fence, and Eric sat on the lower step.

"I began to think you never would come back, Nils," said the boy softly.

"Didn't I promise you I would?"

"Yes; but people don't bother about promises they make to babies. Did you really know you were going away for good when you went to Chicago with the cattle that time?"

"I thought it very likely, if I could make my way."

"I don't see how you did it, Nils. Not many fellows could." Eric rubbed his shoulder against his brother's knee.

"The hard thing was leaving home—you and father. It was easy enough, once I got beyond Chicago. Of course I got awful homesick; used to cry myself to sleep. But I'd burned my bridges."

"You had always wanted to go, hadn't you?"

"Always. Do you still sleep in our little room? Is that cottonwood still by the window?"

Eric nodded eagerly and smiled up at his brother in the grey darkness.

"You remember how we always said the leaves were whispering when they rustled at night? Well, they always whispered to me about the sea. Sometimes they said names out of the geography books. In a high wind they had a desperate sound, like someone trying to tear loose."

"How funny, Nils," said Eric dreamily, resting his chin on his hand. "That tree still talks like that, and 'most always it talks to me about you."

They sat a while longer, watching the stars. At last Eric whispered anxiously: "Hadn't we better go back now? Mother will get tired waiting for us." They rose and took a short cut home, through the pasture.

II

The next morning Nils woke with the first flood of light that came with dawn. The white-plastered walls of his room reflected the glare that shone through the thin window shades, and he found it impossible to sleep. He dressed hurriedly and slipped down the hall and up the back stairs to the half-story room which he used to share with his little brother. Eric, in a skimpy nightshirt, was sitting on the edge of the bed, rubbing his eyes, his pale yellow hair standing up in tufts all over his head. When he saw Nils, he murmured something confusedly and hustled his long legs into his trousers. "I didn't expect you'd be up so early, Nils," he said, as his head emerged from his blue shirt.

"Oh, you thought I was a dude, did you?" Nils gave him a playful tap which bent the tall boy up like a clasp knife. "See here; I must teach you to box." Nils thrust his hands into his pockets and walked about. "You haven't changed things much up here. Got most of my old traps, haven't you?"

He took down a bent, withered piece of sapling that hung over the dresser. "If this isn't the stick Lou Sandberg killed himself with!"

The boy looked up from his shoe-lacing.

"Yes; you never used to let me play with that. Just how did he do it, Nils? You were with father when he found Lou, weren't you?"

"Yes. Father was going off to preach somewhere, and, as we drove along, Lou's place looked sort of forlorn, and we thought we'd stop and cheer him up. When we found him father said he'd been dead a couple days. He'd tied a piece of binding twine round his neck, made a noose in each end, fixed the nooses over the ends of a bent stick, and let the stick spring straight; strangled himself."

"What made him kill himself such a silly way?"

The simplicity of the boy's question set Nils laughing. He clapped little Eric on the shoulder. "What made him such a silly as to kill himself at all, I should say!"

"Oh, well! But his hogs had the cholera, and all up and died on him, didn't they?"

"Sure they did; but he didn't have cholera; and there were plenty of hogs left in the world, weren't there?"

"Well, but, if they weren't his, how could they do him any good?" Eric asked, in astonishment.

"Oh, scat! He could have had lots of fun with other people's hogs. He was a chump, Lou Sandberg. To kill yourself for a pig—think of that, now!" Nils laughed all the way downstairs, and quite embarrassed little Eric, who fell to scrubbing his face and hands at the tin basin. While he was parting his wet hair at the kitchen looking glass, a heavy tread sounded on the stairs. The boy dropped his comb. "Gracious, there's Mother. We must have talked too long." He hurried out to the shed, slipped on his overalls, and disappeared with the milking pails.

Mrs. Ericson came in, wearing a clean white apron, her black hair shining from the application of a wet brush.

"Good morning, Mother. Can't I make the fire for you?"

"No, thank you, Nils. It's no trouble to make a cob fire, and I like to manage the kitchen stove myself." Mrs. Ericson paused with a shovel full of ashes in her hand. "I expect you will be wanting to see your brothers as soon as possible. I'll take you up to Anders' place this morning. He's threshing, and most of our boys are over there."

"Will Olaf be there?"

Mrs. Ericson went on taking out the ashes, and spoke between shovels. "No; Olaf's wheat is all in, put away in his new barn. He got six thousand bushel this year. He's going to town today to get men to finish roofing his barn."

"So Olaf is building a new barn?" Nils asked absently.

"Biggest one in the county, and almost done. You'll likely be here for the barn-raising. He's going to have a supper and a dance as soon as everybody's done threshing. Says it keeps the voters in good humour. I tell him that's all nonsense; but Olaf has a head for politics."

"Does Olaf farm all Cousin Henrik's land?"

Mrs. Ericson frowned as she blew into the faint smoke curling up about the cobs. "Yes; he holds it in trust for the children, Hilda and her brothers. He keeps strict account of everything he raises on it, and puts the proceeds out at compound interest for them."

Nils smiled as he watched the little flames shoot up. The door of the back stairs opened, and Hilda emerged, her arms behind her, buttoning up her long gingham apron as she came. He nodded to her gaily, and she twinkled at him out of her little blue eyes, set far apart over her wide cheekbones.

"There, Hilda, you grind the coffee—and just put in an extra handful; I expect your Cousin Nils likes his strong," said Mrs. Ericson, as she went out to the shed.

Nils turned to look at the little girl, who gripped the coffee grinder between her knees and ground so hard that her two braids bobbed and her face flushed under its broad spattering of freckles. He noticed on her middle finger something that had not been there last night, and that had evidently been put on for company: a tiny gold ring with a clumsily set garnet stone. As her hand went round and round he touched the ring with the tip of his finger, smiling.

Hilda glanced toward the shed door through which Mrs. Ericson had disappeared. "My Cousin Clara gave me that," she whispered bashfully. "She's Cousin Olaf's wife."

III

Mrs. Olaf Ericson—Clara Vavrika, as many people still called her—was moving restlessly about her big bare house that morning. Her husband had left for the county town before his wife was out of bed—her lateness in rising was one of the many things the Ericson family had against her. Clara seldom came downstairs before eight o'clock, and this morning she was even later, for she had dressed with unusual care. She put on, however, only a tight-fitting black dress, which people thereabouts thought very plain. She was a tall, dark woman of thirty, with a rather sallow complexion and a touch of dull salmon red in her cheeks, where the blood seemed to burn under her brown skin. Her hair, parted evenly above her low forehead, was so black that there were distinctly blue lights in it. Her black eyebrows were delicate half-moons and her lashes were long and heavy. Her eyes slanted a little, as if she had a strain of Tartar or gypsy blood, and were sometimes full of fiery determination and sometimes dull and opaque. Her expression was never altogether amiable; was often, indeed, distinctly sullen, or, when she was animated, sarcastic. She was most attractive in profile, for then one saw to advantage her small, well-shaped head and delicate ears, and felt at once that here was a very positive, if not an altogether pleasing, personality.

The entire management of Mrs. Olaf's household devolved upon her aunt, Johanna Vavrika, a superstitious, doting woman of fifty. When Clara was a little girl her mother died, and Johanna's life had been spent in ungrudging service to her niece. Clara, like many self-willed and discontented persons, was really very apt, without knowing it, to do as other people told her, and to let her destiny be decided for her by intelligences much below her own. It was her Aunt Johanna who had humoured and spoiled her in her girlhood, who had got her off to Chicago to study piano, and who had finally persuaded her to marry Olaf Ericson as the best match she would be likely to make in that part of the country. Johanna Vavrika had been deeply scarred by smallpox in the old country. She was short and fat, homely and jolly and sentimental. She was so broad, and took such short steps when she walked, that her brother, Joe Vavrika, always called her his duck. She adored her niece because of her talent, because of her good looks and masterful ways, but most of all because of her selfishness.

Clara's marriage with Olaf Ericson was Johanna's particular triumph. She was inordinately proud of Olaf's position, and she found a sufficiently exciting career in managing Clara's house, in keeping it above the criticism of the Ericsons, in pampering Olaf to keep him from finding fault with his wife, and in concealing from every one Clara's domestic infelicities. While Clara slept of a morning, Johanna Vavrika was bustling about, seeing that Olaf and the men had their breakfast, and that the cleaning or the butter-making or the washing was properly begun by the two girls in the kitchen. Then, at about eight o'clock, she would take Clara's coffee up to her, and chat with her while she drank it, telling her what was going on in the house. Old Mrs. Ericson frequently said that her daughter-in-law would not know what day of the week it was if Johanna did not tell her every morning. Mrs. Ericson despised and pitied Johanna, but did not wholly dislike her. The one thing she hated in her daughter-in-law above everything else was the way in which Clara could come it over people. It enraged her that the affairs of her son's big, barnlike house went on as well as they did, and she used to feel that in this world we have to wait overlong to see the guilty punished. "Suppose Johanna Vavrika died or got sick?" the old lady used to say to Olaf. "Your wife wouldn't know where to look for her own dish-cloth." Olaf only shrugged his shoulders. The fact remained that Johanna did not die, and, although Mrs. Ericson often told her she was looking poorly, she was never ill. She seldom left the house, and she slept in a little room off the kitchen. No Ericson, by night or day, could come prying about there to find fault without her knowing it. Her one weakness was that she was an incurable talker, and she sometimes made trouble without meaning to.

This morning Clara was tying a wine-coloured ribbon about her throat when Johanna appeared with her coffee. After putting the tray on a sewing table, she began to make Clara's bed, chattering the while in Bohemian.

"Well, Olaf got off early, and the girls are baking. I'm going down presently to make some poppy-seed bread for Olaf. He asked for prune preserves at breakfast, and I told him I was out of them, and to bring some prunes and honey and cloves from town."

Clara poured her coffee. "Ugh! I don't see how men can eat so much sweet stuff. In the morning, too!"

Her aunt chuckled knowingly. "Bait a bear with honey, as we say in the old country."

"Was he cross?" her niece asked indifferently.

"Olaf? Oh, no! He was in fine spirits. He's never cross if you know how to take him. I never knew a man to make so little fuss about bills. I gave him a list of things to get a yard long, and he didn't say a word; just folded it up and put it in his pocket."

"I can well believe he didn't say a word," Clara remarked with a shrug. "Some day he'll forget how to talk."

"Oh, but they say he's a grand speaker in the Legislature. He knows when to keep quiet. That's why he's got such influence in politics. The people have confidence in him." Johanna beat up a pillow and held it under her fat chin while she slipped on the case. Her niece laughed.

"Maybe we could make people believe we were wise, Aunty, if we held our tongues. Why did you tell Mrs. Ericson that Norman threw me again last Saturday and turned my foot? She's been talking to Olaf."

Johanna fell into great confusion. "Oh, but, my precious, the old lady asked for you, and she's always so angry if I can't give an excuse. Anyhow, she needn't talk; she's always tearing up something with that motor of hers."

When her aunt clattered down to the kitchen, Clara went to dust the parlour. Since there was not much there to dust, this did not take very long. Olaf had built the house new for her before their marriage, but her interest in furnishing it had been short-lived. It went, indeed, little beyond a bathtub and her piano. They had disagreed about almost every other article of furniture, and Clara had said she would rather have her house empty than full of things she didn't want. The house was set in a hillside, and the west windows of the parlour looked out above the kitchen yard thirty feet below. The east windows opened directly into the front yard. At one of the latter, Clara, while she was dusting, heard a low whistle. She did not turn at once, but listened intently as she drew her cloth slowly along the round of a chair. Yes, there it was:

I dreamt that I dwelt in ma-a-arble halls.

She turned and saw Nils Ericson laughing in the sunlight, his hat in his hand, just outside the window. As she crossed the room he leaned against the wire screen. "Aren't you at all surprised to see me, Clara Vavrika?"

"No; I was expecting to see you. Mother Ericson telephoned Olaf last night that you were here."

Nils squinted and gave a long whistle. "Telephoned? That must have been while Eric and I were out walking. Isn't she enterprising? Lift this screen, won't you?"

Clara lifted the screen, and Nils swung his leg across the window-sill. As he stepped into the room she said: "You didn't think you were going to get ahead of your mother, did you?"

He threw his hat on the piano. "Oh, I do sometimes. You see, I'm ahead of her now. I'm supposed to be in Anders' wheat-field. But, as we were leaving, Mother ran her car into a soft place beside the road and sank up to the hubs. While they were going for the horses to pull her out, I cut away behind the stacks and escaped." Nils chuckled. Clara's dull eyes lit up as she looked at him admiringly.

"You've got them guessing already. I don't know what your mother said to Olaf over the telephone, but he came back looking as if he'd seen a ghost, and he didn't go to bed until a dreadful hour—ten o'clock, I should think. He sat out on the porch in the dark like a graven image. It had been one of his talkative days, too." They both laughed, easily and lightly, like people who have laughed a great deal together; but they remained standing.

"Anders and Otto and Peter looked as if they had seen ghosts, too, over in the threshing field. What's the matter with them all?"

Clara gave him a quick, searching look. "Well, for one thing, they've always been afraid you have the other will."

Nils looked interested. "The other will?"

"Yes. A later one. They knew your father made another, but they never knew what he did with it. They almost tore the old house to pieces looking for it. They always suspected that he carried on a clandestine correspondence with you, for the one thing he would do was to get his own mail himself. So they thought he might have sent the new will to you for safekeeping. The old one, leaving everything to your mother, was made long before you went away, and it's understood among them that it cuts you out—that she will leave all the property to the others. Your father made the second will to prevent that. I've been hoping you had it. It would be such fun to spring it on them." Clara laughed mirthfully, a thing she did not often do now.

Nils shook his head reprovingly. "Come, now, you're malicious."

"No, I'm not. But I'd like something to happen to stir them all up, just for once. There never was such a family for having nothing ever happen to them but dinner and threshing. I'd almost be willing to die, just to have a funeral. *You* wouldn't stand it for three weeks."

Nils bent over the piano and began pecking at the keys with the finger of one hand. "I wouldn't? My dear young lady, how do you know what I can stand? *You* wouldn't wait to find out."

Clara flushed darkly and frowned. "I didn't believe you would ever come back—" she said defiantly.

"Eric believed I would, and he was only a baby when I went away. However, all's well that ends well, and I haven't come back to be a skeleton at the feast. We mustn't quarrel. Mother will be here with a search warrant pretty soon." He swung round and faced her, thrusting his hands into his coat pockets. "Come, you ought to be glad to see me, if you want something to happen. I'm something, even without a will. We can have a little fun, can't we? I think we can!"

She echoed him, "I think we can!" They both laughed and their eyes sparkled. Clara Vavrika looked ten years younger than when she had put the velvet ribbon about her throat that morning.

"You know, I'm so tickled to see mother," Nils went on. "I didn't know I was so proud of her. A regular pile driver. How about little pigtails, down at the house? Is Olaf doing the square thing by those children?"

Clara frowned pensively. "Olaf has to do something that looks like the square thing, now that he's a public man!" She glanced drolly at Nils. "But he makes a good commission out of it. On Sundays they all get together here and figure. He lets Peter and Anders put in big bills for the keep of the two boys, and he pays them out of the estate. They are always having what they call accountings. Olaf gets something out of it, too. I don't know just how they do it, but it's entirely a family matter, as they say. And when the Ericsons say that—" Clara lifted her eyebrows.

Just then the angry *honk-honk* of an approaching motor sounded from down the road. Their eyes met and they began to laugh. They laughed as children do when they can not contain themselves, and can not explain the cause of their mirth to grown people, but share it perfectly together. When Clara Vavrika sat down at the piano after he was gone, she felt that she had laughed away a dozen years. She practised as if the house were burning over her head.

When Nils greeted his mother and climbed into the front seat of the motor beside her, Mrs. Ericson looked grim, but she made no comment upon his truancy until she had turned her car and was retracing her revolutions along the road that ran by Olaf's big pasture. Then she remarked dryly:

"If I were you I wouldn't see too much of Olaf's wife while you are here. She's the kind of woman who can't see much of men without getting herself talked about. She was a good deal talked about before he married her."

"Hasn't Olaf tamed her?" Nils asked indifferently.

Mrs. Ericson shrugged her massive shoulders. "Olaf don't seem to have much luck, when it comes to wives. The first one was meek enough, but she was always ailing. And this one has her own way. He says if he quarreled with her she'd go back to her father, and then he'd lose the Bohemian vote. There are a great many Bohunks in this district. But when you find a man under his wife's thumb you can always be sure there's a soft spot in him somewhere."

Nils thought of his own father, and smiled. "She brought him a good deal of money, didn't she, besides the Bohemian vote?"

Mrs. Ericson sniffed. "Well, she has a fair half section in her own name, but I can't see as that does Olaf much good. She will have a good deal of property some day, if old Vavrika don't marry again. But I don't consider a saloonkeeper's money as good as other people's money."

Nils laughed outright. "Come, Mother, don't let your prejudices carry you that far. Money's money. Old Vavrika's a mighty decent sort of saloonkeeper. Nothing rowdy about him."

Mrs. Ericson spoke up angrily. "Oh, I know you always stood up for them! But hanging around there when you were a boy never did you any good, Nils, nor any of the other boys who went there. There weren't so many after her when she married Olaf, let me tell you. She knew enough to grab her chance."

Nils settled back in his seat. "Of course I liked to go there, Mother, and you were always cross about it. You never took the trouble to find out that it was the one jolly house in this country for a boy to go to. All the rest of you were working yourselves to death, and the houses were mostly a mess, full of babies and washing and flies. Oh, it was all right—I understand that; but you are young only once, and I happened to be young then. Now, Vavrika's was always jolly. He played the violin, and I used to take my flute, and Clara played the piano, and Johanna used to sing Bohemian songs. She always had a big supper for us—herrings and pickles and poppy-seed bread, and lots of cake and preserves. Old Joe had been in the army in the old country, and he could tell lots of good stories. I can see him cutting bread, at the head of the table, now. I don't know what I'd have done when I was a kid if it hadn't been for the Vavrikas, really."

"And all the time he was taking money that other people had worked hard in the fields for," Mrs. Ericson observed.

"So do the circuses, Mother, and they're a good thing. People ought to get fun for some of their money. Even father liked old Joe."

"Your father," Mrs. Ericson said grimly, "liked everybody."

As they crossed the sand creek and turned into her own place, Mrs. Ericson observed, "There's Olaf's buggy. He's stopped on his way from town." Nils shook himself and prepared to greet his brother, who was waiting on the porch.

Olaf was a big, heavy Norwegian, slow of speech and movement. His head was large and square, like a block of wood. When Nils, at a distance, tried to remember what his brother looked like, he could recall only his heavy head, high forehead, large nostrils, and pale blue eyes, set far apart. Olaf's features were rudimentary: the thing one noticed was the face itself, wide and flat and pale; devoid of any expression, betraying his fifty years as little as it betrayed anything else, and powerful by reason of its very stolidness. When Olaf shook hands with Nils he looked at him from under his light eyebrows, but Nils felt that no one could ever say what that pale look might mean. The one thing he had always felt in Olaf was a heavy stubbornness, like the unyielding stickiness of wet loam against the plow. He had always found Olaf the most difficult of his brothers.

"How do you do, Nils? Expect to stay with us long?"

"Oh, I may stay forever," Nils answered gaily. "I like this country better than I used to."

"There's been some work put into it since you left," Olaf remarked.

"Exactly. I think it's about ready to live in now—and I'm about ready to settle down." Nils saw his brother lower his big head ("Exactly like a bull," he thought.) "Mother's been persuading me to slow down now, and go in for farming," he went on lightly.

Olaf made a deep sound in his throat. "Farming ain't learned in a day," he brought out, still looking at the ground.

"Oh, I know! But I pick things up quickly." Nils had not meant to antagonize his brother, and he did not know now why he was doing it. "Of course," he went on, "I shouldn't expect to make a big success, as you fellows have done. But then, I'm not ambitious. I won't want much. A little land, and some cattle, maybe."

Olaf still stared at the ground, his head down. He wanted to ask Nils what he had been doing all these years, that he didn't have a business somewhere he couldn't afford to leave; why he hadn't more pride than to come back with only a little sole-leather trunk to show for himself, and to present himself as the only failure in the family. He did not ask one of these questions, but he made them all felt distinctly.

"Humph!" Nils thought. "No wonder the man never talks, when he can butt his ideas into you like that without ever saying a word. I suppose he uses that kind of smokeless powder on his wife all the time. But I guess she has her innings." He chuckled, and Olaf looked up. "Never mind me, Olaf. I laugh without knowing why, like little Eric. He's another cheerful dog."

"Eric," said Olaf slowly, "is a spoiled kid. He's just let his mother's best cow go dry because he don't milk her right. I was hoping you'd take him away somewhere and put him into business. If he don't do any good among strangers, he never will." This was a long speech for Olaf, and as he finished it he climbed into his buggy.

Nils shrugged his shoulders. "Same old tricks," he

thought. "Hits from behind you every time. What a whale of a man!" He turned and went round to the kitchen, where his mother was scolding little Eric for letting the gasoline get low.

IV

Joe Vavrika's saloon was not in the county seat, where Olaf and Mrs. Ericson did their trading, but in a cheerfuller place, a little Bohemian settlement which lay at the other end of the county, ten level miles north of Olaf's farm. Clara rode up to see her father almost every day. Vavrika's house was, so to speak, in the back yard of his saloon. The garden between the two buildings was inclosed by a high board fence as tight as a partition, and in summer Joe kept beer tables and wooden benches among the gooseberry bushes under his little cherry tree. At one of these tables Nils Ericson was seated in the late afternoon, three days after his return home. Joe had gone in to serve a customer, and Nils was lounging on his elbows, looking rather mournfully into his half-emptied pitcher, when he heard a laugh across the little garden. Clara, in her riding habit, was standing at the back door of the house, under the grapevine trellis that old Joe had grown there long ago. Nils rose.

"Come out and keep your father and me company. We've been gossiping all afternoon. Nobody to bother us but the flies."

She shook her head. "No, I never come out here any more. Olaf doesn't like it. I must live up to my position, you know."

"You mean to tell me you never come out and chat with the boys, as you used to? He *has* tamed you! Who keeps up these flower-beds?"

"I come out on Sundays, when father is alone, and read the Bohemian papers to him. But I am never here when the bar is open. What have you two been doing?"

"Talking, as I told you. I've been telling him about my travels. I find I can't talk much at home, not even to Eric."

Clara reached up and poked with her riding-whip at a white moth that was fluttering in the sunlight among the vine leaves. "I suppose you will never tell me about all those things."

"Where can I tell them? Not in Olaf's house, certainly. What's the matter with our talking here?" He pointed persuasively with his hat to the bushes and the green table, where the flies were singing lazily above the empty beer glasses.

Clara shook her head weakly. "No, it wouldn't do. Besides, I am going now."

"I'm on Eric's mare. Would you be angry if I overtook you?"

Clara looked back and laughed. "You might try and see. I can leave you if I don't want you. Eric's mare can't keep up with Norman."

Nils went into the bar and attempted to pay his score. Big Joe, six feet four, with curly yellow hair and mustache, clapped him on the shoulder. "Not a Goddamn a your money go in my drawer, you hear? Only next time you bring your flute, te-te-te-te-te-ty." Joe wagged his fingers in imitation of the flute player's position. "My Clara, she come all-a-time Sundays an' play for me. She not like to play at Ericson's place." He shook his yellow curls and laughed. "Not a Goddamn a fun at Ericson's. You come a Sunday. You like-a fun. No forget de flute." Joe talked very rapidly and always tumbled over his English. He seldom spoke it to his customers, and had never learned much.

Nils swung himself into the saddle and trotted to the west of the village, where the houses and gardens scattered into prairie land and the road turned south. Far ahead of him, in the declining light, he saw Clara Vavrika's slender figure, loitering on horseback. He touched his mare with the whip, and shot along the white, level road, under the reddening sky. When he overtook Olaf's wife he saw that she had been crying. "What's the matter, Clara Vavrika?" he asked kindly.

"Oh, I get blue sometimes. It was awfully jolly living there with father. I wonder why I ever went away."

Nils spoke in a low, kind tone that he sometimes used

with women: "That's what I've been wondering these many years. You were the last girl in the country I'd have picked for a wife for Olaf. What made you do it, Clara?"

"I suppose I really did it to oblige the neighbours" —Clara tossed her head. "People were beginning to wonder."

"To wonder?"

"Yes—why I didn't get married. I suppose I didn't like to keep them in suspense. I've discovered that most girls marry out of consideration for the neighbourhood."

Nils bent his head toward her and his white teeth flashed. "I'd have gambled that one girl I knew would say, 'Let the neighbourhood be damned.'"

Clara shook her head mournfully. "You see, they have it on you, Nils; that is, if you're a woman. They say you're beginning to go off. That's what makes us get married: we can't stand the laugh."

Nils looked sidewise at her. He had never seen her head droop before. Resignation was the last thing he would have expected of her. "In your case, there wasn't something else?"

"Something else?"

"I mean, you didn't do it to spite somebody? Somebody who didn't come back?"

Clara drew herself up. "Oh, I never thought you'd come back. Not after I stopped writing to you, at least. *That* was all over, long before I married Olaf."

"It never occurred to you, then, that the meanest thing you could do to me was to marry Olaf?"

Clara laughed. "No; I didn't know you were so fond of Olaf."

Nils smoothed his horse's mane with his glove. "You know, Clara Vavrika, you are never going to stick it out. You'll cut away some day, and I've been thinking you might as well cut away with me."

Clara threw up her chin. "Oh, you don't know me as well as you think. I won't cut away. Sometimes, when I'm with father, I feel like it. But I can hold out as long as the Ericsons can. They've never got the best of me yet, and one can live, so long as one isn't beaten. If I go back to father, it's all up with Olaf in politics. He knows that, and he never goes much beyond sulking. I've as much wit as the Ericsons. I'll never leave them unless I can show them a thing or two."

"You mean unless you can come it over them?"

"Yes—unless I go away with a man who is cleverer than they are, and who has more money."

Nils whistled. "Dear me, you are demanding a good deal. The Ericsons, take the lot of them, are a bunch to beat. But I should think the excitement of tormenting them would have worn off by this time."

"It has, I'm afraid," Clara admitted mournfully.

"Then why don't you cut away? There are more amusing games than this in the world. When I came home I thought it might amuse me to bully a few quarter sections out of the Ericsons; but I've almost decided I can get more fun for my money somewhere else."

Clara took in her breath sharply. "Ah, you have got the other will! That was why you came home!"

"No, it wasn't. I came home to see how you were getting on with Olaf."

Clara struck her horse with the whip, and in a bound she was far ahead of him. Nils dropped one word, "Damn!" and whipped after her; but she leaned forward in her saddle and fairly cut the wind. Her long riding skirt rippled in the still air behind her. The sun was just sinking behind the stubble in a vast, clear sky, and the shadows drew across the fields so rapidly that Nils could scarcely keep in sight the dark figure on the road. When he overtook her he caught her horse by the bridle. Norman reared, and Nils was frightened for her; but Clara kept her seat.

"Let me go, Nils Ericson!" she cried. "I hate you more than any of them. You were created to torture me, the whole tribe of you—to make me suffer in every possible way."

She struck her horse again and galloped away from him. Nils set his teeth and looked thoughtful. He rode slowly home along the deserted road, watching the stars come out in the clear violet sky. They flashed softly into the limpid heavens, like jewels let fall into clear water. They were a reproach, he felt, to a sordid world. As he

turned across the sand creek, he looked up at the North
Star and smiled, as if there were an understanding between them. His mother scolded him for being late for
supper.

V

On Sunday afternoon Joe Vavrika, in his shirt sleeves
and carpet slippers, was sitting in his garden, smoking a
long-tasseled porcelain pipe with a hunting scene painted
on the bowl. Clara sat under the cherry tree, reading
aloud to him from the weekly Bohemian papers. She had
worn a white muslin dress under her riding habit, and the
leaves of the cherry tree threw a pattern of sharp shadows
over her skirt. The black cat was dozing in the sunlight at
her feet, and Joe's dachshund was scratching a hole under
the scarlet geraniums and dreaming of badgers. Joe was
filling his pipe for the third time since dinner, when he
heard a knocking on the fence. He broke into a loud
guffaw and unlatched the little door that led into the
street. He did not call Nils by name, but caught him by
the hand and dragged him in. Clara stiffened and the
colour deepened under her dark skin. Nils, too, felt a little
awkward. He had not seen her since the night when she
rode away from him and left him alone on the level road
between the fields. Joe dragged him to the wooden bench
beside the green table.

"You bring de flute," he cried, tapping the leather
case under Nils' arm. "Ah, das-a good! Now we have some
liddle fun like old times. I got somet'ing good for you."
Joe shook his finger at Nils and winked his blue eye, a
bright clear eye, full of fire, though the tiny bloodvessels
on the ball were always a little distended. "I got somet'ing
for you from"—he paused and waved his hand—"Hongarie.
You know Hongarie? You wait!" He pushed Nils down on
the bench, and went through the back door of his saloon.

Nils looked at Clara, who sat frigidly with her white
skirts drawn tight about her. "He didn't tell you he had
asked me to come, did he? He wanted a party and pro-

ceeded to arrange it. Isn't he fun? Don't be cross; let's give him a good time."

Clara smiled and shook out her skirt. "Isn't that like Father? And he has sat here so meekly all day. Well, I won't pout. I'm glad you came. He doesn't have very many good times now any more. There are so few of his kind left. The second generation are a tame lot."

Joe came back with a flask in one hand and three wine glasses caught by the stems between the fingers of the other. These he placed on the table with an air of ceremony, and, going behind Nils, held the flask between him and the sun, squinting into it admiringly. "You know dis, Tokai? A great friend of mine, he bring dis to me, a present out of Hongarie. You know how much it cost, dis wine? Chust so much what it weigh in gold. Nobody but de nobles drink him in Bohemie. Many, many years I save him up, dis Tokai." Joe whipped out his official corkscrew and delicately removed the cork. "De old man die what bring him to me, an' dis wine he lay on his belly in my cellar an' sleep. An' now," carefully pouring out the heavy yellow wine, "an' now he wake up; and maybe he wake us up, too!" He carried one of the glasses to his daughter and presented it with great gallantry.

Clara shook her head, but, seeing her father's disappointment, relented. "You taste it first. I don't want so much."

Joe sampled it with a beatific expression, and turned to Nils. "You drink him slow, dis wine. He very soft, but he go down hot. You see!"

After a second glass Nils declared that he couldn't take any more without getting sleepy. "Now get your fiddle, Vavrika," he said as he opened his flute case.

But Joe settled back in his wooden rocker and wagged his big carpet slipper. "No-no-no-no-no-no-no! No play fiddle now any more: too much ache in de finger," waving them, "all-a-time rheumatiz. You play de flute, te-tety-te-tety-te. Bohemie songs."

"I've forgotten all the Bohemian songs I used to play with you and Johanna. But here's one that will make Clara pout. You remember how her eyes used to snap when we called her the Bohemian Girl?" Nils lifted his flute and began "When Other Lips and Other Hearts," and Joe hummed the air in a husky baritone, waving his carpet slipper. "Oh-h-h, das-a fine music," he cried, clapping his hands as Nils finished. "Now 'Marble Halls, Marble Halls'! Clara, you sing him."

Clara smiled and leaned back in her chair, beginning softly:

> "I dreamt that I dwelt in ma-a-arble halls,
> With vassals and serfs at my knee,"

and Joe hummed like a big bumblebee.

"There's one more you always played," Clara said quietly, "I remember that best." She locked her hands over her knee and began "The Heart Bowed Down," and sang it through without groping for the words. She was singing with a good deal of warmth when she came to the end of the old song:

> "For memory is the only friend
> That grief can call its own."

Joe flashed out his red silk handkerchief and blew his nose, shaking his head. "No-no-no-no-no-no-no! Too sad, too sad! I not like-a dat. Play quick somet'ing gay now."

Nils put his lips to the instrument, and Joe lay back in his chair, laughing and singing, "Oh, Evelina, Sweet Evelina!" Clara laughed, too. Long ago, when she and Nils went to high school, the model student of their class was a very homely girl in thick spectacles. Her name was Evelina Oleson; she had a long, swinging walk which somehow suggested the measure of that song, and they used mercilessly to sing it at her.

"Dat ugly Oleson girl, she teach in de school," Joe gasped, "an' she still walks chust like dat, yup-a, yup-a, yup-a, chust like a camel she go! Now, Nils, we have some more li'l drink. Oh, yes-yes-yes-yes-yes-yes-*yes*! Dis time you haf to drink, and Clara she haf to, so she show she not jealous. So, we all drink to your girl. You not tell her name, eh? No-no-no, I no make you tell. She pretty, eh? She make good sweetheart? I bet!" Joe winked and lifted his glass. "How soon you get married?"

Nils screwed up his eyes. "That I don't know. When she says."

Joe threw out his chest. "Das-a way boys talks. No way for mans. Mans say, 'You come to de church, an' get a hurry on you.' Das-a way mans talks."

"Maybe Nils hasn't got enough to keep a wife," put in Clara ironically. "How about that, Nils?" she asked him frankly, as if she wanted to know.

Nils looked at her coolly, raising one eyebrow. "Oh, I can keep her, all right."

"The way she wants to be kept?"

"With my wife, I'll decide that," replied Nils calmly. "I'll give her what's good for her."

Clara made a wry face. "You'll give her the strap, I expect, like old Peter Oleson gave his wife."

"When she needs it," said Nils lazily, locking his hands behind his head and squinting up through the leaves of the cherry tree. "Do you remember the time I squeezed the cherries all over your clean dress, and Aunt Johanna boxed my ears for me? My gracious, weren't you mad! You had both hands full of cherries, and I squeezed 'em and made the juice fly all over you. I liked to have fun with you; you'd get so mad."

"We *did* have fun, didn't we? None of the other kids ever had so much fun. We knew how to play."

Nils dropped his elbows on the table and looked steadily across at her. "I've played with lots of girls since, but I haven't found one who was such good fun."

Clara laughed. The late afternoon sun was shining full in her face, and deep in the back of her eyes there shone something fiery, like the yellow drops of Tokai in the brown glass bottle. "Can you still play, or are you only pretending?"

"I can play better than I used to, and harder."

"Don't you ever work, then?" She had not intended to say it. It slipped out because she was confused enough to say just the wrong thing.

"I work between times." Nils' steady gaze still beat upon her. "Don't you worry about my working, Mrs. Ericson. You're getting like all the rest of them." He reached his brown, warm hand across the table and dropped it on Clara's, which was cold as an icicle. "Last call for play, Mrs. Ericson!" Clara shivered, and suddenly her hands and cheeks grew warm. Her fingers lingered in his a moment, and they looked at each other earnestly. Joe Vavrika had put the mouth of the bottle to his lips and was swallowing the last drops of the Tokai, standing. The sun, just about to sink behind his shop, glistened on the bright glass, on his flushed face and curly yellow hair. "Look," Clara whispered, "that's the way I want to grow old."

VI

On the day of Olaf Ericson's barn-raising, his wife, for once in a way, rose early. Johanna Vavrika had been baking cakes and frying and boiling and spicing meats for a week beforehand, but it was not until the day before the party was to take place that Clara showed any interest in it. Then she was seized with one of her fitful spasms of energy, and took the wagon and little Eric and spent the day on Plum Creek, gathering vines and swamp goldenrod to decorate the barn.

By four o'clock in the afternoon buggies and wagons began to arrive at the big unpainted building in front of Olaf's house. When Nils and his mother came at five, there were more than fifty people in the barn, and a great drove of children. On the ground floor stood six long tables, set with the crockery of seven flourishing Ericson families, lent for the occasion. In the middle of each table was a big yellow pumpkin, hollowed out and filled with woodbine. In one corner of the barn, behind a pile of green-and-white striped watermelons, was a circle of chairs for the old people; the younger guests sat on bushel measures or barbed-wire spools, and the children tumbled about in the haymow. The box stalls Clara had converted into booths. The framework was hidden by goldenrod and sheaves of wheat, and the partitions were covered with wild grapevines full of fruit. At one of these Johanna Vavrika watched over her cooked meats, enough to provision an army; and at the next her kitchen girls had ranged the ice-cream freezers, and Clara was already cutting pies and cakes against the hour of serving. At the third stall, little Hilda, in a bright pink lawn dress, dispensed lemonade throughout the afternoon. Olaf, as a public man, had thought it inadvisable to serve beer in his barn; but Joe Vavrika had come over with two demijohns concealed in his buggy, and after his arrival the wagon shed was much frequented by the men.

"Hasn't Cousin Clara fixed things lovely?" little Hilda whispered, when Nils went up to her stall and asked for lemonade.

Nils leaned against the booth, talking to the excited little girl and watching the people. The barn faced the west, and the sun, pouring in at the big doors, filled the whole interior with a golden light, through which filtered fine particles of dust from the haymow, where the children were romping. There was a great chattering from the stall where Johanna Vavrika exhibited to the admiring women her platters heaped with fried chicken, her roasts of beef, boiled tongues, and baked hams with cloves stuck in the crisp brown fat and garnished with tansy and parsley. The older women, having assured themselves that there were twenty kinds of cake, not counting cookies, and three dozen fat pies, repaired to the corner behind the pile of watermelons, put on their white aprons, and fell to their knitting and fancywork. They were a fine company of old women, and a Dutch painter would have loved to find them there together, where the sun made bright patches on the floor and sent long, quivering shafts of gold through the dusky shade up among the rafters. There were fat, rosy old women who looked hot in their best black dresses; spare, alert old women with brown, dark-veined hands; and several of almost heroic frame, not less massive than old Mrs. Ericson herself. Few of them wore glasses, and old Mrs. Svendsen, a Danish woman, who was quite bald, wore the only cap among them. Mrs. Oleson, who had twelve big grandchildren, could still show two braids of yellow hair as thick as her own wrists. Among all these grandmothers there were more brown heads than white. They all had a pleased, prosperous air, as if they were more than satisfied with themselves and with life. Nils, leaning against Hilda's lemonade stand, watched them as they sat chattering in four languages, their fingers never lagging behind their tongues.

"Look at them over there," he whispered, detaining Clara as she passed him. "Aren't they the Old Guard? I've just counted thirty hands. I guess they've wrung many a chicken's neck and warmed many a boy's jacket for him in their time."

In reality he fell into amazement when he thought of the Herculean labours those fifteen pairs of hands had performed: of the cows they had milked, the butter they had made, the gardens they had planted, the children and grandchildren they had tended, the brooms they had worn out, the mountains of food they had cooked. It made him dizzy. Clara Vavrika smiled a hard, enigmatical smile at him and walked rapidly away. Nils' eyes followed her white figure as she went toward the house. He watched her walking alone in the sunlight, looked at her slender, defiant shoulders and her little hard-set head with its coils of blue-black hair. "No," he reflected; "she'd never be like them, not if she lived here a hundred years. She'd only grow more bitter. You can't tame a wild thing; you can only chain it. People aren't all alike. I mustn't lose my nerve." He gave Hilda's pigtail a parting tweak and set out after Clara. "Where to?" he asked, as he came upon her in the kitchen.

"I'm going to the cellar for preserves."

"Let me go with you. I never get a moment alone with you. Why do you keep out of my way?"

Clara laughed. "I don't usually get in anybody's way."

Nils followed her down the stairs and to the far corner of the cellar, where a basement window let in a stream of light. From a swinging shelf Clara selected several glass jars, each labeled in Johanna's careful hand. Nils took up a brown flask. "What's this? It looks good."

"It is. It's some French brandy father gave me when I was married. Would you like some? Have you a corkscrew? I'll get glasses."

When she brought them, Nils took them from her and put them down on the window-sill. "Clara Vavrika, do you remember how crazy I used to be about you?"

Clara shrugged her shoulders. "Boys are always crazy

about somebody or another. I dare say some silly has been crazy about Evelina Oleson. You got over it in a hurry."

"Because I didn't come back, you mean? I had to get on, you know, and it was hard sledding at first. Then I heard you'd married Olaf."

"And then you stayed away from a broken heart," Clara laughed.

"And then I began to think about you more than I had since I first went away. I began to wonder if you were really as you had seemed to me when I was a boy. I thought I'd like to see. I've had lots of girls, but no one ever pulled me the same way. The more I thought about you, the more I remembered how it used to be—like hearing a wild tune you can't resist, calling you out at night. It had been a long while since anything had pulled me out of my boots, and I wondered whether anything ever could again." Nils thrust his hands into his coat pockets and squared his shoulders, as his mother sometimes squared hers, as Olaf, in a clumsier manner, squared his. "So I thought I'd come back and see. Of course the family have tried to do me, and I rather thought I'd bring out father's will and make a fuss. But they can have their old land; they've put enough sweat into it." He took the flask and filled the two glasses carefully to the brim. "I've found out what I want from the Ericsons. Drink *skoal*, Clara." He lifted his glass, and Clara took hers with downcast eyes. "Look at me, Clara Vavrika. *Skoal!*"

She raised her burning eyes and answered fiercely: "*Skoal!*"

The barn supper began at six o'clock and lasted for two hilarious hours. Yense Nelson had made a wager that he could eat two whole fried chickens, and he did. Eli Swanson stowed away two whole custard pies, and Nick Hermanson ate a chocolate layer cake to the last crumb. There was even a cooky contest among the children, and one thin, slablike Bohemian boy consumed sixteen and won the prize, a gingerbread pig which Johanna Vavrika had carefully decorated with red candies and burnt sugar. Fritz Sweiheart, the German carpenter, won in the pickle contest, but he disappeared soon after supper and was not seen for the rest of the evening. Joe Vavrika said that Fritz could have managed the pickles all right, but he had sampled the demijohn in his buggy too often before sitting down to the table.

While the supper was being cleared away the two fiddlers began to tune up for the dance. Clara was to accompany them on her old upright piano, which had been brought down from her father's. By this time Nils had renewed old acquaintances. Since his interview with Clara in the cellar, he had been busy telling all the old women how young they looked, and all the young ones how pretty they were, and assuring the men that they had here the best farmland in the world. He had made himself so agreeable that old Mrs. Ericson's friends began to come up to her and tell how lucky she was to get her smart son back again, and please to get him to play his flute. Joe Vavrika, who could still play very well when he forgot that he had rheumatism, caught up a fiddle from Johnny Oleson and played a crazy Bohemian dance tune that set the wheels going. When he dropped the bow every one was ready to dance.

Olaf, in a frock coat and a solemn made-up necktie, led the grand march with his mother. Clara had kept well out of *that* by sticking to the piano. She played the march with a pompous solemnity which greatly amused the prodigal son, who went over and stood behind her.

"Oh, aren't you rubbing it into them, Clara Vavrika? And aren't you lucky to have me here, or all your wit would be thrown away."

"I'm used to being witty for myself. It saves my life."

The fiddles struck up a polka, and Nils convulsed Joe Vavrika by leading out Evelina Oleson, the homely school-teacher. His next partner was a very fat Swedish girl, who, although she was an heiress, had not been asked for the first dance, but had stood against the wall in her tight, high-heeled shoes, nervously fingering a lace handkerchief. She was soon out of breath, so Nils led her, pleased and panting, to her seat, and went over to the piano, from which Clara had been watching his gallantry. "Ask Olena Yenson," she whispered. "She waltzes beautifully."

Olena, too, was rather inconveniently plump, handsome in a smooth, heavy way, with a fine colour and good-natured, sleepy eyes. She was redolent of violet sachet powder, and had warm, soft, white hands, but she danced divinely, moving as smoothly as the tide coming in. "There, that's something like," Nils said as he released her. "You'll give me the next waltz, won't you? Now I must go and dance with my little cousin."

Hilda was greatly excited when Nils went up to her stall and held out his arm. Her little eyes sparkled, but she declared that she could not leave her lemonade. Old Mrs. Ericson, who happened along at this moment, said she would attend to that, and Hilda came out, as pink as her pink dress. The dance was a schottische, and in a moment her yellow braids were fairly standing on end. "Bravo!" Nils cried encouragingly. "Where did you learn to dance so nicely?"

"My Cousin Clara taught me," the little girl panted.

Nils found Eric sitting with a group of boys who were too awkward or too shy to dance, and told him that he must dance the next waltz with Hilda.

The boy screwed up his shoulders. "Aw, Nils, I can't dance. My feet are too big; I look silly."

"Don't be thinking about yourself. It doesn't matter how boys look."

Nils had never spoken to him so sharply before, and Eric made haste to scramble out of his corner and brush the straw from his coat.

Clara nodded approvingly. "Good for you, Nils. I've been trying to get hold of him. They dance very nicely together; I sometimes play for them."

"I'm obliged to you for teaching him. There's no reason why he should grow up to be a lout."

"He'll never be that. He's more like you than any of them. Only he hasn't your courage." From her slanting eyes Clara shot forth one of those keen glances, admiring and at the same time challenging, which she seldom bestowed on any one, and which seemed to say, "Yes, I admire you, but I am your equal."

Clara was proving a much better host than Olaf, who, once the supper was over, seemed to feel no interest in anything but the lanterns. He had brought a locomotive headlight from town to light the revels, and he kept skulking about as if he feared the mere light from it might set his new barn on fire. His wife, on the contrary, was cordial to every one, was animated and even gay. The deep salmon colour in her cheeks burned vividly, and her eyes were full of life. She gave the piano over to the fat Swedish heiress, pulled her father away from the corner where he sat gossiping with his cronies, and made him dance a Bohemian dance with her. In his youth Joe had been a famous dancer, and his daughter got him so limbered up that every one sat around and applauded them. The old ladies were particularly delighted, and made them go through the dance again. From their corner where they watched and commented, the old women kept time with their feet and hands, and whenever the fiddles struck up a new air old Mrs. Svendsen's white cap would begin to bob.

Clara was waltzing with little Eric when Nils came up to them, brushed his brother aside, and swung her out among the dancers. "Remember how we used to waltz on rollers at the old skating rink in town? I suppose people don't do that any more. We used to keep it up for hours. You know, we never did moon around as other boys and girls did. It was dead serious with us from the beginning. When we were most in love with each other, we used to fight. You were always pinching people; your fingers were like little nippers. A regular snapping turtle, you were. Lord, how you'd like Stockholm! Sit out in the streets in front of cafés and talk all night in summer. Just like a reception—officers and ladies and funny English people. Jolliest people in the world, the Swedes, once you get them going. Always drinking things—champagne and stout mixed, half-and-half; serve it out of big pitchers, and serve plenty. Slow pulse, you know; they can stand a lot. Once they light up, they're glowworms, I can tell you."

"All the same, you don't really like gay people."

"*I* don't?"

"No; I could tell that when you were looking at the old women there this afternoon. They're the kind you really admire, after all; women like your mother. And that's the kind you'll marry."

"Is it, Miss Wisdom? You'll see who I'll marry, and she won't have a domestic virtue to bless herself with. She'll be a snapping turtle, and she'll be a match for me. All the same, they're a fine bunch of old dames over there. You admire them yourself."

"No, I don't; I detest them."

"You won't, when you look back on them from Stockholm or Budapest. Freedom settles all that. Oh, but you're the real Bohemian Girl, Clara Vavrika!" Nils laughed down at her sullen frown and began mockingly to sing:

> "Oh, how could a poor gypsy maiden like me
> Expect the proud bride of a baron to be?"

Clara clutched his shoulder. "Hush, Nils; every one is looking at you."

"I don't care. They can't gossip. It's all in the family, as the Ericsons say when they divide up little Hilda's patrimony amongst them. Besides, we'll give them something to talk about when we hit the trail. Lord, it will be a godsend to them! They haven't had anything so interesting to chatter about since the grasshopper year. It'll give them a new lease of life. And Olaf won't lose the Bohemian vote, either. They'll have the laugh on him so that they'll vote two apiece. They'll send him to Congress. They'll never forget his barn party, or us. They'll always remember us as we're dancing together now. We're making a legend. Where's my waltz, boys?" he called as they whirled past the fiddlers.

The musicians grinned, looked at each other, hesitated, and began a new air; and Nils sang with them, as the couples fell from a quick waltz to a long, slow glide:

> "When other lips and other hearts
> Their tale of love shall tell,
> In language whose excess imparts
> The power they feel so well."

The old women applauded vigorously. "What a gay one he is, that Nils!" And old Mrs. Svendsen's cap lurched dreamily from side to side to the flowing measure of the dance.

> "Of days that have as ha-a-p-py been,
>   And you'll remember me."

VII

The moonlight flooded that great, silent land. The reaped fields lay yellow in it. The straw stacks and poplar windbreaks threw sharp black shadows. The roads were white rivers of dust. The sky was a deep, crystalline blue, and the stars were few and faint. Everything seemed to have succumbed, to have sunk to sleep, under the great, golden, tender, midsummer moon. The splendour of it seemed to transcend human life and human fate. The senses were too feeble to take it in, and every time one looked up at the sky one felt unequal to it, as if one were sitting deaf under the waves of a great river of melody. Near the road, Nils Ericson was lying against a straw stack in Olaf's wheat field. His own life seemed strange and unfamiliar to him, as if it were something he had read about, or dreamed, and forgotten. He lay very still, watching the white road that ran in front of him, lost itself among the fields, and then, at a distance, reappeared over a little hill. At last, against this white band he saw something moving rapidly, and he got up and walked to the edge of the field. "She is passing the row of poplars now," he thought. He heard the padded beat of hoofs along the dusty road, and as she came into sight he stepped out and waved his arms. Then, for fear of frightening the horse, he drew back and waited. Clara had seen him, and she came up at a walk. Nils took the horse by the bit and stroked his neck.

"What are you doing out so late, Clara Vavrika? I went to the house, but Johanna told me you had gone to your father's."

"Who can stay in the house on a night like this? Aren't you out yourself?"

"Ah, but that's another matter."

Nils turned the horse into the field.

"What are you doing? Where are you taking Norman?"

"Not far, but I want to talk to you tonight; I have something to say to you. I can't talk to you at the house, with Olaf sitting there on the porch, weighing a thousand tons."

Clara laughed. "He won't be sitting there now. He's in bed by this time, and asleep—weighing a thousand tons."

Nils plodded on across the stubble. "Are you really going to spend the rest of your life like this, night after night, summer after summer? Haven't you anything better to do on a night like this than to wear yourself and Norman out tearing across the country to your father's and back? Besides, your father won't live forever, you know. His little place will be shut up or sold, and then you'll have nobody but the Ericsons. You'll have to fasten down the hatches for the winter then."

Clara moved her head restlessly. "Don't talk about that. I try never to think of it. If I lost Father I'd lose everything, even my hold over the Ericsons."

"Bah! You'd lose a good deal more than that. You'd lose your race, everything that makes you yourself. You've lost a good deal of it now."

"Of what?"

"Of your love of life, your capacity for delight."

Clara put her hands up to her face. "I haven't, Nils Ericson, I haven't! Say anything to me but that. I won't have it!" she declared vehemently.

Nils led the horse up to a straw stack, and turned to Clara, looking at her intently, as he had looked at her that Sunday afternoon at Vavrika's. "But why do you fight for that so? What good is the power to enjoy, if you never enjoy? Your hands are cold again; what are you afraid of all the time? Ah, you're afraid of losing it; that's what's the matter with you! And you will, Clara Vavrika, you will! When I used to know you—listen; you've caught a wild bird in your hand, haven't you, and felt its heart beat so hard that you were afraid it would shatter its little body to pieces? Well, you used to be just like that, a slender, eager thing with a wild delight inside you. That is how I

remembered you. And I come back and find you—a bitter
woman. This is a perfect ferret fight here; you live by
biting and being bitten. Can't you remember what life
used to be? Can't you remember that old delight? I've
never forgotten it, or known its like, on land or sea."

He drew the horse under the shadow of the straw
stack. Clara felt him take her foot out of the stirrup, and
she slid softly down into his arms. He kissed her slowly.
He was a deliberate man, but his nerves were steel when
he wanted anything. Something flashed out from him like
a knife out of a sheath. Clara felt everything slipping away
from her; she was flooded by the summer night. He thrust
his hand into his pocket, and then held it out at arm's
length. "Look," he said. The shadow of the straw stack fell
sharp across his wrist, and in the palm of his hand she saw
a silver dollar shining. "That's my pile," he muttered;
"will you go with me?"

Clara nodded, and dropped her forehead on his
shoulder.

Nils took a deep breath. "Will you go with me tonight?"

"Where?" she whispered softly.

"To town, to catch the midnight flyer."

Clara lifted her head and pulled herself together.
"Are you crazy, Nils? We couldn't go away like that."

"That's the only way we ever will go. You can't sit on
the bank and think about it. You have to plunge. That's
the way I've always done, and it's the right way for people
like you and me. There's nothing so dangerous as sitting
still. You've only got one life, one youth, and you can let it
slip through your fingers if you want to; nothing easier.
Most people do that. You'd be better off tramping the
roads with me than you are here." Nils held back her head
and looked into her eyes. "But I'm not that kind of a
tramp, Clara. You won't have to take in sewing. I'm with a
Norwegian shipping line; came over on business with the
New York offices, but now I'm going straight back to
Bergen. I expect I've got as much money as the Ericsons.
Father sent me a little to get started. They never knew
about that. There, I hadn't meant to tell you; I wanted you
to come on your own nerve."

Clara looked off across the fields. "It isn't that, Nils, but something seems to hold me. I'm afraid to pull against it. It comes out of the ground, I think."

"I know all about that. One has to tear loose. You're not needed here. Your father will understand; he's made like us. As for Olaf, Johanna will take better care of him than ever you could. It's now or never, Clara Vavrika. My bag's at the station; I smuggled it there yesterday."

Clara clung to him and hid her face against his shoulder. "Not tonight," she whispered. "Sit here and talk to me tonight. I don't want to go anywhere tonight. I may never love you like this again."

Nils laughed through his teeth. "You can't come that on me. That's not my way, Clara Vavrika. Eric's mare is over there behind the stacks, and I'm off on the midnight. It's goodbye, or off across the world with me. My carriage won't wait. I've written a letter to Olaf; I'll mail it in town. When he reads it he won't bother us—not if I know him. He'd rather have the land. Besides, I could demand an investigation of his administration of Cousin Henrik's estate, and that would be bad for a public man. You've no clothes, I know; but you can sit up tonight, and we can get everything on the way. Where's your old dash, Clara Vavrika? What's become of your Bohemian blood? I used to think you had courage enough for anything. Where's your nerve—what are you waiting for?"

Clara drew back her head, and he saw the slumberous fire in her eyes. "For you to say one thing, Nils Ericson."

"I never say that thing to any woman, Clara Vavrika." He leaned back, lifted her gently from the ground, and whispered through his teeth: "But I'll never, never let you go, not to any man on earth but me! Do you understand me? Now, wait here."

Clara sank down on a sheaf of wheat and covered her face with her hands. She did not know what she was going to do—whether she would go or stay. The great, silent country seemed to lay a spell upon her. The ground seemed to hold her as if by roots. Her knees were soft under her. She felt as if she could not bear separation from her old sorrows, from her old discontent. They were

dear to her, they had kept her alive, they were a part of
her. There would be nothing left of her if she were
wrenched away from them. Never could she pass beyond
that skyline against which her restlessness had beat so
many times. She felt as if her soul had built itself a nest
there on that horizon at which she looked every morning
and every evening, and it was dear to her, inexpressibly
dear. She pressed her fingers against her eyeballs to shut
it out. Beside her she heard the tramping of horses in the
soft earth. Nils said nothing to her. He put his hands
under her arms and lifted her lightly to her saddle. Then
he swung himself into his own.

"We shall have to ride fast to catch the midnight
train. A last gallop, Clara Vavrika. Forward!"

There was a start, a thud of hoofs along the moonlit
road, two dark shadows going over the hill; and then the
great, still land stretched untroubled under the azure
night. Two shadows had passed.

VII

A year after the flight of Olaf Ericson's wife, the night
train was steaming across the plains of Iowa. The conductor was hurrying through one of the day coaches, his
lantern on his arm, when a lank, fair-haired boy sat up in
one of the plush seats and tweaked him by the coat.

"What is the next stop, please, sir?"

"Red Oak, Iowa. But you go through to Chicago,
don't you?" He looked down, and noticed that the boy's
eyes were red and his face was drawn, as if he were in
trouble.

"Yes. But I was wondering whether I could get off at
the next place and get a train back to Omaha."

"Well, I suppose you could. Live in Omaha?"

"No. In the western part of the State. How soon do
we get to Red Oak?"

"Forty minutes. You'd better make up your mind, so
I can tell the baggageman to put your trunk off."

"Oh, never mind about that! I mean, I haven't got
any," the boy added, blushing.

"Run away," the conductor thought, as he slammed the coach door behind him.

Eric Ericson crumpled down in his seat and put his brown hand to his forehead. He had been crying, and he had had no supper, and his head was aching violently. "Oh, what shall I do?" he thought, as he looked dully down at his big shoes. "Nils will be ashamed of me; I haven't got any spunk."

Ever since Nils had run away with his brother's wife, life at home had been hard for little Eric. His mother and Olaf both suspected him of complicity. Mrs. Ericson was harsh and faultfinding, constantly wounding the boy's pride; and Olaf was always setting her against him.

Joe Vavrika heard often from his daughter. Clara had always been fond of her father, and happiness made her kinder. She wrote him long accounts of the voyage to Bergen, and of the trip she and Nils took through Bohemia to the little town where her father had grown up and where she herself was born. She visited all her kinsmen there, and sent her father news of his brother, who was a priest; of his sister, who had married a horse-breeder—of their big farm and their many children. These letters Joe always managed to read to little Eric. They contained messages for Eric and Hilda. Clara sent presents, too, which Eric never dared to take home and which poor little Hilda never even saw, though she loved to hear Eric tell about them when they were out getting the eggs together. But Olaf once saw Eric coming out of Vavrika's house —the old man had never asked the boy to come into his saloon—and Olaf went straight to his mother and told her. That night Mrs. Ericson came to Eric's room after he was in bed and made a terrible scene. She could be very terrifying when she was really angry. She forbade him ever to speak to Vavrika again, and after that night she would not allow him to go to town alone. So it was a long while before Eric got any more news of his brother. But old Joe suspected what was going on, and he carried Clara's letters about in his pocket. One Sunday he drove out to see a German friend of his, and chanced to catch sight of Eric, sitting by the cattle pond in the big pasture. They went together into Fritz Oberlies' barn, and read the letters and talked things over. Eric admitted that things were getting hard for him at home. That very night old Joe sat down and laboriously penned a statement of the case to his daughter.

Things got no better for Eric. His mother and Olaf felt that, however closely he was watched, he still, as they said, "heard." Mrs. Ericson could not admit neutrality. She had sent Johanna Vavrika packing back to her brother's, though Olaf would much rather have kept her than Anders' eldest daughter, whom Mrs. Ericson installed in her place. He was not so highhanded as his mother, and he once sulkily told her that she might better have taught her granddaughter to cook before she sent Johanna away. Olaf could have borne a good deal for the sake of prunes spiced in honey, the secret of which Johanna had taken away with her.

At last two letters came to Joe Vavrika: one from Nils, inclosing a postal order for money to pay Eric's passage to Bergen, and one from Clara, saying that Nils had a place for Eric in the offices of his company, that he was to live with them, and that they were only waiting for him to come. He was to leave New York on one of the boats of Nils' own line; the captain was one of their friends, and Eric was to make himself known at once.

Nils' directions were so explicit that a baby could have followed them, Eric felt. And here he was, nearing Red Oak, Iowa, and rocking backward and forward in despair. Never had he loved his brother so much, and never had the big world called to him so hard. But there was a lump in his throat which would not go down. Ever since nightfall he had been tormented by the thought of his mother, alone in that big house that had sent forth so many men. Her unkindness now seemed so little, and her loneliness so great. He remembered everything she had ever done for him: how frightened she had been when he tore his hand in the corn-sheller, and how she wouldn't let Olaf scold him. When Nils went away he didn't leave his mother all alone, or he would never have gone. Eric felt sure of that.

The train whistled. The conductor came in, smiling

not unkindly. "Well, young man, what are you going to do? We stop at Red Oak in three minutes."

"Yes, thank you. I'll let you know." The conductor went out, and the boy doubled up with misery. He couldn't let his one chance go like this. He felt for his breast pocket and crackled Nils' letter to give him courage. He didn't want Nils to be ashamed of him. The train stopped. Suddenly he remembered his brother's kind, twinkling eyes, that always looked at you as if from far away. The lump in his throat softened. "Ah, but Nils, Nils would *understand*!" he thought. "That's just it about Nils; he always understands."

A lank, pale boy with a canvas telescope stumbled off the train to the Red Oak siding, just as the conductor called, "All aboard!"

The next night Mrs. Ericson was sitting alone in her wooden rocking-chair on the front porch. Little Hilda had been sent to bed and had cried herself to sleep. The old woman's knitting was on her lap, but her hands lay motionless on top of it. For more than an hour she had not moved a muscle. She simply sat, as only the Ericsons and the mountains can sit. The house was dark, and there was no sound but the croaking of the frogs down in the pond of the little pasture.

Eric did not come home by the road, but across the fields, where no one could see him. He set his telescope down softly in the kitchen shed, and slipped noiselessly along the path to the front porch. He sat down on the step without saying anything. Mrs. Ericson made no sign, and the frogs croaked on. At last the boy spoke timidly.

"I've come back, Mother."

"Very well," said Mrs. Ericson.

Eric leaned over and picked up a little stick out of the grass.

"How about the milking?" he faltered.

"That's been done, hours ago."

"Who did you get?"

"Get? I did it myself. I can milk as good as any of you."

Eric slid along the step nearer to her. "Oh, Mother,

why did you?" he asked sorrowfully. "Why didn't you get
one of Otto's boys?"

"I didn't want anybody to know I was in need of a
boy," said Mrs. Ericson bitterly. She looked straight in
front of her and her mouth tightened. "I always meant to
give you the home farm," she added.

The boy stared and slid closer. "Oh, Mother," he
faltered, "I don't care about the farm. I came back because
I thought you might be needing me, maybe." He hung his
head and got no further.

"Very well," said Mrs. Ericson. Her hand went out
from her suddenly and rested on his head. Her fingers
twined themselves in his soft, pale hair. His tears splashed
down on the boards; happiness filled his heart.

The Troll Garden

Flavia and Her Artists

As the train neared Tarrytown, Imogen Willard began to wonder why she had consented to be one of Flavia's house party at all. She had not felt enthusiastic about it since leaving the city, and was experiencing a prolonged ebb of purpose, a current of chilling indecision, under which she vainly sought for the motive which had induced her to accept Flavia's invitation.

Perhaps it was a vague curiosity to see Flavia's husband, who had been the magician of her childhood and the hero of innumerable Arabian fairy tales. Perhaps it was a desire to see M. Roux, whom Flavia had announced as the especial attraction of the occasion. Perhaps it was a wish to study that remarkable woman in her own setting.

Imogen admitted a mild curiosity concerning Flavia. She was in the habit of taking people rather seriously, but somehow found it impossible to take Flavia so, because of the very vehemence and insistence with which Flavia demanded it. Submerged in her studies, Imogen had, of late years, seen very little of Flavia; but Flavia, in her hurried visits to New York, between her excursions from studio to studio—her luncheons with this lady who had to play at a matinee, and her dinners with that singer who had an evening concert—had seen enough of her friend's handsome daughter to conceive for her an inclination of such violence and assurance as only Flavia could afford. The fact that Imogen had shown rather marked capacity in certain esoteric lines of scholarship, and had decided to specialize in a well-sounding branch of philology at the Ecole des Chartes, had fairly placed her in that category of "interesting people" whom Flavia considered her natural affinities, and lawful prey.

When Imogen stepped upon the station platform she was immediately appropriated by her hostess, whose commanding figure and assurance of attire she had recognized from a distance. She was hurried into a high tilbury and Flavia, taking the driver's cushion beside her, gathered up the reins with an experienced hand.

"My dear girl," she remarked, as she turned the horses up the street, "I was afraid the train might be late. M. Roux insisted upon coming up by boat and did not arrive until after seven."

"To think of M. Roux's being in this part of the world at all, and subject to the vicissitudes of river boats! Why in the world did he come over?" queried Imogen with lively interest. "He is the sort of man who must dissolve and become a shadow outside of Paris."

"Oh, we have a houseful of the most interesting people," said Flavia, professionally. "We have actually managed to get Ivan Schemetzkin. He was ill in California at the close of his concert tour, you know, and he is recuperating with us, after his wearing journey from the coast. Then there is Jules Martel, the painter; Signor Donati, the tenor; Professor Schotte, who has dug up Assyria, you know; Restzhoff, the Russian chemist; Alcée Buisson, the philologist; Frank Wellington, the novelist; and Will Maidenwood, the editor of *Woman*. Then there is my second cousin, Jemima Broadwood, who made such a hit in Pinero's comedy last winter, and Frau Lichtenfeld. *Have* you read her?"

Imogen confessed her utter ignorance of Frau Lichtenfeld, and Flavia went on.

"Well, she is a most remarkable person; one of those advanced German women, a militant iconoclast, and this drive will not be long enough to permit of my telling you her history. Such a story! Her novels were the talk of all Germany when I was there last, and several of them have been suppressed—an honor in Germany, I understand. 'At Whose Door' has been translated. I am so unfortunate as not to read German."

"I'm all excitement at the prospect of meeting Miss Broadwood," said Imogen. "I've seen her in nearly everything she does. Her stage personality is delightful. She always reminds me of a nice, clean, pink-and-white boy who has just had his cold bath, and come down all aglow for a run before breakfast."

"Yes, but isn't it unfortunate that she will limit herself to those minor comedy parts that are so little appreciated in this country? One ought to be satisfied with nothing less than the best, ought one?" The peculiar, breathy tone in which Flavia always uttered that word "best," the most worn in her vocabulary, always jarred on Imogen and always made her obdurate.

"I don't at all agree with you," she said reservedly. "I thought everyone admitted that the most remarkable thing about Miss Broadwood is her admirable sense of fitness, which is rare enough in her profession."

Flavia could not endure being contradicted; she always seemed to regard it in the light of a defeat, and usually colored unbecomingly. Now she changed the subject.

"Look, my dear," she cried, "there is Frau Lichtenfeld now, coming to meet us. Doesn't she look as if she had just escaped out of Valhalla? She is actually over six feet."

Imogen saw a woman of immense stature, in a very short skirt and a broad, flapping sun hat, striding down the hillside at a long, swinging gait. The refugee from Valhalla approached, panting. Her heavy, Teutonic features were scarlet from the rigor of her exercise, and her hair, under her flapping sun hat, was tightly befrizzled about her brow. She fixed her sharp little eyes upon Imogen and extended both her hands.

"So this is the little friend?" she cried, in a rolling baritone.

Imogen was quite as tall as her hostess; but everything, she reflected, is comparative. After the introduction Flavia apologized.

"I wish I could ask you to drive up with us, Frau Lichtenfeld."

"Ah, no!" cried the giantess, drooping her head in humorous caricature of a time-honored pose of the heroines of sentimental romances. "It has never been my fate to be fitted into corners. I have never known the sweet privileges of the tiny."

Laughing, Flavia started the ponies, and the colossal woman, standing in the middle of the dusty road, took off her wide hat and waved them a farewell which, in scope of gesture, recalled the salute of a plumed cavalier.

When they arrived at the house, Imogen looked about her with keen curiosity, for this was veritably the work of Flavia's hands, the materialization of hopes long deferred. They passed directly into a large, square hall with a gallery on three sides, studio fashion. This opened at one end into a Dutch breakfast room, beyond which was the large dining room. At the other end of the hall was the music room. There was a smoking room, which one entered through the library behind the staircase. On the second floor there was the same general arrangement: a square hall, and, opening from it, the guest chambers, or, as Miss Broadwood termed them, the "cages."

When Imogen went to her room, the guests had begun to return from their various afternoon excursions. Boys were gliding through the halls with ice water, covered trays, and flowers, colliding with maids and valets who carried shoes and other articles of wearing apparel. Yet, all this was done in response to inaudible bells, on felt soles, and in hushed voices, so that there was very little confusion about it.

Flavia had at last built her house and hewn out her seven pillars; there could be no doubt, now, that the asylum for talent, the sanatorium of the arts, so long projected, was an accomplished fact. Her ambition had long ago outgrown the dimensions of her house on Prairie Avenue; besides, she had bitterly complained that in Chicago traditions were against her. Her project had been delayed by Arthur's doggedly standing out for the Michigan woods, but Flavia knew well enough that certain of the *rarae aves*—"the best"—could not be lured so far away from the seaport, so she declared herself for the historic Hudson and knew no retreat. The establishing of a New York office had at length overthrown Arthur's last valid objection to quitting the lake country for three months of the year; and Arthur could be wearied into anything, as those who knew him knew.

Flavia's house was the mirror of her exultation; it was

a temple to the gods of Victory, a sort of triumphal arch. In her earlier days she had swallowed experiences that would have unmanned one of less torrential enthusiasm or blind pertinacity. But, of late years, her determination had told; she saw less and less of those mysterious persons with mysterious obstacles in their path and mysterious grievances against the world, who had once frequented her house on Prairie Avenue. In the stead of this multitude of the unarrived, she had now the few, the select, "the best." Of all that band of indigent retainers who had once fed at her board like the suitors in the halls of Penelope, only Alcée Buisson still retained his right of entrée. He alone had remembered that ambition hath a knapsack at his back, wherein he puts alms to oblivion, and he alone had been considerate enough to do what Flavia had expected of him, and give his name a current value in the world. Then, as Miss Broadwood put it, "he was her first real one,"—and Flavia, like Mohammed, could remember her first believer.

"The House of Song," as Miss Broadwood had called it, was the outcome of Flavia's more exalted strategies. A woman who made less a point of sympathizing with their delicate organisms, might have sought to plunge these phosphorescent pieces into the tepid bath of domestic life; but Flavia's discernment was deeper. This must be a refuge where the shrinking soul, the sensitive brain, should be unconstrained; where the caprice of fancy should outweigh the civil code, if necessary. She considered that this much Arthur owed her; for she, in her turn, had made concessions. Flavia had, indeed, quite an equipment of epigrams to the effect that our century creates the iron genii which evolve its fairy tales: but the fact that her husband's name was annually painted upon some ten thousand threshing machines in reality contributed very little to her happiness.

Arthur Hamilton was born and had spent his boyhood in the West Indies, and physically he had never lost the brand of the tropics. His father, after inventing the machine which bore his name, had returned to the States to patent and manufacture it. After leaving college, Arthur had spent five years ranching in the West and traveling abroad. Upon his father's death he had returned to Chicago and, to the astonishment of all his friends, had taken up the business—without any demonstration of enthusiasm, but with quiet perseverance, marked ability, and amazing industry. Why or how a self-sufficient, rather ascetic man of thirty, indifferent in manner, wholly negative in all other personal relations, should have doggedly wooed and finally married Flavia Malcolm was a problem that had vexed older heads than Imogen's.

While Imogen was dressing she heard a knock at her door, and a young woman entered whom she at once recognized as Jemima Broadwood—"Jimmy" Broadwood she was called by people in her own profession. While there was something unmistakably professional in her frank *savoir-faire*, "Jimmy's" was one of those faces to which the rouge never seems to stick. Her eyes were keen and gray as a windy April sky, and so far from having been seared by calcium lights, you might have fancied they had never looked on anything less bucolic than growing fields and country fairs. She wore her thick, brown hair short and parted at the side; and, rather than hinting at freakishness, this seemed admirably in keeping with her fresh, boyish countenance. She extended to Imogen a large, well-shaped hand which it was a pleasure to clasp.

"Ah! You are Miss Willard, and I see I need not introduce myself. Flavia said you were kind enough to express a wish to meet me, and I preferred to meet you alone. Do you mind if I smoke?"

"Why, certainly not," said Imogen, somewhat disconcerted and looking hurriedly about for matches.

"There, be calm, I'm always prepared," said Miss Broadwood, checking Imogen's flurry with a soothing gesture, and producing an oddly fashioned silver match-case from some mysterious recess in her dinner gown. She sat down in a deep chair, crossed her patent-leather Oxfords, and lit her cigarette. "This matchbox," she went on meditatively, "once belonged to a Prussian officer. He shot himself in his bathtub, and I bought it at the sale of his effects."

Imogen had not yet found any suitable reply to make to this rather irrelevant confidence, when Miss Broadwood turned to her cordially: "I'm awfully glad you've come, Miss Willard, though I've not quite decided why you did it. I wanted very much to meet you. Flavia gave me your thesis to read."

"Why, how funny!" ejaculated Imogen.

"On the contrary," remarked Miss Broadwood. "I thought it decidedly lacked humor."

"I meant," stammered Imogen, beginning to feel very much like Alice in Wonderland, "I meant that I thought it rather strange Mrs. Hamilton should fancy you would be interested."

Miss Broadwood laughed heartily. "Now, don't let my rudeness frighten you. Really, I found it very interesting, and no end impressive. You see, most people in my profession are good for absolutely nothing else, and, therefore, they have a deep and abiding conviction that in some other line they might have shone. Strange to say, scholarship is the object of our envious and particular admiration. Anything in type impresses us greatly; that's why so many of us marry authors or newspapermen and lead miserable lives." Miss Broadwood saw that she had rather disconcerted Imogen, and blithely tacked in another direction. "You see," she went on, tossing aside her half-consumed cigarette, "some years ago Flavia would not have deemed me worthy to open the pages of your thesis—nor to be one of her house party of the chosen, for that matter. I've Pinero to thank for both pleasures. It all depends on the class of business I'm playing whether I'm in favor or not. Flavia is my second cousin, you know, so I can say whatever disagreeable things I choose with perfect good grace. I'm quite desperate for someone to laugh with, so I'm going to fasten myself upon you—for, of course, one can't expect any of these gypsy-dago people to see anything funny. I don't intend you shall lose the humor of the situation. What do you think of Flavia's infirmary for the arts, anyway?"

"Well, it's rather too soon for me to have any opinion at all," said Imogen, as she again turned to her dressing. "So far, you are the only one of the artists I've met."

"One of them?" echoed Miss Broadwood. "One of the *artists*? My offense may be rank, my dear, but I really don't deserve that. Come, now, whatever badges of my tribe I may bear upon me, just let me divest you of any notion that I take myself seriously."

Imogen turned from the mirror in blank astonishment and sat down on the arm of a chair, facing her visitor. "I can't fathom you at all, Miss Broadwood," she said frankly. "Why shouldn't you take yourself seriously? What's the use of beating about the bush? Surely you know that you are one of the few players on this side of the water who have at all the spirit of natural or ingenuous comedy?"

"Thank you, my dear. Now we are quite even about the thesis, aren't we? Oh, did you mean it? Well, you *are* a clever girl. But you see it doesn't do to permit oneself to look at it in that light. If we do, we always go to pieces and waste our substance astarring as the unhappy daughter of the Capulets. But there, I hear Flavia coming to take you down; and just remember I'm not one of them—the artists, I mean."

Flavia conducted Imogen and Miss Broadwood downstairs. As they reached the lower hall they heard voices from the music room, and dim figures were lurking in the shadows under the gallery, but their hostess led straight to the smoking room. The June evening was chilly, and a fire had been lighted in the fireplace. Through the deepening dusk, the firelight flickered upon the pipes and curious weapons on the wall and threw an orange glow over the Turkish hangings. One side of the smoking room was entirely of glass, separating it from the conservatory, which was flooded with white light from the electric bulbs. There was about the darkened room some suggestion of certain chambers in the Arabian Nights, opening on a court of palms. Perhaps it was partially this memory-evoking suggestion that caused Imogen to start so violently when she saw dimly, in a blur of shadow, the figure of a man, who sat smoking in a low, deep chair before the fire. He was long, and thin, and brown. His long, nerveless hands drooped from the arms of his chair. A brown mustache shaded his mouth, and his eyes were sleepy and apathetic. When Imogen entered he rose indolently and gave her his hand, his manner barely courteous.

"I am glad you arrived promptly, Miss Willard," he said with an indifferent drawl. "Flavia was afraid you might be late. You had a pleasant ride up, I hope?"

"Oh, very, thank you, Mr. Hamilton," she replied, feeling that he did not particularly care whether she replied at all.

Flavia explained that she had not yet had time to dress for dinner, as she had been attending to Mr. Will Maidenwood, who had become faint after hurting his finger in an obdurate window, and immediately excused herself. As she left, Hamilton turned to Miss Broadwood with a rather spiritless smile.

"Well, Jimmy," he remarked, "I brought up a piano box full of fireworks for the boys. How do you suppose we'll manage to keep them until the Fourth?"

"We can't, unless we steel ourselves to deny there are any on the premises," said Miss Broadwood, seating herself on a low stool by Hamilton's chair and leaning back against the mantel. "Have you seen Helen, and has she told you the tragedy of the tooth?"

"She met me at the station, with her tooth wrapped up in tissue paper. I had tea with her an hour ago. Better sit down, Miss Willard;" he rose and pushed a chair toward Imogen, who was standing peering into the conservatory. "We are scheduled to dine at seven, but they seldom get around before eight."

By this time Imogen had made out that here the plural pronoun, third person, always referred to the artists. As Hamilton's manner did not spur one to cordial intercourse, and as his attention seemed directed to Miss Broadwood, insofar as it could be said to be directed to anyone, she sat down facing the conservatory and watched him, unable to decide in how far he was identical with the man who had first met Flavia Malcolm in her mother's house, twelve years ago. Did he at all remember having known her as a little girl, and why did his indifference hurt her so, after all these years? Had some remnant of her childish affection for him gone on living, somewhere down in the sealed caves of her consciousness, and had she really expected to find it possible to be fond of him again? Suddenly she saw a light in the man's sleepy eyes, an unmistakable expression of interest and pleasure that fairly startled her. She turned quickly in the direction of his glance, and saw Flavia, just entering, dressed for dinner and lit by the effulgence of her most radiant manner. Most people considered Flavia handsome, and there was no gainsaying that she carried her five-and-thirty years splendidly. Her figure had never grown matronly, and her face was of the sort that does not show wear. Its blond tints were as fresh and enduring as enamel—and quite as hard. Its usual expression was one of tense, often strained, animation, which compressed her lips nervously. A perfect scream of animation, Miss Broadwood had called it, created and maintained by sheer, indomitable force of will. Flavia's appearance on any scene whatever made a ripple, caused a certain agitation and recognition, and, among impressionable people, a certain uneasiness. For all her sparkling assurance of manner, Flavia was certainly always ill at ease and, even more certainly, anxious. She seemed not convinced of the established order of material things, seemed always trying to conceal her feeling that walls might crumble, chasms open, or the fabric of her life fly to the winds in irretrievable entanglement. At least this was the impression Imogen got from that note in Flavia which was so manifestly false.

Hamilton's keen, quick, satisfied glance at his wife had recalled to Imogen all her inventory of speculations about them. She looked at him with compassionate surprise. As a child she had never permitted herself to believe that Hamilton cared at all for the woman who had taken him away from her; and since she had begun to think about them again, it had never occurred to her that anyone could become attached to Flavia in that deeply personal and exclusive sense. It seemed quite as irrational as trying to possess oneself of Broadway at noon.

When they went out to dinner Imogen realized the completeness of Flavia's triumph. They were people of one name, mostly, like kings; people whose names stirred the imagination like a romance or a melody. With the notable exception of M. Roux, Imogen had seen most of them before, either in concert halls or lecture rooms; but they looked noticably older and dimmer than she remembered them.

Opposite her sat Schemetzkin, the Russian pianist, a short, corpulent man, with an apoplectic face and purplish skin, his thick, iron-gray hair tossed back from his forehead. Next to the German giantess sat the Italian tenor —the tiniest of men—pale, with soft, light hair, much in disorder, very red lips, and fingers yellowed by cigarettes. Frau Lichtenfeld shone in a gown of emerald green, fitting so closely as to enhance her natural floridness. However, to do the good lady justice, let her attire be never so modest, it gave an effect of barbaric splendor. At her left sat Herr Schotte, the Assyriologist, whose features were effectually concealed by the convergence of his hair and beard, and whose glasses were continually falling into his plate. This gentleman had removed more tons of earth in the course of his explorations than had any of his confreres, and his vigorous attack upon his food seemed to suggest the strenuous nature of his accustomed toil. His eyes were small and deeply set, and his forehead bulged fiercely above his eyes in a bony ridge. His heavy brows completed the leonine suggestion of his face. Even to Imogen, who knew something of his work and greatly respected it, he was entirely too reminiscent of the Stone Age to be altogether an agreeable dinner companion. He seemed, indeed, to have absorbed something of the savagery of those early types of life which he continually studied.

Frank Wellington, the young Kansas man who had been two years out of Harvard and had published three historical novels, sat next to Mr. Will Maidenwood, who was still pale from his recent sufferings and carried his hand bandaged. They took little part in the general conversation, but, like the lion and the unicorn, were always at it, discussing, every time they met, whether there were or were not passages in Mr. Wellington's works which should be eliminated, out of consideration for the Young Person. Wellington had fallen into the hands of a great American syndicate which most effectually befriended struggling authors whose struggles were in the right direction, and which had guaranteed to make him famous before he was thirty. Feeling the security of his position he stoutly defended those passages which jarred upon the sensitive nerves of the young editor of *Woman*. Maidenwood, in the smoothest of voices, urged the necessity of the author's recognizing certain restrictions at the outset, and Miss Broadwood, who joined the argument quite without invitation or encouragement, seconded him with pointed and malicious remarks which caused the young editor manifest discomfort. Restzhoff, the chemist, demanded the attention of the entire company for his exposition of his devices for manufacturing ice cream from vegetable oils and for administering drugs in bonbons.

Flavia, always noticeably restless at dinner, was somewhat apathetic toward the advocate of peptonized chocolate and was plainly concerned about the sudden departure of M. Roux, who had announced that it would be necessary for him to leave tomorrow. M. Emile Roux, who sat at Flavia's right, was a man in middle life and quite bald, clearly without personal vanity, though his publishers preferred to circulate only those of his portraits taken in his ambrosial youth. Imogen was considerably shocked at his unlikeness to the slender, black-stocked Rolla he had looked at twenty. He had declined into the florid, settled heaviness of indifference and approaching age. There was, however, a certain look of durability and solidity about him; the look of a man who has earned the right to be fat and bald, and even silent at dinner if he chooses.

Throughout the discussion between Wellington and Will Maidenwood, though they invited his participation, he remained silent, betraying no sign either of interest or contempt. Since his arrival he had directed most of his conversation to Hamilton, who had never read one of his twelve great novels. This perplexed and troubled Flavia. On the night of his arrival Jules Martel had enthusiastically declared, "There are schools and schools, manners and manners; but Roux is Roux, and Paris sets its watches by his clock." Flavia had already repeated this remark to Imogen. It haunted her, and each time she quoted it she was impressed anew.

Flavia shifted the conversation uneasily, evidently exasperated and excited by her repeated failures to draw the novelist out. "Monsieur Roux," she began abruptly, with her most animated smile, "I remember so well a statement I read some years ago in your 'Mes Etudes des Femmes' to the effect that you had never met a really intellectual woman. May I ask, without being impertinent, whether that assertion still represents your experience?"

"I meant, madam," said the novelist conservatively, "intellectual in a sense very special, as we say of men in whom the purely intellectual functions seem almost independent."

"And you still think a woman so constituted a mythical personage?" persisted Flavia, nodding her head encouragingly.

"*Une Méduse*, madam, who, if she were discovered, would transmute us all into stone," said the novelist, bowing gravely. "If she existed at all," he added deliberately, "it was my business to find her, and she has cost me many a vain pilgrimage. Like Rudel of Tripoli, I have crossed seas and penetrated deserts to seek her out. I have, indeed, encountered women of learning whose industry I have been compelled to respect; many who have possessed beauty and charm and perplexing cleverness; a few with remarkable information and a sort of fatal facility."

"And Mrs. Browning, George Eliot, and your own Mme. Dudevant?" queried Flavia with that fervid enthusiasm with which she could, on occasion, utter things simply incomprehensible for their banality—at her feats of this sort Miss Broadwood was wont to sit breathless with admiration.

"Madam, while the intellect was undeniably present in the performances of those women, it was only the stick of the rocket. Although this woman has eluded me I have studied her conditions and perturbances as astronomers conjecture the orbits of planets they have never seen. If she exists, she is probably neither an artist nor a woman with a mission, but an obscure personage, with imperative intellectual needs, who absorbs rather than produces."

Flavia, still nodding nervously, fixed a strained glance of interrogation upon M. Roux. "Then you think she would be a woman whose first necessity would be to know, whose instincts would be satisfied only with the best, who could draw from others; appreciative, merely?"

The novelist lifted his dull eyes to his interlocutress with an untranslatable smile and a slight inclination of his shoulders. "Exactly so; you are really remarkable, madam," he added, in a tone of cold astonishment.

After dinner the guests took their coffee in the music room, where Schemetzkin sat down at the piano to drum ragtime, and give his celebrated imitation of the boarding-school girl's execution of Chopin. He flatly refused to play anything more serious, and would practice only in the morning, when he had the music room to himself. Hamilton and M. Roux repaired to the smoking room to discuss the necessity of extending the tax on manufactured articles in France—one of those conversations which particularly exasperated Flavia.

After Schemetzkin had grimaced and tortured the keyboard with malicious vulgarities for half an hour, Signor Donati, to put an end to his torture, consented to sing, and Flavia and Imogen went to fetch Arthur to play his accompaniments. Hamilton rose with an annoyed look and placed his cigarette on the mantel. "Why yes, Flavia, I'll accompany him, provided he sings something with a melody, Italian arias or ballads, and provided the recital is not interminable."

"You will join us, M. Roux?"

"Thank you, but I have some letters to write," replied the novelist, bowing.

As Flavia had remarked to Imogen, "Arthur really played accompaniments remarkably well." To hear him recalled vividly the days of her childhood, when he always used to spend his business vacations at her mother's home in Maine. He had possessed for her that almost hypnotic influence which young men sometimes exert upon little girls. It was a sort of phantom love affair, subjective and fanciful, a precocity of instinct, like that tender and maternal concern which some little girls feel for their dolls. Yet this childish infatuation is capable of all the depressions and exaltations of love itself; it has its bitter jealousies, cruel disappointments, its exacting caprices.

Summer after summer she had awaited his coming

and wept at his departure, indifferent to the gayer young men who had called her their sweetheart and laughed at everything she said. Although Hamilton never said so, she had been always quite sure that he was fond of her. When he pulled her up the river to hunt for fairy knolls shut about by low, hanging willows, he was often silent for an hour at a time, yet she never felt he was bored or was neglecting her. He would lie in the sand smoking, his eyes half-closed, watching her play, and she was always conscious that she was entertaining him. Sometimes he would take a copy of "Alice in Wonderland" in his pocket, and no one could read it as he could, laughing at her with his dark eyes, when anything amused him. No one else could laugh so, with just their eyes, and without moving a muscle of their face. Though he usually smiled at passages that seemed not at all funny to the child, she always laughed gleefully, because he was so seldom moved to mirth that any such demonstration delighted her and she took the credit of it entirely to herself. Her own inclination had been for serious stories, with sad endings, like the Little Mermaid, which he had once told her in an unguarded moment when she had a cold, and was put to bed early on her birthday night and cried because she could not have her party. But he highly disapproved of this preference, and had called it a morbid taste, and always shook his finger at her when she asked for the story. When she had been particularly good, or particularly neglected by other people, then he would sometimes melt and tell her the story, and never laugh at her if she enjoyed the "sad ending" even to tears. When Flavia had taken him away and he came no more, she wept inconsolably for the space of two weeks, and refused to learn her lessons. Then she found the story of the Little Mermaid herself, and forgot him.

Imogen had discovered at dinner that he could still smile at one secretly, out of his eyes, and that he had the old manner of outwardly seeming bored, but letting you know that he was not. She was intensely curious about his exact state of feeling toward his wife, and more curious still to catch a sense of his final adjustment to the conditions of life in general. This, she could not help feeling, she might get again—if she could have him alone for an hour, in some place where there was a little river and a sandy cove bordered by drooping willows, and a blue sky seen through white sycamore boughs.

That evening, before retiring, Flavia entered her husband's room, where he sat in his smoking jacket, in one of his favorite low chairs.

"I suppose it's a grave responsibility to bring an ardent, serious young thing like Imogen here among all these fascinating personages," she remarked reflectively. "But, after all, one can never tell. These grave, silent girls have their own charm, even for facile people."

"Oh, so that is your plan?" queried her husband dryly. "I was wondering why you got her up here. She doesn't seem to mix well with the faciles. At least, so it struck me."

Flavia paid no heed to this jeering remark, but repeated, "No, after all, it may not be a bad thing."

"Then do consign her to that shaken reed, the tenor," said her husband yawning. "I remember she used to have a taste for the pathetic."

"And then," remarked Flavia coquettishly, "after all, I owe her mother a return in kind. She was not afraid to trifle with destiny."

But Hamilton was asleep in his chair.

Next morning Imogen found only Miss Broadwood in the breakfast room.

"Good morning, my dear girl, whatever are you doing up so early? They never breakfast before eleven. Most of them take their coffee in their room. Take this place by me."

Miss Broadwood looked particularly fresh and encouraging in her blue serge walking skirt, her open jacket displaying an expanse of stiff, white shirt bosom, dotted with some almost imperceptible figure, and a dark blue-and-white necktie, neatly knotted under her wide, rolling collar. She wore a white rosebud in the lapel of her coat, and decidedly she seemed more than ever like a nice, clean boy on his holiday. Imogen was just hoping that they would breakfast alone when Miss Broadwood exclaimed,

"Ah, there comes Arthur with the children. That's the reward of early rising in this house; you never get to see the youngsters at any other time."

Hamilton entered, followed by two dark, handsome little boys. The girl, who was very tiny, blonde like her mother, and exceedingly frail, he carried in his arms. The boys came up and said good morning with an ease and cheerfulness uncommon, even in well-bred children, but the little girl hid her face on her father's shoulder.

"She's a shy little lady," he explained as he put her gently down in her chair. "I'm afraid she's like her father; she can't seem to get used to meeting people. And you, Miss Willard, did you dream of the White Rabbit or the Little Mermaid?"

"Oh, I dreamed of them all! All the personages of that buried civilization," cried Imogen, delighted that his estranged manner of the night before had entirely vanished and feeling that, somehow, the old confidential relations had been restored during the night.

"Come, William," said Miss Broadwood, turning to the younger of the two boys, "and what did you dream about?"

"We dreamed," said William gravely—he was the more assertive of the two and always spoke for both—"we dreamed that there were fireworks hidden in the basement of the carriage house; lots and lots of fireworks."

His elder brother looked up at him with apprehensive astonishment, while Miss Broadwood hastily put her napkin to her lips and Hamilton dropped his eyes. "If little boys dream things, they are so apt not to come true," he reflected sadly. This shook even the redoubtable William, and he glanced nervously at his brother. "But do things vanish just because they have been dreamed?" he objected.

"Generally that is the very best reason for their vanishing," said Arthur gravely.

"But, Father, people can't help what they dream," remonstrated Edward gently.

"Oh, come! You're making these children talk like a Maeterlinck dialogue," laughed Miss Broadwood.

Flavia presently entered, a book in her hand, and

bade them all good morning. "Come, little people, which story shall it be this morning?" she asked winningly. Greatly excited, the children followed her into the garden. "She does then, sometimes," murmured Imogen as they left the breakfast room.

"Oh, yes, to be sure," said Miss Broadwood cheerfully. "She reads a story to them every morning in the most picturesque part of the garden. The mother of the Gracchi, you know. She does so long, she says, for the time when they will be intellectual companions for her. What do you say to a walk over the hills?"

As they left the house they met Frau Lichtenfeld and the bushy Herr Schotte—the professor cut an astonishing figure in golf stockings—returning from a walk and engaged in an animated conversation on the tendencies of German fiction.

"Aren't they the most attractive little children," exclaimed Imogen as they wound down the road toward the river.

"Yes, and you must not fail to tell Flavia that you think so. She will look at you in a sort of startled way and say, 'Yes, aren't they?' and maybe she will go off and hunt them up and have tea with them, to fully appreciate them. She is awfully afraid of missing anything good, is Flavia. The way those youngsters manage to conceal their guilty presence in the House of Song is a wonder."

"But don't any of the artist-folk fancy children?" asked Imogen.

"Yes, they just fancy them and no more. The chemist remarked the other day that children are like certain salts which need not be actualized because the formulae are quite sufficient for practical purposes. I don't see how even Flavia can endure to have that man about."

"I have always been rather curious to know what Arthur thinks of it all," remarked Imogen cautiously.

"Thinks of it!" ejaculated Miss Broadwood. "Why, my dear, what would any man think of having his house turned into an hotel, habited by freaks who discharge his servants, borrow his money, and insult his neighbors? This place is shunned like a lazaretto!"

"Well, then, why does he—why does he——" persisted Imogen.

"Bah!" interrupted Miss Broadwood impatiently, "why did he in the first place? That's the question."

"Marry her, you mean?" said Imogen coloring.

"Exactly so," said Miss Broadwood sharply, as she snapped the lid of her matchbox.

"I suppose that is a question rather beyond us, and certainly one which we cannot discuss," said Imogen. "But his toleration on this one point puzzles me, quite apart from other complications."

"Toleration? Why this point, as you call it, simply *is* Flavia. Who could conceive of her without it? I don't know where it's all going to end, I'm sure, and I'm equally sure that, if it were not for Arthur, I shouldn't care," declared Miss Broadwood, drawing her shoulders together.

"But will it end at all, now?"

"Such an absurd state of things can't go on indefinitely. A man isn't going to see his wife make a guy of herself forever, is he? Chaos has already begun in the servants' quarters. There are six different languages spoken there now. You see, it's all on an entirely false basis. Flavia hasn't the slightest notion of what these people are really like, their good and their bad alike escape her. They, on the other hand, can't imagine what she is driving at. Now, Arthur is worse off than either faction; he is not in the fairy story in that he sees these people exactly as they are, *but* he is utterly unable to see Flavia as they see her. There you have the situation. Why can't he see her as we do? My dear, that has kept me awake o' nights. This man who has thought so much and lived so much, who is naturally a critic, really takes Flavia at very nearly her own estimate. But now I am entering upon a wilderness. From a brief acquaintance with her you can know nothing of the icy fastnesses of Flavia's self-esteem. It's like St. Peter's; you can't realize its magnitude at once. You have to grow into a sense of it by living under its shadow. It has perplexed even Emile Roux, that merciless dissector of egoism. She has puzzled him the more because he saw at a glance what some of them do not perceive at once, and what will be mercifully concealed from Arthur until the

trump sounds; namely, that all Flavia's artists have done
or ever will do means exactly as much to her as a symphony means to an oyster; that there is no bridge by
which the significance of any work of art could be conveyed to her."

"Then, in the name of goodness, why does she bother?"
gasped Imogen. "She is pretty, wealthy, well-established;
why should she bother?"

"That's what M. Roux has kept asking himself. I can't
pretend to analyze it. She reads papers on the Literary
Landmarks of Paris, the Loves of the Poets, and that sort
of thing, to clubs out in Chicago. To Flavia it is more
necessary to be called clever than to breathe. I would give
a good deal to know that glum Frenchman's diagnosis. He
has been watching her out of those fishy eyes of his as a
biologist watches a hemisphereless frog."

For several days after M. Roux's departure Flavia
gave an embarrassing share of her attention to Imogen.
Embarrassing, because Imogen had the feeling of being
energetically and futilely explored, she knew not for what.
She felt herself under the globe of an air pump, expected
to yield up something. When she confined the conversation to matters of general interest Flavia conveyed to her
with some pique that her one endeavor in life had been to
fit herself to converse with her friends upon those things
which vitally interested them. "One has no right to accept
their best from people unless one gives, isn't it so? I want
to be able to give——!" she declared vaguely. Yet whenever
Imogen strove to pay her tithes and plunged bravely into
her plans for study next winter, Flavia grew absent-minded
and interrupted her by amazing generalizations or by such
embarrassing questions as, "And these grim studies really
have charm for you; you are quite buried in them; they
make other things seem light and ephemeral?"

"I rather feel as though I had got in here under false
pretenses," Imogen confided to Miss Broadwood. "I'm
sure I don't know what it is that she wants of me."

"Ah," chuckled Jemima, "you are not equal to these
heart to heart talks with Flavia. You utterly fail to com-
municate to her the atmosphere of that untroubled joy in
which you dwell. You must remember that she gets no

feeling out of things herself, and she demands that you impart yours to her by some process of psychic transmission. I once met a blind girl, blind from birth, who could discuss the peculiarities of the Barbizon school with just Flavia's glibness and enthusiasm. Ordinarily Flavia knows how to get what she wants from people, and her memory is wonderful. One evening I heard her giving Frau Lichtenfeld some random impressions about Hedda Gabler which she extracted from me five years ago; giving them with an impassioned conviction of which I was never guilty. But I have known other people who could appropriate your stories and opinions; Flavia is infinitely more subtle than that; she can soak up the very thrash and drift of your daydreams, and take the very thrills off your back, as it were."

After some days of unsuccessful effort, Flavia withdrew herself, and Imogen found Hamilton ready to catch her when she was tossed afield. He seemed only to have been awaiting this crisis, and at once their old intimacy reestablished itself as a thing inevitable and beautifully prepared for. She convinced herself that she had not been mistaken in him, despite all the doubts that had come up in later years, and this renewal of faith set more than one question thumping in her brain. "How did he, how can he?" she kept repeating with a tinge of her childish resentment, "what right had he to waste anything so fine?"

When Imogen and Arthur were returning from a walk before luncheon one morning about a week after M. Roux's departure, they noticed an absorbed group before one of the hall windows. Herr Schotte and Restzhoff sat on the window seat with a newspaper between them, while Wellington, Schemetzkin, and Will Maidenwood looked over their shoulders. They seemed intensely interested, Herr Schotte occasionally pounding his knees with his fists in ebullitions of barbaric glee. When Imogen entered the hall, however, the men were all sauntering toward the breakfast room and the paper was lying innocently on the divan. During luncheon the personnel of that window group were unwontedly animated and agreeable—all save Schemetzkin, whose stare was blanker than ever, as though

Roux's mantle of insulting indifference had fallen upon him, in addition to his own oblivious self-absorption. Will Maidenwood seemed embarrassed and annoyed; the chemist employed himself with making polite speeches to Hamilton. Flavia did not come down to lunch—and there was a malicious gleam under Herr Schotte's eyebrows. Frank Wellington announced nervously that an imperative letter from his protecting syndicate summoned him to the city.

After luncheon the men went to the golf links, and Imogen, at the first opportunity, possessed herself of the newspaper which had been left on the divan. One of the first things that caught her eye was an article headed "Roux on Tuft Hunters; The Advanced American Woman as He Sees Her; Aggressive, Superficial, and Insincere." The entire interview was nothing more nor less than a satiric characterization of Flavia, aquiver with irritation and vitriolic malice. No one could mistake it; it was done with all his deftness of portraiture. Imogen had not finished the article when she heard a footstep, and clutching the paper she started precipitately toward the stairway as Arthur entered. He put out his hand, looking critically at her distressed face.

"Wait a moment, Miss Willard," he said peremptorily, "I want to see whether we can find what it was that so interested our friends this morning. Give me the paper, please."

Imogen grew quite white as he opened the journal. She reached forward and crumpled it with her hands. "Please don't, please don't," she pleaded; "it's something I don't want you to see. Oh, why will you? It's just something low and despicable that you can't notice."

Arthur had gently loosed her hands, and he pointed her to a chair. He lit a cigar and read the article through without comment. When he had finished it he walked to the fireplace, struck a match, and tossed the flaming journal between the brass andirons.

"You are right," he remarked as he came back, dusting his hands with his handkerchief. "It's quite impossible to comment. There are extremes of blackguardism for which we have no name. The only thing necessary is to see that Flavia gets no wind of this. This seems to be my cue to act; poor girl."

Imogen looked at him tearfully; she could only murmur, "Oh, why did you read it!"

Hamilton laughed spiritlessly. "Come, don't you worry about it. You always took other people's troubles too seriously. When you were little and all the world was gay and everybody happy, you must needs get the Little Mermaid's troubles to grieve over. Come with me into the music room. You remember the musical setting I once made you for the Lay of the Jabberwock? I was trying it over the other night, long after you were in bed, and I decided it was quite as fine as the Erl-King music. How I wish I could give you some of the cake that Alice ate and make you a little girl again. Then, when you had got through the glass door into the little garden, you could call to me, perhaps, and tell me all the fine things that were going on there. What a pity it is that you ever grew up!" he added, laughing; and Imogen, too, was thinking just that.

At dinner that evening, Flavia, with fatal persistence, insisted upon turning the conversation to M. Roux. She had been reading one of his novels and had remembered anew that Paris set its watches by his clock. Imogen surmised that she was tortured by a feeling that she had not sufficiently appreciated him while she had had him. When she first mentioned his name she was answered only by the pall of silence that fell over the company. Then everyone began to talk at once, as though to correct a false position. They spoke of him with a fervid, defiant admiration, with the sort of hot praise that covers a double purpose. Imogen fancied she could see that they felt a kind of relief at what the man had done, even those who despised him for doing it; that they felt a spiteful hate against Flavia, as though she had tricked them, and a certain contempt for themselves that they had been beguiled. She was reminded of the fury of the crowd in the fairy tale, when once the child had called out that the king was in his night clothes. Surely these people knew no more about Flavia than they had known before, but the mere fact that the thing had been said altered the situation. Flavia, meanwhile, sat chattering amiably, pathetically unconscious of her nakedness.

Hamilton lounged, fingering the stem of his wineglass, gazing down the table at one face after another and studying the various degrees of self-consciousness they exhibited. Imogen's eyes followed his, fearfully. When a lull came in the spasmodic flow of conversation, Arthur, leaning back in his chair, remarked deliberately, "As for M. Roux, his very profession places him in that class of men whom society has never been able to accept unconditionally because it has never been able to assume that they have any ordered notion of taste. He and his ilk remain, with the mountebanks and snake charmers, people indispensable to our civilization, but wholly unreclaimed by it; people whom we receive, but whose invitations we do not accept."

Fortunately for Flavia, this mine was not exploded until just before the coffee was brought. Her laughter was pitiful to hear; it echoed through the silent room as in a vault, while she made some tremulously light remark about her husband's drollery, grim as a jest from the dying. No one responded and she sat nodding her head like a mechanical toy and smiling her white, set smile through her teeth, until Alcée Buisson and Frau Lichtenfeld came to her support.

After dinner the guests retired immediately to their rooms, and Imogen went upstairs on tiptoe, feeling the echo of breakage and the dust of crumbling in the air. She wondered whether Flavia's habitual note of uneasiness were not, in a manner, prophetic, and a sort of unconscious premonition, after all. She sat down to write a letter, but she found herself so nervous, her head so hot and her hands so cold, that she soon abandoned the effort. Just as she was about to seek Miss Broadwood, Flavia entered and embraced her hysterically.

"My dearest girl," she began, "was there ever such an unfortunate and incomprehensible speech made before? Of course it is scarcely necessary to explain to you poor Arthur's lack of tact, and that he meant nothing. But they!

Can they be expected to understand? He will feel wretchedly about it when he realizes what he has done, but in the meantime? And M. Roux, of all men! When we were so fortunate as to get him, and he made himself so unreservedly agreeable, and I fancied that, in his way, Arthur quite admired him. My dear, you have no idea what that speech has done. Schemetzkin and Herr Schotte have already sent me word that they must leave us tomorrow. Such a thing from a host!" Flavia paused, choked by tears of vexation and despair.

Imogen was thoroughly disconcerted; this was the first time she had ever seen Flavia betray any personal emotion which was indubitably genuine. She replied with what consolation she could. "Need they take it personally at all? It was a mere observation upon a class of people——"

"Which he knows nothing whatever about, and with whom he has no sympathy," interrupted Flavia. "Ah, my dear, you could not be *expected* to understand. You can't realize, knowing Arthur as you do, his entire lack of any aesthetic sense whatever. He is absolutely *nil*, stone deaf and stark blind, on that side. He doesn't mean to be brutal, it is just the brutality of utter ignorance. They always feel it—they are so sensitive to unsympathetic influences, you know; they know it the moment they come into the house. I have spent my life apologizing for him and struggling to conceal it; but in spite of me, he wounds them; his very attitude, even in silence, offends them. Heavens! Do I not know? Is it not perpetually and forever wounding me? But there has never been anything so dreadful as this—never! If I could conceive of any possible motive, even!"

"But, surely, Mrs. Hamilton, it was, after all, a mere expression of opinion, such as we are any of us likely to venture upon any subject whatever. It was neither more personal nor more extravagant than many of M. Roux's remarks."

"But, Imogen, certainly M. Roux has the right. It is a part of his art, and that is altogether another matter. Oh, this is not the only instance!" continued Flavia passionately, "I've always had that narrow, bigoted prejudice to contend with. It has always held me back. But this——!"

"I think you mistake his attitude," replied Imogen, feeling a flush that made her ears tingle. "That is, I fancy he is more appreciative than he seems. A man can't be very demonstrative about those things—not if he is a real man. I should not think you would care much about saving the feelings of people who are too narrow to admit of any other point of view than their own." She stopped, finding herself in the impossible position of attempting to explain Hamilton to his wife; a task which, if once begun, would necessitate an entire course of enlightenment which she doubted Flavia's ability to receive, and which she could offer only with very poor grace.

"That's just where it stings most"—here Flavia began pacing the floor—"it is just because they have all shown such tolerance and have treated Arthur with such unfailing consideration that I can find no reasonable pretext for his rancor. How can he fail to see the value of such friendships on the children's account, if for nothing else! What an advantage for them to grow up among such associations! Even though he cares nothing about these things himself he might realize that. Is there nothing I could say by way of explanation? To them, I mean? If someone were to explain to them how unfortunately limited he is in these things——"

"I'm afraid I cannot advise you," said Imogen decidedly, "but that, at least, seems to me impossible."

Flavia took her hand and glanced at her affectionately, nodding nervously. "Of course, dear girl, I can't ask you to be quite frank with me. Poor child, you are trembling and your hands are icy. Poor Arthur! But you must not judge him by this altogether; think how much he misses in life. What a cruel shock you've had. I'll send you some sherry. Good night, my dear."

When Flavia shut the door Imogen burst into a fit of nervous weeping.

Next morning she awoke after a troubled and restless night. At eight o'clock Miss Broadwood entered in a red and white striped bathrobe.

"Up, up, and see the great doom's image!" she cried, her eyes sparkling with excitement. "The hall is full of trunks, they are packing. What bolt has fallen? It's you, *ma chérie*, you've brought Ulysses home again and the slaughter has begun!" she blew a cloud of smoke triumphantly from her lips and threw herself into a chair beside the bed.

Imogen, rising on her elbow, plunged excitedly into the story of the Roux interview, which Miss Broadwood heard with the keenest interest, frequently interrupting her with exclamations of delight. When Imogen reached the dramatic scene which terminated in the destruction of the newspaper, Miss Broadwood rose and took a turn about the room, violently switching the tasselled cords of her bathrobe.

"Stop a moment," she cried, "you mean to tell me that he had such a heaven-sent means to bring her to her senses and didn't use it—that he held such a weapon and threw it away?"

"Use it?" cried Imogen unsteadily. "Of course he didn't! He bared his back to the tormentor, signed himself over to punishment in that speech he made at dinner, which everyone understands but Flavia. She was here for an hour last night and disregarded every limit of taste in her maledictions."

"My dear!" cried Miss Broadwood, catching her hand in inordinate delight at the situation, "do you see what he has done? There'll be no end to it. Why he has sacrificed himself to spare the very vanity that devours him, put rancors in the vessels of his peace, and his eternal jewel given to the common enemy of man, to make them kings, the seed of Banquo kings! He is magnificent!"

"Isn't he always that?" cried Imogen hotly. "He's like a pillar of sanity and law in this house of shams and swollen vanities, where people stalk about with a sort of madhouse dignity, each one fancying himself a king or a pope. If you could have heard that woman talk of him! Why, she thinks him stupid, bigoted, blinded by middle-class prejudices. She talked about his having no aesthetic sense and insisted that her artists had always shown him tolerance. I don't know why it should get on my nerves so, I'm sure, but her stupidity and assurance are enough to drive one to the brink of collapse."

"Yes, as opposed to his singular fineness, they are calculated to do just that," said Miss Broadwood gravely, wisely ignoring Imogen's tears. "But what has been is nothing to what will be. Just wait until Flavia's black swans have flown! You ought not to try to stick it out; that would only make it harder for everyone. Suppose you let me telephone your mother to wire you to come home by the evening train?"

"Anything, rather than have her come at me like that again. It puts me in a perfectly impossible position, and he *is* so fine!"

"Of course it does," said Miss Broadwood sympathetically, "and there is no good to be got from facing it. I will stay because such things interest me, and Frau Lichtenfeld will stay because she has no money to get away, and Buisson will stay because he feels somewhat responsible. These complications are interesting enough to cold-blooded folk like myself who have an eye for the dramatic element, but they are distracting and demoralizing to young people with any serious purpose in life."

Miss Broadwood's counsel was all the more generous seeing that, for her, the most interesting element of this denouement would be eliminated by Imogen's departure. "If she goes now, she'll get over it," soliloquized Miss Broadwood. "If she stays, she'll be wrung for him and the hurt may go deep enough to last. I haven't the heart to see her spoiling things for herself." She telephoned Mrs. Willard and helped Imogen to pack. She even took it upon herself to break the news of Imogen's going to Arthur, who remarked, as he rolled a cigarette in his nerveless fingers:

"Right enough, too. What should she do here with old cynics like you and me, Jimmy? Seeing that she is brim full of dates and formulae and other positivisms, and is so girt about with illusions that she still casts a shadow in the sun. You've been very tender of her, haven't you? I've watched you. And to think it may all be gone when we see her next. 'The common fate of all things rare,' you know. What a good fellow you are, anyway, Jimmy," he added, putting his hands affectionately on her shoulders.

Arthur went with them to the station. Flavia was so prostrated by the concerted action of her guests that she was able to see Imogen only for a moment in her darkened sleeping chamber, where she kissed her hysterically, without lifting her head, bandaged in aromatic vinegar. On the way to the station both Arthur and Imogen threw the burden of keeping up appearances entirely upon Miss Broadwood, who blithely rose to the occasion. When Hamilton carried Imogen's bag into the car, Miss Broadwood detained her for a moment, whispering as she gave her a large, warm handclasp, "I'll come to see you when I get back to town; and, in the meantime, if you meet any of our artists, tell them you have left Caius Marius among the ruins of Carthage."

The Sculptor's Funeral

A group of the townspeople stood on the station siding of a little Kansas town, awaiting the coming of the night train, which was already twenty minutes overdue. The snow had fallen thick over everything; in the pale starlight the line of bluffs across the wide, white meadows south of the town made soft, smoke-colored curves against the clear sky. The men on the siding stood first on one foot and then on the other, their hands thrust deep into their trousers pockets, their overcoats open, their shoulders screwed up with the cold; and they glanced from time to time toward the southeast, where the railroad track wound along the river shore. They conversed in low tones and moved about restlessly, seeming uncertain as to what was expected of them. There was but one of the company who looked as though he knew exactly why he was there; and he kept conspicuously apart; walking to the far end of the platform, returning to the station door, then pacing up the track again, his chin sunk in the high collar of his overcoat, his burly shoulders drooping forward, his gait heavy and dogged. Presently he was approached by a tall, spare, grizzled man clad in a faded Grand Army suit, who shuffled out from the group and advanced with a certain deference, craning his neck forward until his back made the angle of a jackknife three-quarters open.

"I reckon she's agoin' to be pretty late ag'in tonight, Jim," he remarked in a squeaky falsetto. "S'pose it's the snow?"

"I don't know," responded the other man with a shade of annoyance, speaking from out an astonishing cataract of red beard that grew fiercely and thickly in all directions.

The spare man shifted the quill toothpick he was chewing to the other side of his mouth. "It ain't likely that anybody from the East will come with the corpse, I s'pose," he went on reflectively.

"I don't know," responded the other, more curtly than before.

"It's too bad he didn't belong to some lodge or other. I like an order funeral myself. They seem more appropriate for people of some reputation," the spare man continued, with an ingratiating concession in his shrill voice, as he carefully placed his toothpick in his vest pocket. He always carried the flag at the G. A. R. funerals in the town.

The heavy man turned on his heel, without replying, and walked up the siding. The spare man shuffled back to the uneasy group. "Jim's ez full ez a tick, ez ushel," he commented commiseratingly.

Just then a distant whistle sounded, and there was a shuffling of feet on the platform. A number of lanky boys of all ages appeared as suddenly and slimily as eels wakened by the crack of thunder; some came from the waiting room, where they had been warming themselves by the red stove, or half-asleep on the slat benches; others uncoiled themselves from baggage trucks or slid out of express wagons. Two clambered down from the driver's seat of a hearse that stood backed up against the siding. They straightened their stooping shoulders and lifted their heads, and a flash of momentary animation kindled their dull eyes at that cold, vibrant scream, the world-wide call for men. It stirred them like the note of a trumpet; just as it had often stirred the man who was coming home tonight, in his boyhood.

The night express shot, red as a rocket, from out the eastward marsh lands and wound along the river shore under the long lines of shivering poplars that sentineled the meadows, the escaping steam hanging in gray masses against the pale sky and blotting out the Milky Way. In a moment the red glare from the headlight streamed up the snow-covered track before the siding and glittered on the wet, black rails. The burly man with the disheveled red beard walked swiftly up the platform toward the approaching train, uncovering his head as he went. The group of men behind him hesitated, glanced questioningly at one another, and awkwardly followed his example. The train stopped, and the crowd shuffled up to the express car just as the door was thrown open, the spare man in the G. A. R. suit thrusting his head forward with curiosity. The express messenger appeared in the doorway, accompanied by a young man in a long ulster and traveling cap.

"Are Mr. Merrick's friends here?" inquired the young man.

The group on the platform swayed and shuffled uneasily. Philip Phelps, the banker, responded with dignity: "We have come to take charge of the body. Mr. Merrick's father is very feeble and can't be about."

"Send the agent out here," growled the express messenger, "and tell the operator to lend a hand."

The coffin was got out of its rough box and down on the snowy platform. The townspeople drew back enough to make room for it and then formed a close semicircle about it, looking curiously at the palm leaf which lay across the black cover. No one said anything. The baggage man stood by his truck, waiting to get at the trunks. The engine panted heavily, and the fireman dodged in and out among the wheels with his yellow torch and long oilcan, snapping the spindle boxes. The young Bostonian, one of the dead sculptor's pupils who had come with the body, looked about him helplessly. He turned to the banker, the only one of that black, uneasy, stoop-shouldered group who seemed enough of an individual to be addressed.

"None of Mr. Merrick's brothers are here?" he asked uncertainly.

The man with the red beard for the first time stepped up and joined the group. "No, they have not come yet; the family is scattered. The body will be taken directly to the house." He stooped and took hold of one of the handles of the coffin.

"Take the long hill road up, Thompson—it will be easier on the horses," called the liveryman as the undertaker snapped the door of the hearse and prepared to mount to the driver's seat.

Laird, the red-bearded lawyer, turned again to the stranger: "We didn't know whether there would be anyone with him or not," he explained. "It's a long walk, so you'd better go up in the hack." He pointed to a single, battered conveyance, but the young man replied stiffly: "Thank you, but I think I will go up with the hearse. If you don't object," turning to the undertaker, "I'll ride with you."

They clambered up over the wheels and drove off in the starlight up the long, white hill toward the town. The lamps in the still village were shining from under the low, snow-burdened roofs; and beyond, on every side, the plains reached out into emptiness, peaceful and wide as the soft sky itself, and wrapped in a tangible, white silence.

When the hearse backed up to a wooden sidewalk before a naked, weatherbeaten frame house, the same composite, ill-defined group that had stood upon the station siding was huddled about the gate. The front yard was an icy swamp, and a couple of warped planks, extending from the sidewalk to the door, made a sort of rickety footbridge. The gate hung on one hinge and was opened wide with difficulty. Steavens, the young stranger, noticed that something black was tied to the knob of the front door.

The grating sound made by the casket, as it was drawn from the hearse, was answered by a scream from the house; the front door was wrenched open, and a tall, corpulent woman rushed out bareheaded into the snow and flung herself upon the coffin, shrieking: "My boy, my boy! And this is how you've come home to me!"

As Steavens turned away and closed his eyes with a shudder of unutterable repulsion, another woman, also tall, but flat and angular, dressed entirely in black, darted out of the house and caught Mrs. Merrick by the shoulders, crying sharply: "Come, come, Mother; you mustn't go on like this!" Her tone changed to one of obsequious solemnity as she turned to the banker: "The parlor is ready, Mr. Phelps."

The bearers carried the coffin along the narrow boards, while the undertaker ran ahead with the coffin-rests. They bore it into a large, unheated room that smelled of dampness and disuse and furniture polish, and set it down under a hanging lamp ornamented with jingling glass prisms and before a "Rogers group" of John Alden and Priscilla, wreathed with smilax. Henry Steavens stared about him with the sickening conviction that there had been some horrible mistake, and that he had somehow arrived at the wrong destination. He looked painfully about over the clover-green Brussels, the fat plush upholstery, among the hand-painted china plaques and panels, and vases, for some mark of identification, for something that might once conceivably have belonged to Harvey Merrick. It was not until he recognized his friend in the crayon portrait of a little boy in kilts and curls hanging above the piano that he felt willing to let any of these people approach the coffin.

"Take the lid off, Mr. Thompson; let me see my boy's face," wailed the elder woman between her sobs. This time Steavens looked fearfully, almost beseechingly into her face, red and swollen under its masses of strong, black, shiny hair. He flushed, dropped his eyes, and then, almost incredulously, looked again. There was a kind of power about her face—a kind of brutal handsomeness, even, but it was scarred and furrowed by violence, and so colored and coarsened by fiercer passions that grief seemed never to have laid a gentle finger there. The long nose was distended and knobbed at the end, and there were deep lines on either side of it; her heavy, black brows almost met across her forehead; her teeth were large and square and set far apart—teeth that could tear. She filled the room; the men were obliterated, seemed tossed about like twigs in an angry water, and even Steavens felt himself being drawn into the whirlpool.

The daughter—the tall, rawboned woman in crepe, with a mourning comb in her hair which curiously lengthened her long face—sat stiffly upon the sofa, her hands, conspicuous for their large knuckles, folded in her lap, her mouth and eyes drawn down, solemnly awaiting the opening of the coffin. Near the door stood a mulatto woman, evidently a servant in the house, with a timid bearing and an emaciated face pitifully sad and gentle. She was weeping silently, the corner of her calico apron lifted to her eyes, occasionally suppressing a long, quivering sob. Steavens walked over and stood beside her.

Feeble steps were heard on the stairs, and an old man, tall and frail, odorous of pipe smoke, with shaggy, unkept gray hair and a dingy beard, tobacco stained about the mouth, entered uncertainly. He went slowly up to the coffin and stood, rolling a blue cotton handkerchief between his hands, seeming so pained and embarrassed by his wife's orgy of grief that he had no consciousness of anything else.

"There, there, Annie, dear, don't take on so," he quavered timidly, putting out a shaking hand and awkwardly patting her elbow. She turned with a cry and sank upon his shoulder with such violence that he tottered a little. He did not even glance toward the coffin, but continued to look at her with a dull, frightened, appealing expression, as a spaniel looks at the whip. His sunken cheeks slowly reddened and burned with miserable shame. When his wife rushed from the room her daughter strode after her with set lips. The servant stole up to the coffin, bent over it for a moment, and then slipped away to the kitchen, leaving Steavens, the lawyer, and the father to themselves. The old man stood trembling and looking down at his dead son's face. The sculptor's splendid head seemed even more noble in its rigid stillness than in life. The dark hair had crept down upon the wide forehead; the face seemed strangely long, but in it there was not that beautiful and chaste repose which we expect to find in the faces of the dead. The brows were so drawn that there were two deep lines above the beaked nose, and the chin was thrust forward defiantly. It was as though the strain of life had been so sharp and bitter that death could not at once wholly relax the tension and smooth the countenance into perfect peace—as though he were still guarding something precious and holy, which might even yet be wrested from him.

The old man's lips were working under his stained beard. He turned to the lawyer with timid deference:

"Phelps and the rest are comin' back to set up with Harve, ain't they?" he asked. "Thank 'ee, Jim, thank 'ee." He brushed the hair back gently from his son's forehead. "He was a good boy, Jim; always a good boy. He was ez gentle ez a child and the kindest of 'em all—only we didn't none of us ever onderstand him." The tears trickled slowly down his beard and dropped upon the sculptor's coat.

"Martin, Martin. Oh, Martin! come here," his wife wailed from the top of the stairs. The old man started timorously: "Yes, Annie, I'm coming." He turned away, hesitated, stood for a moment in miserable indecision; then he reached back and patted the dead man's hair softly, and stumbled from the room.

"Poor old man, I didn't think he had any tears left. Seems as if his eyes would have gone dry long ago. At his age nothing cuts very deep," remarked the lawyer.

Something in his tone made Steavens glance up. While the mother had been in the room the young man had scarcely seen anyone else; but now, from the moment he first glanced into Jim Laird's florid face and bloodshot eyes, he knew that he had found what he had been heartsick at not finding before—the feeling, the understanding, that must exist in someone, even here.

The man was red as his beard, with features swollen and blurred by dissipation, and a hot, blazing blue eye. His face was strained—that of a man who is controlling himself with difficulty—and he kept plucking at his beard with a sort of fierce resentment. Steavens, sitting by the window, watched him turn down the glaring lamp, still its jangling pendants with an angry gesture, and then stand with his hands locked behind him, staring down into the master's face. He could not help wondering what link there could have been between the porcelain vessel and so sooty a lump of potter's clay.

From the kitchen an uproar was sounding; when the dining-room door opened the import of it was clear. The mother was abusing the maid for having forgotten to make the dressing for the chicken salad which had been prepared for the watchers. Steavens had never heard anything in the least like it; it was injured, emotional, dramatic abuse, unique and masterly in its excruciating cruelty, as violent and unrestrained as had been her grief of twenty minutes before. With a shudder of disgust the lawyer went into the dining room and closed the door into the kitchen.

"Poor Roxy's getting it now," he remarked when he came back. "The Merricks took her out of the poorhouse years ago; and if her loyalty would let her, I guess the poor old thing could tell tales that would curdle your blood. She's the mulatto woman who was standing in here a while ago, with her apron to her eyes. The old woman is a fury; there never was anybody like her for demonstrative piety and ingenious cruelty. She made Harvey's life a hell for him when he lived at home; he was so sick ashamed of it. I never could see how he kept himself so sweet."

"He was wonderful," said Steavens slowly, "wonderful; but until tonight I have never known how wonderful."

"That is the true and eternal wonder of it, anyway; that it can come even from such a dung heap as this," the lawyer cried, with a sweeping gesture which seemed to indicate much more than the four walls within which they stood.

"I think I'll see whether I can get a little air. The room is so close I am beginning to feel rather faint," murmured Steavens, struggling with one of the windows. The sash was stuck, however, and would not yield, so he sat down dejectedly and began pulling at his collar. The lawyer came over, loosened the sash with one blow of his red fist, and sent the window up a few inches. Steavens thanked him, but the nausea which had been gradually climbing into his throat for the last half-hour left him with but one desire—a desperate feeling that he must get away from this place with what was left of Harvey Merrick. Oh, he comprehended well enough now the quiet bitterness of the smile that he had seen so often on his master's lips!

He remembered that once, when Merrick returned from a visit home, he brought with him a singularly feeling and suggestive bas-relief of a thin, faded old woman, sitting and sewing something pinned to her knee; while a full-lipped, full-blooded little urchin, his trousers held up by a single gallows, stood beside her, impatiently twitching her gown to call her attention to a butterfly he had caught. Steavens, impressed by the tender and delicate modeling of the thin, tired face, had asked him if it were his mother. He remembered the dull flush that had burned up in the sculptor's face.

The lawyer was sitting in a rocking chair beside the coffin, his head thrown back and his eyes closed. Steavens looked at him earnestly, puzzled at the line of the chin, and wondering why a man should conceal a feature of such distinction under that disfiguring shock of beard. Suddenly, as though he felt the young sculptor's keen glance, he opened his eyes.

"Was he always a good deal of an oyster?" he asked abruptly. "He was terribly shy as a boy."

"Yes, he was an oyster, since you put it so," rejoined Steavens. "Although he could be very fond of people, he always gave one the impression of being detached. He disliked violent emotion; he was reflective, and rather distrustful of himself—except, of course, as regarded his work. He was surefooted enough there. He distrusted men pretty thoroughly and women even more, yet somehow without believing ill of them. He was determined, indeed, to believe the best, but he seemed afraid to investigate."

"A burnt dog dreads the fire," said the lawyer grimly, and closed his eyes.

Steavens went on and on, reconstructing that whole miserable boyhood. All this raw, biting ugliness had been the portion of the man whose tastes were refined beyond the limits of the reasonable—whose mind was an exhaustless gallery of beautiful impressions, and so sensitive that the mere shadow of a poplar leaf flickering against a sunny wall would be etched and held there forever. Surely, if ever a man had the magic word in his fingertips, it was Merrick. Whatever he touched, he revealed its holiest secret; liberated it from enchantment and restored it to its pristine loveliness, like the Arabian prince who fought the enchantress spell for spell. Upon whatever he had come in contact with, he had left a beautiful record of the experience—a sort of ethereal signature; a scent, a sound, a color that was his own.

Steavens understood now the real tragedy of his master's life; neither love nor wine, as many had conjectured, but a blow which had fallen earlier and cut deeper than these could have done—a shame not his, and yet so unescapably his, to hide in his heart from his very boyhood. And without—the frontier warfare; the yearning of a boy, cast ashore upon a desert of newness and ugliness and sordidness, for all that is chastened and old, and noble with traditions.

At eleven o'clock the tall, flat woman in black crepe entered, announced that the watchers were arriving, and asked them "to step into the dining room." As Steavens rose the lawyer said dryly: "You go on—it'll be a good experience for you, doubtless; as for me, I'm not equal to that crowd tonight; I've had twenty years of them."

As Steavens closed the door after him he glanced back at the lawyer, sitting by the coffin in the dim light, with his chin resting on his hand.

The same misty group that had stood before the door of the express car shuffled into the dining room. In the light of the kerosene lamp they separated and became individuals. The minister, a pale, feeble-looking man with white hair and blond chin-whiskers, took his seat beside a small side table and placed his Bible upon it. The Grand Army man sat down behind the stove and tilted his chair back comfortably against the wall, fishing his quill toothpick from his waistcoat pocket. The two bankers, Phelps and Elder, sat off in a corner behind the dinner table, where they could finish their discussion of the new usury law and its effect on chattel security loans. The real estate agent, an old man with a smiling, hypocritical face, soon joined them. The coal-and-lumber dealer and the cattle shipper sat on opposite sides of the hard coal-burner, their feet on the nickelwork. Steavens took a book from his pocket and began to read. The talk around him ranged through various topics of local interest while the house was quieting down. When it was clear that the members of the family were in bed the Grand Army man hitched his shoulders and, untangling his long legs, caught his heels on the rounds of his chair.

"S'pose there'll be a will, Phelps?" he queried in his weak falsetto.

The banker laughed disagreeably and began trimming his nails with a pearl-handled pocketknife.

"There'll scarcely be any need for one, will there?" he queried in his turn.

The restless Grand Army man shifted his position again, getting his knees still nearer his chin. "Why, the ole man says Harve's done right well lately," he chirped.

The other banker spoke up. "I reckon he means by that Harve ain't asked him to mortgage any more farms lately, so as he could go on with his education."

"Seems like my mind don't reach back to a time when Harve wasn't bein' edycated," tittered the Grand Army man.

There was a general chuckle. The minister took out his handkerchief and blew his nose sonorously. Banker Phelps closed his knife with a snap. "It's too bad the old man's sons didn't turn out better," he remarked with reflective authority. "They never hung together. He spent money enough on Harve to stock a dozen cattle farms and he might as well have poured it into Sand Creek. If Harve had stayed at home and helped nurse what little they had, and gone into stock on the old man's bottom farm, they might all have been well fixed. But the old man had to trust everything to tenants and was cheated right and left."

"Harve never could have handled stock none," interposed the cattleman. "He hadn't it in him to be sharp. Do you remember when he bought Sander's mules for eight-year-olds, when everybody in town knew that Sander's father-in-law give 'em to his wife for a wedding present eighteen years before, an' they was full-grown mules then."

Everyone chuckled, and the Grand Army man rubbed his knees with a spasm of childish delight.

"Harve never was much account for anything practical, and he shore was never fond of work," began the coal-and-lumber dealer. "I mind the last time he was home; the day he left, when the old man was out to the barn helpin' his hand hitch up to take Harve to the train, and Cal Moots was patchin' up the fence, Harve, he come out on the step and sings out, in his ladylike voice: 'Cal Moots, Cal Moots! please come cord my trunk.' "

"That's Harve for you," approved the Grand Army man gleefully. "I kin hear him howlin' yet when he was a big feller in long pants and his mother used to whale him with a rawhide in the barn for lettin' the cows git foundered in the cornfield when he was drivin' 'em home from pasture. He killed a cow of mine that-a-way onc't—a pure Jersey and the best milker I had, an' the ole man had to put up for her. Harve, he was watchin' the sun set acros't the marshes when the anamile got away; he argued that sunset was oncommon fine."

"Where the old man made his mistake was in sending the boy East to school," said Phelps, stroking his goatee and speaking in a deliberate, judicial tone. "There was where he got his head full of traipsing to Paris and all such folly. What Harve needed, of all people, was a course in some first-class Kansas City business college."

The letters were swimming before Steavens's eyes. Was it possible that these men did not understand, that the palm on the coffin meant nothing to them? The very name of their town would have remained forever buried in the postal guide had it not been now and again mentioned in the world in connection with Harvey Merrick's. He remembered what his master had said to him on the day of his death, after the congestion of both lungs had shut off any probability of recovery, and the sculptor had asked his pupil to send his body home. "It's not a pleasant place to be lying while the world is moving and doing and bettering," he had said with a feeble smile, "but it rather seems as though we ought to go back to the place we came from in the end. The townspeople will come in for a look at me; and after they have had their say I shan't have much to fear from the judgment of God. The wings of the Victory, in there"—with a weak gesture toward his studio—"will not shelter me."

The cattleman took up the comment. "Forty's young for a Merrick to cash in; they usually hang on pretty well. Probably he helped it along with whisky."

"His mother's people were not long-lived, and Harvey never had a robust constitution," said the minister mildly. He would have liked to say more. He had been the boy's Sunday-school teacher, and had been fond of him; but he felt that he was not in a position to speak. His own sons had turned out badly, and it was not a year since one of them had made his last trip home in the express car, shot in a gambling house in the Black Hills.

"Nevertheless, there is no disputin' that Harve frequently looked upon the wine when it was red, also variegated, and it shore made an oncommon fool of him," moralized the cattleman.

Just then the door leading into the parlor rattled loudly, and everyone started involuntarily, looking relieved when only Jim Laird came out. His red face was convulsed with anger, and the Grand Army man ducked his head when he saw the spark in his blue, bloodshot eye. They were all afraid of Jim; he was a drunkard, but he could twist the law to suit his client's needs as no other man in all western Kansas could do; and there were many who tried. The lawyer closed the door gently behind him, leaned back against it and folded his arms, cocking his head a little to one side. When he assumed this attitude in the courtroom, ears were always pricked up, as it usually foretold a flood of withering sarcasm.

"I've been with you gentlemen before," he began in a dry, even tone, "when you've sat by the coffins of boys born and raised in this town; and, if I remember rightly, you were never any too well satisfied when you checked them up. What's the matter, anyhow? Why is it that reputable young men are as scarce as millionaires in Sand City? It might almost seem to a stranger that there was some way something the matter with your progressive town. Why did Ruben Sayer, the brightest young lawyer you ever turned out, after he had come home from the university as straight as a die, take to drinking and forge a check and shoot himself? Why did Bill Merrit's son die of the shakes in a saloon in Omaha? Why was Mr. Thomas's son, here, shot in a gambling house? Why did young Adams burn his mill to beat the insurance companies and go to the pen?"

The lawyer paused and unfolded his arms, laying one clenched fist quietly on the table. "I'll tell you why. Because you drummed nothing but money and knavery into their ears from the time they wore knickerbockers; because you carped away at them as you've been carping here tonight, holding our friends Phelps and Elder up to them for their models, as our grandfathers held up George Washington and John Adams. But the boys, worse luck, were young and raw at the business you put them to; and how could they match coppers with such artists as Phelps and Elder? You wanted them to be successful rascals; they were only unsuccessful ones—that's all the difference. There was only one boy ever raised in this borderland between ruffianism and civilization who didn't come to grief, and you hated Harvey Merrick more for winning out than you hated all the other boys who got under the wheels. Lord, Lord, how you did hate him! Phelps, here, is fond of saying that he could buy and sell us all out any time he's a mind to; but he knew Harve wouldn't have given a tinker's damn for his bank and all his cattle farms put together; and a lack of appreciation, that way, goes hard with Phelps.

"Old Nimrod, here, thinks Harve drank too much; and this from such as Nimrod and me!

"Brother Elder says Harve was too free with the old man's money—fell short in filial consideration, maybe. Well, we can all remember the very tone in which brother Elder swore his own father was a liar, in the county court; and we all know that the old man came out of that partnership with his son as bare as a sheared lamb. But maybe I'm getting personal, and I'd better be driving ahead at what I want to say."

The lawyer paused a moment, squared his heavy shoulders, and went on: "Harvey Merrick and I went to school together, back East. We were dead in earnest, and we wanted you all to be proud of us some day. We meant to be great men. Even I, and I haven't lost my sense of humor, gentlemen, I meant to be a great man. I came back here to practice, and I found you didn't in the least want me to be a great man. You wanted me to be a shrewd lawyer—oh, yes! Our veteran here wanted me to get him an increase of pension, because he had dyspepsia; Phelps wanted a new county survey that would put the widow Wilson's little bottom farm inside his south line; Elder wanted to lend money at 5 per cent a month and get it collected; old Stark here wanted to wheedle old women up in Vermont into investing their annuities in real estate mortgages that are not worth the paper they are written on. Oh, you needed me hard enough, and you'll go on needing me; and that's why I'm not afraid to plug the truth home to you this once.

"Well, I came back here and became the damned shyster you wanted me to be. You pretend to have some sort of respect for me; and yet you'll stand up and throw mud at Harvey Merrick, whose soul you couldn't dirty and whose hands you couldn't tie. Oh, you're a discriminating lot of Christians! There have been times when the sight of Harvey's name in some Eastern paper has made me hang my head like a whipped dog; and, again, times when I liked to think of him off there in the world, away from all this hog wallow, doing his great work and climbing the big, clean upgrade he'd set for himself.

"And we? Now that we've fought and lied and sweated and stolen, and hated as only the disappointed strugglers in a bitter, dead little Western town know how to do, what have we got to show for it? Harvey Merrick wouldn't have given one sunset over your marshes for all you've got put together, and you know it. It's not for me to say why, in the inscrutable wisdom of God, a genius should ever have been called from this place of hatred and bitter waters; but I want this Boston man to know that the drivel he's been hearing here tonight is the only tribute any truly great man could ever have from such a lot of sick, side-tracked, burnt-dog, land-poor sharks as the here-present financiers of Sand City—upon which town may God have mercy!"

The lawyer thrust out his hand to Steavens as he passed him, caught up his overcoat in the hall, and had left the house before the Grand Army man had had time to lift his ducked head and crane his long neck about at his fellows.

Next day Jim Laird was drunk and unable to attend the funeral services. Steavens called twice at his office, but was compelled to start East without seeing him. He had a presentiment that he would hear from him again, and left his address on the lawyer's table; but if Laird found it, he never acknowledged it. The thing in him that Harvey Merrick had loved must have gone underground with Harvey Merrick's coffin; for it never spoke again, and Jim got the cold he died of driving across the Colorado mountains to defend one of Phelps's sons, who had got into trouble out there by cutting government timber.

"A Death in the Desert"

Everett Hilgarde was conscious that the man in the seat across the aisle was looking at him intently. He was a large, florid man, wore a conspicuous diamond solitaire upon his third finger, and Everett judged him to be a traveling salesman of some sort. He had the air of an adaptable fellow who had been about the world and who could keep cool and clean under almost any circumstances.

The "High Line Flyer," as this train was derisively called among railroad men, was jerking along through the hot afternoon over the monotonous country between Holdridge and Cheyenne. Besides the blond man and himself the only occupants of the car were two dusty, bedraggled-looking girls who had been to the Exposition at Chicago, and who were earnestly discussing the cost of their first trip out of Colorado. The four uncomfortable passengers were covered with a sediment of fine, yellow dust which clung to their hair and eyebrows like gold powder. It blew up in clouds from the bleak, lifeless country through which they passed, until they were one color with the sagebrush and sandhills. The gray-and-yellow desert was varied only by occasional ruins of deserted towns, and the little red boxes of station houses, where the spindling trees and sickly vines in the blue-grass yards made little green reserves fenced off in that confusing wilderness of sand.

As the slanting rays of the sun beat in stronger and stronger through the car windows, the blond gentleman asked the ladies' permission to remove his coat, and sat in his lavender striped shirt sleeves, with a black silk handkerchief tucked carefully about his collar. He had seemed interested in Everett since they had boarded the train at

Holdridge, and kept glancing at him curiously and then looking reflectively out of the window, as though he were trying to recall something. But wherever Everett went someone was almost sure to look at him with that curious interest, and it had ceased to embarrass or annoy him. Presently the stranger, seeming satisfied with his observation, leaned back in his seat, half-closed his eyes, and began softly to whistle the "Spring Song" from *Proserpine,* the cantata that a dozen years before had made its young composer famous in a night. Everett had heard that air on guitars in Old Mexico, on mandolins at college glees, on cottage organs in New England hamlets, and only two weeks ago he had heard it played on sleighbells at a variety theater in Denver. There was literally no way of escaping his brother's precocity. Adriance could live on the other side of the Atlantic, where his youthful indiscretions were forgotten in his mature achievements, but his brother had never been able to outrun *Proserpine,* and here he found it again in the Colorado sand hills. Not that Everett was exactly ashamed of *Proserpine;* only a man of genius could have written it, but it was the sort of thing that a man of genius outgrows as soon as he can.

Everett unbent a trifle and smiled at his neighbor across the aisle. Immediately the large man rose and, coming over, dropped into the seat facing Hilgarde, extending his card.

"Dusty ride, isn't it? I don't mind it myself; I'm used to it. Born and bred in de briar patch, like Br'er Rabbit. I've been trying to place you for a long time; I think I must have met you before."

"Thank you," said Everett, taking the card; "my name is Hilgarde. You've probably met my brother, Adriance; people often mistake me for him."

The traveling man brought his hand down upon his knee with such vehemence that the solitaire blazed.

"So I was right after all, and if you're not Adriance Hilgarde, you're his double. I thought I couldn't be mistaken. Seen him? Well, I guess! I never missed one of his recitals at the Auditorium, and he played the piano score of *Proserpine* through to us once at the Chicago Press Club. I used to be on the *Commercial* there before I began to travel for the publishing department of the concern. So you're Hilgarde's brother, and here I've run into you at the jumping-off place. Sounds like a newspaper yarn, doesn't it?"

The traveling man laughed and offered Everett a cigar, and plied him with questions on the only subject that people ever seemed to care to talk to Everett about. At length the salesman and the two girls alighted at a Colorado way station, and Everett went on to Cheyenne alone.

The train pulled into Cheyenne at nine o'clock, late by a matter of four hours or so; but no one seemed particularly concerned at its tardiness except the station agent, who grumbled at being kept in the office overtime on a summer night. When Everett alighted from the train he walked down the platform and stopped at the track crossing, uncertain as to what direction he should take to reach a hotel. A phaeton stood near the crossing, and a woman held the reins. She was dressed in white, and her figure was clearly silhouetted against the cushions, though it was too dark to see her face. Everett had scarcely noticed her, when the switch engine came puffing up from the opposite direction, and the headlight threw a strong glare of light on his face. Suddenly the woman in the phaeton uttered a low cry and dropped the reins. Everett started forward and caught the horse's head, but the animal only lifted its ears and whisked its tail in impatient surprise. The woman sat perfectly still, her head sunk between her shoulders and her handkerchief pressed to her face. Another woman came out of the depot and hurried toward the phaeton, crying, "Katharine, dear, what is the matter?"

Everett hesitated a moment in painful embarrassment, then lifted his hat and passed on. He was accustomed to sudden recognitions in the most impossible places, especially by women, but this cry out of the night had shaken him.

While Everett was breakfasting the next morning, the headwaiter leaned over his chair to murmur that there was a gentleman waiting to see him in the parlor. Everett finished his coffee and went in the direction indicated, where he found his visitor restlessly pacing the floor. His whole manner betrayed a high degree of agitation, though his physique was not that of a man whose nerves lie near the surface. He was something below medium height, square-shouldered and solidly built. His thick, closely cut hair was beginning to show gray about the ears, and his bronzed face was heavily lined. His square brown hands were locked behind him, and he held his shoulders like a man conscious of responsibilities; yet, as he turned to greet Everett, there was an incongruous diffidence in his address.

"Good morning, Mr. Hilgarde," he said, extending his hand; "I found your name on the hotel register. My name is Gaylord. I'm afraid my sister startled you at the station last night, Mr. Hilgarde, and I've come around to apologize."

"Ah! The young lady in the phaeton? I'm sure I didn't know whether I had anything to do with her alarm or not. If I did, it is I who owe the apology."

The man colored a little under the dark brown of his face.

"Oh, it's nothing you could help, sir, I fully understand that. You see, my sister used to be a pupil of your brother's, and it seems you favor him; and when the switch engine threw a light on your face it startled her."

Everett wheeled about in his chair. "Oh! *Katharine* Gaylord! Is it possible! Now it's you who have given me a turn. Why, I used to know her when I was a boy. What on earth——"

"Is she doing here?" said Gaylord, grimly filling out the pause. "You've got at the heart of the matter. You knew my sister had been in bad health for a long time?"

"No, I had never heard a word of that. The last I knew of her she was singing in London. My brother and I correspond infrequently and seldom get beyond family matters. I am deeply sorry to hear this. There are more reasons why I am concerned than I can tell you."

The lines in Charley Gaylord's brow relaxed a little.

"What I'm trying to say, Mr. Hilgarde, is that she wants to see you. I hate to ask you, but she's so set on it.

We live several miles out of town, but my rig's below, and I can take you out anytime you can go."

"I can go now, and it will give me real pleasure to do so," said Everett, quickly. "I'll get my hat and be with you in a moment."

When he came downstairs Everett found a cart at the door, and Charley Gaylord drew a long sigh of relief as he gathered up the reins and settled back into his own element.

"You see, I think I'd better tell you something about my sister before you see her, and I don't know just where to begin. She traveled in Europe with your brother and his wife, and sang at a lot of his concerts; but I don't know just how much you know about her."

"Very little, except that my brother always thought her the most gifted of his pupils, and that when I knew her she was very young and very beautiful and turned my head sadly for a while."

Everett saw that Gaylord's mind was quite engrossed by his grief. He was wrought up to the point where his reserve and sense of proportion had quite left him, and his trouble was the one vital thing in the world. "That's the whole thing," he went on, flicking his horses with the whip.

"She was a great woman, as you say, and she didn't come of a great family. She had to fight her own way from the first. She got to Chicago, and then to New York, and then to Europe, where she went up like lightning, and got a taste for it all; and now she's dying here like a rat in a hole, out of her own world, and she can't fall back into ours. We've grown apart, some way—miles and miles apart—and I'm afraid she's fearfully unhappy."

"It's a very tragic story that you are telling me, Gaylord," said Everett. They were well out into the country now, spinning along over the dusty plains of red grass, with the ragged-blue outline of the mountains before them.

"Tragic!" cried Gaylord, starting up in his seat, "my God, man, nobody will ever know how tragic. It's a tragedy I live with and eat with and sleep with, until I've lost my grip on everything. You see she had made a good bit of money, but she spent it all going to health resorts. It's her lungs, you know. I've got money enough to send her anywhere, but the doctors all say it's no use. She hasn't the ghost of a chance. It's just getting through the days now. I had no notion she was half so bad before she came to me. She just wrote that she was all run down. Now that she's here, I think she'd be happier anywhere under the sun, but she won't leave. She says it's easier to let go of life here, and that to go East would be dying twice. There was a time when I was a brakeman with a run out of Bird City, Iowa, and she was a little thing I could carry on my shoulder, when I could get her everything on earth she wanted, and she hadn't a wish my $80 a month didn't cover; and now, when I've got a little property together, I can't buy her a night's sleep!"

Everett saw that, whatever Charley Gaylord's present status in the world might be, he had brought the brakeman's heart up the ladder with him, and the brakeman's frank avowal of sentiment. Presently Gaylord went on:

"You can understand how she has outgrown her family. We're all a pretty common sort, railroaders from away back. My father was a conductor. He died when we were kids. Maggie, my other sister, who lives with me, was a telegraph operator here while I was getting my grip on things. We had no education to speak of. I have to hire a stenographer because I can't spell straight—the Almighty couldn't teach me to spell. The things that make up life to Kate are all Greek to me, and there's scarcely a point where we touch any more, except in our recollections of the old times when we were all young and happy together, and Kate sang in a church choir in Bird City. But I believe, Mr. Hilgarde, that if she can see just one person like you, who knows about the things and people she's interested in, it will give her about the only comfort she can have now."

The reins slackened in Charley Gaylord's hand as they drew up before a showily painted house with many gables and a round tower. "Here we are," he said, turning to Everett, "and I guess we understand each other."

They were met at the door by a thin, colorless woman, whom Gaylord introduced as "my sister, Maggie." She asked her brother to show Mr. Hilgarde into the music room, where Katharine wished to see him alone.

When Everett entered the music room he gave a little start of surprise, feeling that he had stepped from the glaring Wyoming sunlight into some New York studio that he had always known. He wondered which it was of those countless studios, high up under the roofs, over banks and shops and wholesale houses, that this room resembled, and he looked incredulously out of the window at the gray plain that ended in the great upheaval of the Rockies.

The haunting air of familiarity about the room perplexed him. Was it a copy of some particular studio he knew, or was it merely the studio atmosphere that seemed so individual and poignantly reminiscent here in Wyoming? He sat down in a reading chair and looked keenly about him. Suddenly his eye fell upon a large photograph of his brother above the piano. Then it all became clear to him: this was veritably his brother's room. If it were not an exact copy of one of the many studios that Adriance had fitted up in various parts of the world, wearying of them and leaving almost before the renovator's varnish had dried, it was at least in the same tone. In every detail Adriance's taste was so manifest that the room seemed to exhale his personality.

Among the photographs on the wall there was one of Katharine Gaylord, taken in the days when Everett had known her, and when the flash of her eye or the flutter of her skirt was enough to set his boyish heart in a tumult. Even now, he stood before the portrait with a certain degree of embarrassment. It was the face of a woman already old in her first youth, thoroughly sophisticated and a trifle hard, and it told of what her brother had called her fight. The camaraderie of her frank, confident eyes was qualified by the deep lines about her mouth and the curve of the lips, which was both sad and cynical. Certainly she had more good will than confidence toward the world, and the bravado of her smile could not conceal the shadow of an unrest that was almost discontent. The chief charm of the woman, as Everett had known her, lay in her superb figure and in her eyes, which possessed a warm, life-giving quality like the sunlight; eyes which glowed with a sort of perpetual *salutat* to the world. Her head, Everett remembered as peculiarly well-shaped and proudly poised.

There had been always a little of the imperatrix about her, and her pose in the photograph revived all his old impressions of her unattachedness, of how absolutely and valiantly she stood alone.

Everett was still standing before the picture, his hands behind him and his head inclined, when he heard the door open. A very tall woman advanced toward him, holding out her hand. As she started to speak, she coughed slightly; then, laughing, said, in a low, rich voice, a trifle husky: "You see I make the traditional Camille entrance—with the cough. How good of you to come, Mr. Hilgarde."

Everett was acutely conscious that while addressing him she was not looking at him at all, and, as he assured her of his pleasure in coming, he was glad to have an opportunity to collect himself. He had not reckoned upon the ravages of a long illness. The long, loose folds of her white gown had been especially designed to conceal the sharp outlines of her emaciated body, but the stamp of her disease was there; simple and ugly and obtrusive, a pitiless fact that could not be disguised or evaded. The splendid shoulders were stooped, there was a swaying unevenness in her gait, her arms seemed disproportionately long, and her hands were transparently white and cold to the touch. The changes in her face were less obvious; the proud carriage of the head, the warm, clear eyes, even the delicate flush of color in her cheeks, all defiantly remained, though they were all in a lower key—older, sadder, softer.

She sat down upon the divan and began nervously to arrange the pillows. "I know I'm not an inspiring object to look upon, but you must be quite frank and sensible about that and get used to it at once, for we've no time to lose. And if I'm a trifle irritable you won't mind?—for I'm more than usually nervous."

"Don't bother with me this morning, if you are tired," urged Everett. "I can come quite as well tomorrow."

"Gracious, no!" she protested, with a flash of that quick, keen humor that he remembered as a part of her. "It's solitude that I'm tired to death of—solitude and the wrong kind of people. You see, the minister, not content with reading the prayers for the sick, called on me this morning. He happened to be riding by on his bicycle and felt it his duty to stop. Of course, he disapproves of my profession, and I think he takes it for granted that I have a dark past. The funniest feature of his conversation is that he is always excusing my own vocation to me—condoning it, you know—and trying to patch up my peace with my conscience by suggesting possible noble uses for what he kindly calls my talent."

Everett laughed. "Oh! I'm afraid I'm not the person to call after such a serious gentleman—I can't sustain the situation. At my best I don't reach higher than low comedy. Have you decided to which one of the noble uses you will devote yourself?"

Katharine lifted her hands in a gesture of renunciation and exclaimed: "I'm not equal to any of them, not even the least noble. I didn't study that method."

She laughed and went on nervously: "The parson's not so bad. His English never offends me, and he has read Gibbon's *Decline and Fall*, all five volumes, and that's something. Then, he has been to New York, and that's a great deal. But how we are losing time! Do tell me about New York; Charley says you're just on from there. How does it look and taste and smell just now? I think a whiff of the Jersey ferry would be as flagons of cod-liver oil to me. Who conspicuously walks the Rialto now, and what does he or she wear? Are the trees still green in Madison Square, or have they grown brown and dusty? Does the chaste Diana on the Garden Theatre still keep her vestal vows through all the exasperating changes of weather? Who has your brother's old studio now, and what misguided aspirants practice their scales in the rookeries about Carnegie Hall? What do people go to see at the theaters, and what do they eat and drink there in the world nowadays? You see, I'm homesick for it all, from the Battery to Riverside. Oh, let me die in Harlem!" She was interrupted by a violent attack of coughing, and Everett, embarrassed by her discomfort, plunged into gossip about the professional people he had met in town during the summer and the musical outlook for the winter. He was diagraming with his pencil, on the back of an old envelope he found in his pocket, some new mechanical device to be used at the Metropolitan in the production of the *Rheingold*, when he became conscious that she was looking at him intently, and that he was talking to the four walls.

Katharine was lying back among the pillows, watching him through half-closed eyes, as a painter looks at a picture. He finished his explanation vaguely enough and put the envelope back in his pocket. As he did so she said, quietly: "How wonderfully like Adriance you are!" and he felt as though a crisis of some sort had been met and tided over.

He laughed, looking up at her with a touch of pride in his eyes that made them seem quite boyish. "Yes, isn't it absurd? It's almost as awkward as looking like Napoleon —but, after all, there are some advantages. It has made some of his friends like me, and I hope it will make you."

Katharine smiled and gave him a quick, meaning glance from under her lashes. "Oh, it did that long ago. What a haughty, reserved youth you were then, and how you used to stare at people and then blush and look cross if they paid you back in your own coin. Do you remember that night when you took me home from a rehearsal and scarcely spoke a word to me?"

"It was the silence of admiration," protested Everett, "very crude and boyish, but very sincere and not a little painful. Perhaps you suspected something of the sort? I remember you saw fit to be very grown-up and worldly."

"I believe I suspected a pose; the one that college boys usually affect with singers—'an earthen vessel in love with a star,' you know. But it rather surprised me in you, for you must have seen a good deal of your brother's pupils. Or had you an omnivorous capacity, and elasticity that always met the occasion?"

"Don't ask a man to confess the follies of his youth," said Everett, smiling a little sadly; "I am sensitive about some of them even now. But I was not so sophisticated as you imagined. I saw my brother's pupils come and go, but that was about all. Sometimes I was called on to play accompaniments, or to fill out a vacancy at a rehearsal, or to order a carriage for an infuriated soprano who had thrown up her part. But they never spent any time on me, unless it was to notice the resemblance you speak of."

"Yes," observed Katharine, thoughtfully, "I noticed it then, too; but it has grown as you have grown older. That is rather strange, when you have lived such different lives. It's not merely an ordinary family likeness of feature, you know, but a sort of interchangeable individuality; the suggestion of the other man's personality in your face—like an air transposed to another key. But I'm not attempting to define it; it's beyond me; something altogether unusual and a trifle—well, uncanny," she finished, laughing.

"I remember," Everett said seriously, twirling the pencil between his fingers and looking, as he sat with his head thrown back, out under the red window blind which was raised just a little, and as it swung back and forth in the wind revealed the glaring panorama of the desert—a blinding stretch of yellow, flat as the sea in dead calm, splotched here and there with deep purple shadows; and, beyond, the ragged-blue outline of the mountains and the peaks of snow, white as the white clouds—"I remember, when I was a little fellow I used to be very sensitive about it. I don't think it exactly displeased me, or that I would have had it otherwise if I could, but it seemed to me like a birthmark, or something not to be lightly spoken of. People were naturally always fonder of Ad than of me, and I used to feel the chill of reflected light pretty often. It came into even my relations with my mother. Ad went abroad to study when he was absurdly young, you know, and mother was all broken up over it. She did her whole duty by each of us, but it was sort of generally understood among us that she'd have made burnt offerings of us all for Ad any day. I was a little fellow then, and when she sat alone on the porch in the summer dusk she used sometimes to call me to her and turn my face up in the light that streamed out through the shutters and kiss me, and then I always knew she was thinking of Adriance."

"Poor little chap," said Katharine, and her tone was a trifle huskier than usual. "How fond people have always been of Adriance! Now tell me the latest news of him. I haven't heard, except through the press, for a year or more. He was in Algeria then, in the valley of the Chelif, riding horseback night and day in an Arabian costume, and in his usual enthusiastic fashion he had quite made up his mind to adopt the Mohammedan faith and become as nearly an Arab as possible. How many countries and faiths has he adopted, I wonder? Probably he was playing Arab to himself all the time. I remember he was a sixteenth-century duke in Florence once for weeks together."

"Oh, that's Adriance," chuckled Everett. "He is himself barely long enough to write checks and be measured for his clothes. I didn't hear from him while he was an Arab; I missed that."

"He was writing an Algerian suite for the piano then; it must be in the publisher's hands by this time. I have been too ill to answer his letter, and have lost touch with him."

Everett drew a letter from his pocket. "This came about a month ago. It's chiefly about his new opera, which is to be brought out in London next winter. Read it at your leisure."

"I think I shall keep it as a hostage, so that I may be sure you will come again. Now I want you to play for me. Whatever you like; but if there is anything new in the world, in mercy let me hear it. For nine months I have heard nothing but 'The Baggage Coach Ahead' and 'She Is My Baby's Mother.'"

He sat down at the piano, and Katharine sat near him, absorbed in his remarkable physical likeness to his brother and trying to discover in just what it consisted. She told herself that it was very much as though a sculptor's finished work had been rudely copied in wood. He was of a larger build than Adriance, and his shoulders were broad and heavy, while those of his brother were slender and rather girlish. His face was of the same oval mold, but it was gray and darkened about the mouth by continual shaving. His eyes were of the same inconstant April color, but they were reflective and rather dull; while Adriance's were always points of highlight, and always meaning another thing than the thing they meant yesterday. But it was hard to see why this earnest man should so continually suggest that lyric, youthful face that was as gay as his was grave. For Adriance, though he was ten years the elder, and though his hair was streaked with silver, had the face of a boy of twenty, so mobile that it told his thoughts before he could put them into words. A contralto, famous for the extravagance of her vocal methods and of her affections, had once said to him that the shepherd boys who sang in the Vale of Tempe must certainly have looked like young Hilgarde; and the comparison had been appropriated by a hundred shyer women who preferred to quote.

As Everett sat smoking on the veranda of the Inter-Ocean House that night, he was a victim to random recollections. His infatuation for Katharine Gaylord, visionary as it was, had been the most serious of his boyish love affairs, and had long disturbed his bachelor dreams. He was painfully timid in everything relating to the emotions, and his hurt had withdrawn him from the society of women. The fact that it was all so done and dead and far behind him, and that the woman had lived her life out since then, gave him an oppressive sense of age and loss. He bethought himself of something he had read about "sitting by the hearth and remembering the faces of women without desire," and felt himself an octogenarian.

He remembered how bitter and morose he had grown during his stay at his brother's studio when Katharine Gaylord was working there, and how he had wounded Adriance on the night of his last concert in New York. He had sat there in the box while his brother and Katharine were called back again and again after the last number, watching the roses go up over the footlights until they were stacked half as high as the piano, brooding, in his sullen boy's heart, upon the pride those two felt in each other's work—spurring each other to their best and beautifully contending in song. The footlights had seemed a hard, glittering line drawn sharply between their life and his; a circle of flame set about those splendid children of genius. He walked back to his hotel alone and sat in his window staring out on Madison Square until long after midnight, resolving to beat no more at doors that he could never enter and realizing more keenly than ever before how far this glorious world of beautiful creations lay from the paths of men like himself. He told himself that he had in common with this woman only the baser uses of life.

* * *

Everett's week in Cheyenne stretched to three, and he saw no prospect of release except through the thing he dreaded. The bright, windy days of the Wyoming autumn passed swiftly. Letters and telegrams came urging him to hasten his trip to the coast, but he resolutely postponed his business engagements. The mornings he spent on one of Charley Gaylord's ponies, or fishing in the mountains, and in the evenings he sat in his room writing letters or reading. In the afternoon he was usually at his post of duty. Destiny, he reflected, seems to have very positive notions about the sort of parts we are fitted to play. The scene changes and the compensation varies, but in the end we usually find that we have played the same class of business from first to last. Everett had been a stopgap all his life. He remembered going through a looking glass labyrinth when he was a boy and trying gallery after gallery, only at every turn to bump his nose against his own face—which, indeed, was not his own, but his brother's. No matter what his mission, east or west, by land or sea, he was sure to find himself employed in his brother's business, one of the tributary lives which helped to swell the shining current of Adriance Hilgarde's. It was not the first time that his duty had been to comfort, as best he could, one of the broken things his brother's imperious speed had cast aside and forgotten. He made no attempt to analyze the situation or to state it in exact terms; but he felt Katharine Gaylord's need for him, and he accepted it as a commission from his brother to help this woman to die. Day by day he felt her demands on him grow more imperious, her need for him grow more acute and positive; and day by day he felt that in his peculiar relation to her his own individuality played a smaller and smaller part. His power to minister to her comfort, he saw, lay solely in his link with his brother's life. He understood all that his physical resemblance meant to her. He knew that she sat by him always watching for some common trick of gesture, some familiar play of expression, some illusion of light and shadow, in which he should seem wholly Adriance. He knew that she lived upon this and that her disease fed upon it; that it sent shudders of remembrance through her and that in the exhaustion which followed this turmoil of her dying senses, she slept deep and sweet and dreamed of youth and art and days in a certain old Florentine garden, and not of bitterness and death.

The question which most perplexed him was, "How much shall I know? How much does she wish me to know?" A few days after his first meeting with Katharine Gaylord, he had cabled his brother to write her. He had merely said that she was mortally ill; he could depend on Adriance to say the right thing—that was a part of his gift. Adriance always said not only the right thing, but the opportune, graceful, exquisite thing. His phrases took the color of the moment and the then-present condition, so that they never savored of perfunctory compliment or frequent usage. He always caught the lyric essence of the moment, the poetic suggestion of every situation. Moreover, he usually did the right thing, the opportune, graceful, exquisite thing—except, when he did very cruel things —bent upon making people happy when their existence touched his, just as he insisted that his material environment should be beautiful; lavishing upon those near him all the warmth and radiance of his rich nature, all the homage of the poet and troubadour, and, when they were no longer near, forgetting—for that also was a part of Adriance's gift.

Three weeks after Everett had sent his cable, when he made his daily call at the gaily painted ranch house, he found Katharine laughing like a schoolgirl. "Have you ever thought," she said, as he entered the music room, "how much these seances of ours are like Heine's 'Florentine Nights,' except that I don't give you an opportunity to monopolize the conversation as Heine did?" She held his hand longer than usual, as she greeted him, and looked searchingly up into his face. "You are the kindest man living; the kindest," she added, softly.

Everett's gray face colored faintly as he drew his hand away, for he felt that this time she was looking at him and not at a whimsical caricature of his brother. "Why, what have I done now?" he asked, lamely. "I can't remember having sent you any stale candy or champagne since yesterday."

She drew a letter with a foreign postmark from between the leaves of a book and held it out, smiling. "You got him to write it. Don't say you didn't, for it came direct, you see, and the last address I gave him was a place in Florida. This deed shall be remembered of you when I am with the just in Paradise. But one thing you did not ask him to do, for you didn't know about it. He has sent me his latest work, the new sonata, the most ambitious thing he has ever done, and you are to play it for me directly, though it looks horribly intricate. But first for the letter; I think you would better read it aloud to me."

Everett sat down in a low chair facing the window seat in which she reclined with a barricade of pillows behind her. He opened the letter, his lashes half-veiling his kind eyes, and saw to his satisfaction that it was a long one—wonderfully tactful and tender, even for Adriance, who was tender with his valet and his stable boy, with his old gondolier and the beggar-women who prayed to the saints for him.

The letter was from Granada, written in the Alhambra, as he sat by the fountain of the Patio di Lindaraxa. The air was heavy, with the warm fragrance of the South and full of the sound of splashing, running water, as it had been in a certain old garden in Florence, long ago. The sky was one great turquoise, heated until it glowed. The wonderful Moorish arches threw graceful blue shadows all about him. He had sketched an outline of them on the margin of his notepaper. The subtleties of Arabic decoration had cast an unholy spell over him, and the brutal exaggerations of Gothic art were a bad dream, easily forgotten. The Alhambra itself had, from the first, seemed perfectly familiar to him, and he knew that he must have trod that court, sleek and brown and obsequious, centuries before Ferdinand rode into Andalusia. The letter was full of confidences about his work, and delicate allusions to their old happy days of study and comradeship, and of her own work, still so warmly remembered and appreciatively discussed everywhere he went.

As Everett folded the letter he felt that Adriance had divined the thing needed and had risen to it in his own wonderful way. The letter was consistently egotistical and seemed to him even a trifle patronizing, yet it was just

what she had wanted. A strong realization of his brother's
charm and intensity and power came over him; he felt the
breath of that whirlwind of flame in which Adriance passed,
consuming all in his path, and himself even more resolutely than he consumed others. Then he looked down at
this white, burnt-out brand that lay before him. "Like
him, isn't it?" she said, quietly.

"I think I can scarcely answer his letter, but when
you see him next you can do that for me. I want you to tell
him many things for me, yet they can all be summed up in
this: I want him to grow wholly into his best and greatest
self, even at the cost of the dear boyishness that is half his
charm to you and me. Do you understand me?"

"I know perfectly well what you mean," answered
Everett, thoughtfully. "I have often felt so about him
myself. And yet it's difficult to prescribe for those fellows;
so little makes, so little mars."

Katharine raised herself upon her elbow, and her face
flushed with feverish earnestness. "Ah, but it is the waste
of himself that I mean; his lashing himself out on stupid
and uncomprehending people until they take him at their
own estimate. He can kindle marble, strike fire from
putty, but is it worth what it costs him?"

"Come, come," expostulated Everett, alarmed at her
excitement. "Where is the new sonata? Let him speak for
himself."

He sat down at the piano and began playing the first
movement, which was indeed the voice of Adriance, his
proper speech. The sonata was the most ambitious work
he had done up to that time and marked the transition
from his purely lyric vein to a deeper and nobler style.
Everett played intelligently and with that sympathetic
comprehension which seems peculiar to a certain lovable
class of men who never accomplish anything in particular.
When he had finished he turned to Katharine.

"How he has grown!" she cried. "What the three last
years have done for him! He used to write only the tragedies of passion; but this is the tragedy of the soul, the
shadow coexistent with the soul. This is the tragedy of
effort and failure, the thing Keats called hell. This is my
tragedy, as I lie here spent by the racecourse, listening to

the feet of the runners as they pass me. Ah, God! The swift feet of the runners!"

She turned her face away and covered it with her straining hands. Everett crossed over to her quickly and knelt beside her. In all the days he had known her she had never before, beyond an occasional ironical jest, given voice to the bitterness of her own defeat. Her courage had become a point of pride with him, and to see it going sickened him.

"Don't do it," he gasped. "I can't stand it, I really can't, I feel it too much. We mustn't speak of that; it's too tragic and too vast."

When she turned her face back to him there was a ghost of the old, brave, cynical smile on it, more bitter than the tears she could not shed. "No, I won't be so ungenerous; I will save that for the watches of the night when I have no better company. Now you may mix me another drink of some sort. Formerly, when it was not *if* I should ever sing Brunnhilde, but quite simply when I *should* sing Brunnhilde, I was always starving myself and thinking what I might drink and what I might not. But broken music boxes may drink whatsoever they list, and no one cares whether they lose their figure. Run over that theme at the beginning again. That, at least, is not new. It was running in his head when we were in Venice years ago, and he used to drum it on his glass at the dinner table. He had just begun to work it out when the late autumn came on, and the paleness of the Adriatic oppressed him, and he decided to go to Florence for the winter, and lost touch with the theme during his illness. Do you remember those frightful days? All the people who have loved him are not strong enough to save him from himself! When I got word from Florence that he had been ill I was in Nice filling a concert engagement. His wife was hurrying to him from Paris, but I reached him first. I arrived at dusk, in a terrific storm. They had taken an old palace there for the winter, and I found him in the library—a long, dark room full of old Latin books and heavy furniture and bronzes. He was sitting by a wood fire at one end of the room, looking, oh, so worn and pale!—as he always does when he is ill, you know. Ah, it is so good that you *do* know! Even his red smoking jacket lent no color to his face. His first words were not to tell me how ill he had been, but that that morning he had been well enough to put the last strokes to the score of his *Souvenirs d'Automne*. He was as I most like to remember him: so calm and happy and tired; not gay, as he usually is, but just contented and tired with that heavenly tiredness that comes after a good work done at last. Outside, the rain poured down in torrents, and the wind moaned for the pain of all the world and sobbed in the branches of the shivering olives and about the walls of that desolated old palace. How that night comes back to me! There were no lights in the room, only the wood fire which glowed upon the hard features of the bronze Dante, like the reflection of purgatorial flames, and threw long black shadows about us; beyond us it scarcely penetrated the gloom at all. Adriance sat staring at the fire with the weariness of all his life in his eyes, and of all the other lives that must aspire and suffer to make up one such life as his. Somehow the wind with all its world-pain had got into the room, and the cold rain was in our eyes, and the wave came up in both of us at once—that awful, vague, universal pain, that cold fear of life and death and God and hope—and we were like two clinging together on a spar in midocean after the shipwreck of everything. Then we heard the front door open with a great gust of wind that shook even the walls, and the servants came running with lights, announcing that Madam had returned, '*and in the book we read no more that night.*'"

She gave the old line with a certain bitter humor, and with the hard, bright smile in which of old she had wrapped her weakness as in a glittering garment. That ironical smile, worn like a mask through so many years, had gradually changed even the lines of her face completely, and when she looked in the mirror she saw not herself, but the scathing critic, the amused observer and satirist of herself. Everett dropped his head upon his hand and sat looking at the rug. "How much you have cared!" he said.

"Ah, yes, I cared," she replied, closing her eyes with a long-drawn sigh of relief; and lying perfectly still, she went on: "You can't imagine what a comfort it is to have you know how I cared, what a relief it is to be able to tell it to someone. I used to want to shriek it out to the world in the long nights when I could not sleep. It seemed to me that I could not die with it. It demanded some sort of expression. And now that you know, you would scarcely believe how much less sharp the anguish of it is."

Everett continued to look helplessly at the floor. "I was not sure how much you wanted me to know," he said.

"Oh, I intended you should know from the first time I looked into your face, when you came that day with Charley. I flatter myself that I have been able to conceal it when I chose, though I suppose women always think that. The more observing ones may have seen, but discerning people are usually discreet and often kind, for we usually bleed a little before we begin to discern. But I wanted you to know; you are so like him that it is almost like telling him himself. At least, I feel now that he will know some day, and then I will be quite sacred from his compassion, for we none of us dare pity the dead. Since it was what my life has chiefly meant, I should like him to know. On the whole I am not ashamed of it. I have fought a good fight."

"And has he never known at all?" asked Everett, in a thick voice.

"Oh! Never at all in the way that you mean. Of course, he is accustomed to looking into the eyes of women and finding love there; when he doesn't find it there he thinks he must have been guilty of some discourtesy and is miserable about it. He has a genuine fondness for everyone who is not stupid or gloomy, or old or preternaturally ugly. Granted youth and cheerfulness, and a moderate amount of wit and some tact, and Adriance will always be glad to see you coming around the corner. I shared with the rest; shared the smiles and the gallantries and the droll little sermons. It was quite like a Sunday-school picnic; we wore our best clothes and a smile and took our turns. It was his kindness that was hardest. I have pretty well used my life up at standing punishment."

"Don't; you'll make me hate him," groaned Everett.

Katharine laughed and began to play nervously with her fan. "It wasn't in the slightest degree his fault; that is the most grotesque part of it. Why, it had really begun before I ever met him. I fought my way to him, and I drank my doom greedily enough."

Everett rose and stood hesitating. "I think I must go. You ought to be quiet, and I don't think I can hear any more just now."

She put out her hand and took his playfully. "You've put in three weeks at this sort of thing, haven't you? Well, it may never be to your glory in this world, perhaps, but it's been the mercy of heaven to me, and it ought to square accounts for a much worse life than yours will ever be."

Everett knelt beside her, saying, brokenly: "I stayed because I wanted to be with you, that's all. I have never cared about other women since I met you in New York when I was a lad. You are a part of my destiny, and I could not leave you if I would."

She put her hands on his shoulders and shook her head. "No, no; don't tell me that. I have seen enough of tragedy, God knows. Don't show me any more just as the curtain is going down. No, no, it was only a boy's fancy, and your divine pity and my utter pitiableness have recalled it for a moment. One does not love the dying, dear friend. If some fancy of that sort had been left over from boyhood, this would rid you of it, and that were well. Now go, and you will come again tomorrow, as long as there are tomorrows, will you not?" She took his hand with a smile that lifted the mask from her soul, that was both courage and despair, and full of infinite loyalty and tenderness, as she said softly:

> For ever and for ever, farewell, Cassius;
> If we do meet again, why, we shall smile;
> If not, why then, this parting was well made.

The courage in her eyes was like the clear light of a star to him as he went out.

On the night of Adriance Hilgarde's opening concert in Paris Everett sat by the bed in the ranch house in Wyoming, watching over the last battle that we have with the flesh before we are done with it and free of it forever. At times it seemed that the serene soul of her must have left already and found some refuge from the storm, and only the tenacious animal life were left to do battle with death. She labored under a delusion at once pitiful and merciful, thinking that she was in the Pullman on her way to New York, going back to her life and her work. When she aroused from her stupor it was only to ask the porter to waken her half an hour out of Jersey City, or to remonstrate with him about the delays and the roughness of the road. At midnight Everett and the nurse were left alone with her. Poor Charley Gaylord had lain down on a couch outside the door. Everett sat looking at the sputtering night lamp until it made his eyes ache. His head dropped forward on the foot of the bed, and he sank into a heavy, distressful slumber. He was dreaming of Adriance's concert in Paris, and of Adriance, the troubadour, smiling and debonair, with his boyish face and the touch of silver gray in his hair. He heard the applause and he saw the roses going up over the footlights until they were stacked half as high as the piano, and the petals fell and scattered, making crimson splotches on the floor. Down this crimson pathway came Adriance with his youthful step, leading his prima donna by the hand; a dark woman this time, with Spanish eyes.

The nurse touched him on the shoulder; he started and awoke. She screened the lamp with her hand. Everett saw that Katharine was awake and conscious, and struggling a little. He lifted her gently on his arm and began to fan her. She laid her hands lightly on his hair and looked into his face with eyes that seemed never to have wept or doubted. "Ah, dear Adriance, dear, dear," she whispered.

Everett went to call her brother, but when they came back the madness of art was over for Katharine.

Two days later Everett was pacing the station siding, waiting for the westbound train. Charley Gaylord walked beside him, but the two men had nothing to say to each other. Everett's bags were piled on the truck, and his step was hurried and his eyes were full of impatience, as he gazed again and again up the track, watching for the train. Gaylord's impatience was not less than his own; these two, who had grown so close, had now become painful and impossible to each other, and longed for the wrench of farewell.

As the train pulled in Everett wrung Gaylord's hand among the crowd of alighting passengers. The people of a German opera company, en route to the coast, rushed by them in frantic haste to snatch their breakfast during the stop. Everett heard an exclamation in a broad German dialect, and a massive woman whose figure persistently escaped from her stays in the most improbable places rushed up to him, her blond hair disordered by the wind, and glowing with joyful surprise she caught his coat sleeve with her tightly gloved hands.

"Herr Gott, Adriance, *lieber Freund,"* she cried, emotionally.

Everett quickly withdrew his arm and lifted his hat, blushing. "Pardon me, madam, but I see that you have mistaken me for Adriance Hilgarde. I am his brother," he said quietly, and turning from the crestfallen singer, he hurried into the car.

The Garden Lodge

When Caroline Noble's friends learned that Raymond d'Esquerré was to spend a month at her place on the Sound before he sailed to fill his engagement for the London opera season, they considered it another striking instance of the perversity of things. That the month was May, and the most mild and florescent of all the blue-and-white Mays the middle coast had known in years, but added to their sense of wrong. D'Esquerré, they learned, was ensconced in the lodge in the apple orchard, just beyond Caroline's glorious garden, and report went that at almost any hour the sound of the tenor's voice and of Caroline's crashing accompaniment could be heard floating through the open windows, out among the snowy apple boughs. The Sound, steel-blue and dotted with white sails, was splendidly seen from the windows of the lodge. The garden to the left and the orchard to the right had never been so riotous with spring, and had burst into impassioned bloom, as if to accommodate Caroline, though she was certainly the last woman to whom the witchery of Freya could be attributed; the last woman, as her friends affirmed, to at all adequately appreciate and make the most of such a setting for the great tenor.

Of course, they admitted, Caroline was musical—well, she ought to be!—but in that, as in everything, she was paramountly cool-headed, slow of impulse, and disgustingly practical; in that, as in everything else, she had herself so provokingly well in hand. Of course, it would be she, always mistress of herself in any situation, she, who would never be lifted one inch from the ground by it, and who would go on superintending her gardeners and workmen as usual—it would be she who got him. Perhaps some of them suspected that this was exactly why she did get him, and it but nettled them the more.

Caroline's coolness, her capableness, her general success, especially exasperated people because they felt that, for the most part, she had made herself what she was; that she had cold-bloodedly set about complying with the demands of life and making her position comfortable and masterful. That was why, everyone said, she had married Howard Noble. Women who did not get through life so well as Caroline, who could not make such good terms either with fortune or their husbands, who did not find their health so unfailingly good, or hold their looks so well, or manage their children so easily, or give such distinction to all they did, were fond of stamping Caroline as a materialist, and called her hard.

The impression of cold calculation, of having a definite policy, which Caroline gave, was far from a false one; but there was this to be said for her—that there were extenuating circumstances which her friends could not know.

If Caroline held determinedly to the middle course, if she was apt to regard with distrust everything which inclined toward extravagance, it was not because she was unacquainted with other standards than her own, or had never seen another side of life. She had grown up in Brooklyn, in a shabby little house under the vacillating administration of her father, a music teacher who usually neglected his duties to write orchestral compositions for which the world seemed to have no especial need. His spirit was warped by bitter vindictiveness and puerile self-commiseration, and he spent his days in scorn of the labor that brought him bread and in pitiful devotion to the labor that brought him only disappointment, writing interminable scores which demanded of the orchestra everything under heaven except melody.

It was not a cheerful home for a girl to grow up in. The mother, who idolized her husband as the music lord of the future, was left to a lifelong battle with broom and dustpan, to never-ending conciliatory overtures to the butcher and grocer, to the making of her own gowns and of Caroline's, and to the delicate task of mollifying Auguste's neglected pupils.

The son, Heinrich, a painter, Caroline's only brother, had inherited all his father's vindictive sensitiveness without his capacity for slavish application. His little studio on the third floor had been much frequented by young men as unsuccessful as himself, who met there to give themselves over to contemptuous derision of this or that artist whose industry and stupidity had won him recognition. Heinrich, when he worked at all, did newspaper sketches at twenty-five dollars a week. He was too indolent and vacillating to set himself seriously to his art, too irascible and poignantly self-conscious to make a living, too much addicted to lying late in bed, to the incontinent reading of poetry, and to the use of chloral to be anything very positive except painful. At twenty-six he shot himself in a frenzy, and the whole wretched affair had effectually shattered his mother's health and brought on the decline of which she died. Caroline had been fond of him, but she felt a certain relief when he no longer wandered about the little house, commenting ironically upon its shabbiness, a Turkish cap on his head and a cigarette hanging from between his long, tremulous fingers.

After her mother's death Caroline assumed the management of that bankrupt establishment. The funeral expenses were unpaid, and Auguste's pupils had been frightened away by the shock of successive disasters and the general atmosphere of wretchedness that pervaded the house. Auguste himself was writing a symphonic poem, Icarus, dedicated to the memory of his son. Caroline was barely twenty when she was called upon to face this tangle of difficulties, but she reviewed the situation candidly. The house had served its time at the shrine of idealism; vague, distressing, unsatisfied yearnings had brought it low enough. Her mother, thirty years before, had eloped and left Germany with her music teacher, to give herself over to lifelong, drudging bondage at the kitchen range. Ever since Caroline could remember, the law in the house had been a sort of mystic worship of things distant, intangible and unattainable. The family had lived in successive ebullitions of generous enthusiasm, in talk of masters and masterpieces, only to come down to the cold facts in the case; to boiled mutton and to the necessity of turning the dining-room carpet. All these emotional pyrotechnics had ended in petty jealousies, in neglected duties, and in cowardly fear of the little grocer on the corner.

From her childhood she had hated it, that humiliating and uncertain existence, with its glib tongue and empty pockets, its poetic ideals and sordid realities, its indolence and poverty tricked out in paper roses. Even as a little girl, when vague dreams beset her, when she wanted to lie late in bed and commune with visions, or to leap and sing because the sooty little trees along the street were putting out their first pale leaves in the sunshine, she would clench her hands and go to help her mother sponge the spots from her father's waistcoat or press Heinrich's trousers. Her mother never permitted the slightest question concerning anything Auguste or Heinrich saw fit to do, but from the time Caroline could reason at all she could not help thinking that many things went wrong at home. She knew, for example, that her father's pupils ought not to be kept waiting half an hour while he discussed Schopenhauer with some bearded socialist over a dish of herrings and a spotted tablecloth. She knew that Heinrich ought not to give a dinner on Heine's birthday, when the laundress had not been paid for a month and when he frequently had to ask his mother for carfare. Certainly Caroline had served her apprenticeship to idealism and to all the embarrassing inconsistencies which it sometimes entails, and she decided to deny herself this diffuse, ineffectual answer to the sharp questions of life.

When she came into the control of herself and the house she refused to proceed any further with her musical education. Her father, who had intended to make a concert pianist of her, set this down as another item in his long list of disappointments and his grievances against the world. She was young and pretty, and she had worn turned gowns and soiled gloves and improvised hats all her life. She wanted the luxury of being like other people, of being honest from her hat to her boots, of having nothing to hide, not even in the matter of stockings, and she was willing to work for it. She rented a little studio away from that house of misfortune and began to give lessons. She managed well and was the sort of girl people liked to help. The bills were paid and Auguste went on composing, growing indignant only when she refused to insist that her pupils should study his compositions for the piano. She began to get engagements in New York to play accompaniments at song recitals. She dressed well, made herself agreeable, and gave herself a chance. She never permitted herself to look further than a step ahead, and set herself with all the strength of her will to see things as they are and meet them squarely in the broad day. There were two things she feared even more than poverty: the part of one that sets up an idol and the part of one that bows down and worships it.

When Caroline was twenty-four she married Howard Noble, then a widower of forty, who had been for ten years a power in Wall Street. Then, for the first time, she had paused to take breath. It took a substantialness as unquestionable as his; his money, his position, his energy, the big vigor of his robust person, to satisfy her that she was entirely safe. Then she relaxed a little, feeling that there was a barrier to be counted upon between her and that world of visions and quagmires and failure.

Caroline had been married for six years when Raymond d'Esquerré came to stay with them. He came chiefly because Caroline was what she was; because he, too, felt occasionally the need of getting out of Klingsor's garden, of dropping down somewhere for a time near a quiet nature, a cool head, a strong hand. The hours he had spent in the garden lodge were hours of such concentrated study as, in his fevered life, he seldom got in anywhere. She had, as he told Noble, a fine appreciation of the seriousness of work.

One evening two weeks after d'Esquerré had sailed, Caroline was in the library giving her husband an account of the work she had laid out for the gardeners. She superintended the care of the grounds herself. Her garden, indeed, had become quite a part of her; a sort of beautiful adjunct, like gowns or jewels. It was a famous spot, and Noble was very proud of it.

"What do you think, Caroline, of having the garden lodge torn down and putting a new summer house there at the end of the arbor; a big rustic affair where you could have tea served in midsummer?" he asked.

"The lodge?" repeated Caroline looking at him quickly. "Why, that seems almost a shame, doesn't it, after d'Esquerré has used it?"

Noble put down his book with a smile of amusement.

"Are you going to be sentimental about it? Why, I'd sacrifice the whole place to see that come to pass. But I don't believe you could do it for an hour together."

"I don't believe so, either," said his wife, smiling.

Noble took up his book again and Caroline went into the music room to practice. She was not ready to have the lodge torn down. She had gone there for a quiet hour every day during the two weeks since d'Esquerré had left them. It was the sheerest sentiment she had ever permitted herself. She was ashamed of it, but she was childishly unwilling to let it go.

Caroline went to bed soon after her husband; but she was not able to sleep. The night was close and warm, presaging storm. The wind had fallen, and the water slept, fixed and motionless as the sand. She rose and thrust her feet into slippers and, putting a dressing gown over her shoulders, opened the door of her husband's room; he was sleeping soundly. She went into the hall and down the stairs; then, leaving the house through a side door, stepped into the vine-covered arbor that led to the garden lodge. The scent of the June roses was heavy in the still air, and the stones that paved the path felt pleasantly cool through the thin soles of her slippers. Heat-lightning flashed continuously from the bank of clouds that had gathered over the sea, but the shore was flooded with moonlight and, beyond, the rim of the Sound lay smooth and shining. Caroline had the key of the lodge, and the door creaked as she opened it. She stepped into the long, low room radiant with the moonlight which streamed through the bow window and lay in a silvery pool along the waxed floor. Even that part of the room which lay in the shadow was vaguely illuminated; the piano, the tall candlesticks, the picture frames and white casts standing out as clearly in the half-light as did the sycamores and black poplars of the garden against the still, expectant night sky. Caroline sat down to think it all over. She had come here to do just that every day of the two weeks since d'Esquerré's departure, but, far from ever having reached a conclusion, she had succeeded only in losing her way in a maze of memories—sometimes bewilderingly confused, sometimes too acutely distinct—where there was neither path, nor clue, nor any hope of finality. She had, she realized, defeated a lifelong regimen; completely confounded herself by falling unaware and incontinently into that luxury of reverie which, even as a little girl, she had so determinedly denied herself; she had been developing with alarming celerity that part of one which sets up an idol and that part of one which bows down and worships it.

It was a mistake, she felt, ever to have asked d'Esquerré to come at all. She had an angry feeling that she had done it rather in self-defiance, to rid herself finally of that instinctive fear of him which had always troubled and perplexed her. She knew that she had reckoned with herself before he came; but she had been equal to so much that she had never really doubted she would be equal to this. She had come to believe, indeed, almost arrogantly in her own malleability and endurance; she had done so much with herself that she had come to think that there was nothing which she could not do; like swimmers, overbold, who reckon upon their strength and their power to hoard it, forgetting the ever-changing moods of their adversary, the sea.

And d'Esquerré was a man to reckon with. Caroline did not deceive herself now upon that score. She admitted it humbly enough, and since she had said good-by to him she had not been free for a moment from the sense of his formidable power. It formed the undercurrent of her consciousness; whatever she might be doing or thinking, it went on, involuntarily, like her breathing, sometimes welling up until suddenly she found herself suffocating. There was a moment of this tonight, and Caroline rose and stood shuddering, looking about her in the blue duskiness of the silent room. She had not been here at night before, and the spirit of the place seemed more troubled and insistent than ever it had in the quiet of the afternoons. Caroline brushed her hair back from her damp forehead and went over to the bow window. After raising it she sat down upon the low seat. Leaning her head against the sill, and loosening her nightgown at the throat, she half-closed her eyes and looked off into the troubled night, watching the play of the heat-lightning upon the massing clouds between the pointed tops of the poplars.

Yes, she knew, she knew well enough, of what absurdities this spell was woven; she mocked, even while she winced. His power, she knew, lay not so much in anything that he actually had—though he had so much—or in anything that he actually was, but in what he suggested, in what he seemed picturesque enough to have or be—and that was just anything that one chose to believe or to desire. His appeal was all the more persuasive and alluring in that it was to the imagination alone, in that it was as indefinite and impersonal as those cults of idealism which so have their way with women. What he had was that, in his mere personality, he quickened and in a measure gratified that something without which—to women—life is no better than sawdust, and to the desire for which most of their mistakes and tragedies and astonishingly poor bargains are due.

D'Esquerré had become the center of a movement, and the Metropolitan had become the temple of a cult. When he could be induced to cross the Atlantic, the opera season in New York was successful; when he could not, the management lost money; so much everyone knew. It was understood, too, that his superb art had disproportionately little to do with his peculiar position. Women swayed the balance this way or that; the opera, the orchestra, even his own glorious art, achieved at such a cost, were but the accessories of himself; like the scenery and costumes and even the soprano, they all went to produce atmosphere, were the mere mechanics of the beautiful illusion.

Caroline understood all this; tonight was not the first time that she had put it to herself so. She had seen the same feeling in other people, watched for it in her friends, studied it in the house night after night when he sang, candidly putting herself among a thousand others.

D'Esquerré's arrival in the early winter was the signal for a feminine hegira toward New York. On the nights when he sang women flocked to the Metropolitan from mansions and hotels, from typewriter desks, schoolrooms, shops, and fitting rooms. They were of all conditions and complexions. Women of the world who accepted him knowingly as they sometimes took champagne for its agreeable effect; sisters of charity and overworked shopgirls, who received him devoutly; withered women who had taken doctorate degrees and who worshipped furtively through prism spectacles; business women and women of affairs, the Amazons who dwelt afar from men in the stony fastnesses of apartment houses. They all entered into the same romance; dreamed, in terms as various as the hues of fantasy, the same dream; drew the same quick breath when he stepped upon the stage, and, at his exit, felt the same dull pain of shouldering the pack again.

There were the maimed, even; those who came on crutches, who were pitted by smallpox or grotesquely painted by cruel birth stains. These, too, entered with him into enchantment. Stout matrons became slender girls again; worn spinsters felt their cheeks flush with the tenderness of their lost youth. Young and old, however hideous, however fair, they yielded up their heat—whether quick or latent—sat hungering for the mystic bread wherewith he fed them at this eucharist of sentiment.

Sometimes, when the house was crowded from the orchestra to the last row of the gallery, when the air was charged with this ecstasy of fancy, he himself was the victim of the burning reflection of his power. They acted upon him in turn; he felt their fervent and despairing appeal to him; it stirred him as the spring drives the sap up into an old tree; he, too, burst into bloom. For the moment he, too, believed again, desired again, he knew not what, but something.

But it was not in these exalted moments that Caroline had learned to fear him most. It was in the quiet, tired reserve, the dullness, even, that kept him company between these outbursts that she found that exhausting drain upon her sympathies which was the very pith and substance of their alliance. It was the tacit admission of disappointment under all this glamour of success—the helplessness of the enchanter to at all enchant himself—that awoke in her an illogical, womanish desire to in some way compensate, to make it up to him.

She had observed drastically to herself that it was her eighteenth year he awoke in her—those hard years she had spent in turning gowns and placating tradesmen, and which she had never had time to live. After all, she reflected, it was better to allow one's self a little youth—to dance a little at the carnival and to live these things when they are natural and lovely, not to have them coming back on one and demanding arrears when they are humiliating and impossible. She went over tonight all the catalogue of her self-deprivations; recalled how, in the light of her father's example, she had even refused to humor her innocent taste for improvising at the piano; how, when she began to teach, after her mother's death, she had struck out one little indulgence after another, reducing her life to a relentless routine, unvarying as clockwork. It seemed to her that ever since d'Esquerré first came into the house she had been haunted by an imploring little girlish ghost that followed her about, wringing its hands and entreating for an hour of life.

The storm had held off unconscionably long; the air within the lodge was stifling, and without the garden waited, breathless. Everything seemed pervaded by a poignant distress; the hush of feverish, intolerable expectation. The still earth, the heavy flowers, even the growing darkness, breathed the exhaustion of protracted waiting. Caroline felt that she ought to go; that it was wrong to stay; that the hour and the place were as treacherous as her own reflections. She rose and began to pace the floor, stepping softly, as though in fear of awakening someone, her figure, in its thin drapery, diaphanously vague and white. Still unable to shake off the obsession of the intense stillness, she sat down at the piano and began to run over the first act of the *Walküre*, the last of his roles they had practiced together; playing listlessly and absently at first, but with gradually increasing seriousness. Perhaps it was the still heat of the summer night, perhaps it was the heavy odors from the garden that came in through the open windows; but as she played there grew and grew the feeling that he was there, beside her, standing in his accustomed place. In the duet at the end of the first act she heard him clearly: *"Thou art the Spring for which I sighed in Winter's cold embraces."* Once as he sang it, he had put his arm about her, his one hand under her heart, while with the other he took her right from the keyboard, holding her as he always held *Sieglinde* when he drew her toward the window. She had been wonderfully the mistress of herself at the time; neither repellent nor acquiescent. She remembered that she had rather exulted, then, in her self-control—which he had seemed to take for granted, though there was perhaps the whisper of a question from the hand under her heart. *"Thou art the Spring for which I sighed in Winter's cold embraces."* Caroline lifted her hands quickly from the keyboard, and she bowed her head in them, sobbing.

The storm broke and the rain beat in, spattering her nightdress until she rose and lowered the windows. She dropped upon the couch and began fighting over again the battles of other days, while the ghosts of the slain rose as from a sowing of dragon's teeth. The shadows of things, always so scorned and flouted, bore down upon her merciless and triumphant. It was not enough; this happy, useful, well-ordered life was not enough. It did not satisfy, it was not even real. No, the other things, the shadows—they were the realities. Her father, poor Heinrich, even her mother, who had been able to sustain her poor romance and keep her little illusions amid the tasks of a scullion, were nearer happiness than she. Her sure foundation was but made ground, after all, and the people in Klingsor's garden were more fortunate, however barren the sands from which they conjured their paradise.

The lodge was still and silent; her fit of weeping over, Caroline made no sound, and within the room, as without in the garden, was the blackness of storm. Only now and then a flash of lightning showed a woman's slender figure rigid on the couch, her face buried in her hands.

Toward morning, when the occasional rumbling of thunder was heard no more and the beat of the raindrops upon the orchard leaves was steadier, she fell asleep and

did not waken until the first red streaks of dawn shone
through the twisted boughs of the apple trees. There was
a moment between world and world, when, neither asleep
nor awake, she felt her dream grow thin, melting away
from her, felt the warmth under her heart growing cold.
Something seemed to slip from the clinging hold of her
arms, and she groaned protestingly through her parted
lips, following it a little way with fluttering hands. Then
her eyes opened wide and she sprang up and sat holding
dizzily to the cushions of the couch, staring down at her
bare, cold feet, at her laboring breast, rising and falling
under her open nightdress.

The dream was gone, but the feverish reality of it still
pervaded her and she held it as the vibrating string holds
a tone. In the last hour the shadows had had their way
with Caroline. They had shown her the nothingness of
time and space, of system and discipline, of closed doors
and broad waters. Shuddering, she thought of the Arabian
fairy tale in which the genie brought the princess of China
to the sleeping prince of Damascus and carried her through
the air back to her palace at dawn. Caroline closed her
eyes and dropped her elbows weakly upon her knees, her
shoulders sinking together. The horror was that it had not
come from without, but from within. The dream was no
blind chance; it was the expression of something she had
kept so close a prisoner that she had never seen it herself;
it was the wail from the donjon deeps when the watch
slept. Only as the outcome of such a night of sorcery could
the thing have been loosed to straighten its limbs and
measure itself with her; so heavy were the chains upon it,
so many a fathom deep, it was crushed down into darkness. The fact that d'Esquerré happened to be on the
other side of the world meant nothing; had he been here,
beside her, it could scarcely have hurt her self-respect so
much. As it was, she was without even the extenuation of
an outer impulse, and she could scarcely have despised
herself more had she come to him here in the night three
weeks ago and thrown herself down upon the stone slab at
the door there.

Caroline rose unsteadily and crept guiltily from the
lodge and along the path under the arbor, terrified lest the

servants should be stirring, trembling with the chill air, while the wet shrubbery, brushing against her, drenched her nightdress until it clung about her limbs.

At breakfast her husband looked across the table at her with concern. "It seems to me that you are looking rather fagged, Caroline. It was a beastly night to sleep. Why don't you go up to the mountains until this hot weather is over? By the way, were you in earnest about letting the lodge stand?"

Caroline laughed quietly. "No, I find I was not very serious. I haven't sentiment enough to forego a summer house. Will you tell Baker to come tomorrow to talk it over with me? If we are to have a house party, I should like to put him to work on it at once."

Noble gave her a glance, half-humorous, half-vexed. "Do you know I am rather disappointed?" he said. "I had almost hoped that, just for once, you know, you would be a little bit foolish."

"Not now that I've slept over it," replied Caroline, and they both rose from the table, laughing.

The Marriage of Phaedra

The sequence of events was such that MacMaster did not make his pilgrimage to Hugh Treffinger's studio until three years after that painter's death. MacMaster was himself a painter, an American of the Gallicized type, who spent his winters in New York, his summers in Paris, and no inconsiderable amount of time on the broad waters between. He had often contemplated stopping in London on one of his return trips in the late autumn, but he had always deferred leaving Paris until the prick of necessity drove him home by the quickest and shortest route.

Treffinger was a comparatively young man at the time of his death, and there had seemed no occasion for haste until haste was of no avail. Then, possibly, though there had been some correspondence between them, MacMaster felt certain qualms about meeting in the flesh a man who in the flesh was so diversely reported. His intercourse with Treffinger's work had been so deep and satisfying, so apart from other appreciations, that he rather dreaded a critical juncture of any sort. He had always felt himself singularly inept in personal relations, and in this case he had avoided the issue until it was no longer to be feared or hoped for. There still remained, however, Treffinger's great unfinished picture, the *Marriage of Phaedra*, which had never left his studio, and of which MacMaster's friends had now and again brought report that it was the painter's most characteristic production.

The young man arrived in London in the evening, and the next morning went out to Kensington to find Treffinger's studio. It lay in one of the perplexing by-streets off Holland Road, and the number he found on a door set in a high garden wall, the top of which was

covered with broken green glass and over which a bud-
ding lilac bush nodded. Treffinger's plate was still there,
and a card requesting visitors to ring for the attendant. In
response to MacMaster's ring, the door was opened by a
cleanly built little man, clad in a shooting jacket and
trousers that had been made for an ampler figure. He had
a fresh complexion, eyes of that common uncertain shade
of gray, and was closely shaven except for the incipient
muttonchops on his ruddy cheeks. He bore himself in a
manner strikingly capable, and there was a sort of trim-
ness and alertness about him, despite the too-generous
shoulders of his coat. In one hand he held a bulldog pipe,
and in the other a copy of *Sporting Life*. While MacMaster
was explaining the purpose of his call he noticed that the
man surveyed him critically, though not impertinently.
He was admitted into a little tank of a lodge made of
whitewashed stone, the back door and windows opening
upon a garden. A visitor's book and a pile of catalogues lay
on a deal table, together with a bottle of ink and some
rusty pens. The wall was ornamented with photographs
and colored prints of racing favorites.

"The studio is h'only open to the public on Saturdays
and Sundays," explained the man—he referred to himself
as "Jymes"—"but of course we make exceptions in the
case of pynters. Lydy Elling Treffinger 'erself is on the
Continent, but Sir 'Ugh's orders was that pynters was to
'ave the run of the place." He selected a key from his
pocket and threw open the door into the studio which,
like the lodge, was built against the wall of the garden.

MacMaster entered a long, narrow room, built of
smoothed planks, painted a light green; cold and damp
even on that fine May morning. The room was utterly
bare of furniture—unless a stepladder, a model throne,
and a rack laden with large leather portfolios could be
accounted such—and was windowless, without other open-
ings than the door and the skylight, under which hung the
unfinished picture itself. MacMaster had never seen so
many of Treffinger's paintings together. He knew the painter
had married a woman with money and had been able to
keep such of his pictures as he wished. These, with all of

his replicas and studies, he had left as a sort of common legacy to the younger men of the school he had originated.

As soon as he was left alone MacMaster sat down on the edge of the model throne before the unfinished picture. Here indeed was what he had come for; it rather paralyzed his receptivity for the moment, but gradually the thing found its way to him.

At one o'clock he was standing before the collection of studies done for *Boccaccio's Garden* when he heard a voice at his elbow.

"Pardon, sir, but I was just about to lock up and go to lunch. Are you lookin' for the figure study of Boccaccio 'imself?" James queried respectfully. "Lydy Elling Treffinger give it to Mr. Rossiter to take down to Oxford for some lectures he's been agiving there."

"Did he never paint out his studies, then?" asked MacMaster with perplexity. "Here are two completed ones for this picture. Why did he keep them?"

"I don't know as I could say as to that, sir," replied James, smiling indulgently, "but that was 'is way. That is to say, 'e pynted out very frequent, but 'e always made two studies to stand; one in watercolors and one in oils, before 'e went at the final picture—to say nothink of all the pose studies 'e made in pencil before he begun on the composition proper at all. He was that particular. You see, 'e wasn't so keen for the final effect as for the proper pyntin' of 'is pictures. 'E used to say they ought to be well made, the same as any other h'article of trade. I can lay my 'and on the pose studies for you, sir." He rummaged in one of the portfolios and produced half a dozen drawings, "These three," he continued, "was discarded; these two was the pose he finally accepted; this one without alteration, as it were.

"That's in Paris, as I remember," James continued reflectively. "It went with the *Saint Cecilia* into the Baron H—'s collection. Could you tell me, sir, 'as 'e it still? I don't like to lose account of them, but some 'as changed 'ands since Sir 'Ugh's death."

"H—'s collection is still intact, I believe," replied MacMaster. "You were with Treffinger long?"

"From my boyhood, sir," replied James with gravity. "I was a stable boy when 'e took me."

"You were his man, then?"

"That's it, sir. Nobody else ever done anything around the studio. I always mixed 'is colors and 'e taught me to do a share of the varnishin'; 'e said as 'ow there wasn't a 'ouse in England as could do it proper. You ayn't looked at the *Marriage* yet, sir?" he asked abruptly, glancing doubtfully at MacMaster, and indicating with his thumb the picture under the north light.

"Not very closely. I prefer to begin with something simpler; that's rather appalling, at first glance," replied MacMaster.

"Well may you say that, sir," said James warmly. "That one regular killed Sir 'Ugh; it regular broke 'im up, and nothink will ever convince me as 'ow it didn't bring on 'is second stroke."

When MacMaster walked back to High Street to take his bus his mind was divided between two exultant convictions. He felt that he had not only found Treffinger's greatest picture, but that, in James, he had discovered a kind of cryptic index to the painter's personality—a clue which, if tactfully followed, might lead to much.

Several days after his first visit to the studio, MacMaster wrote to Lady Mary Percy, telling her that he would be in London for some time and asking her if he might call. Lady Mary was an only sister of Lady Ellen Treffinger, the painter's widow, and MacMaster had known her during one winter he spent at Nice. He had known her, indeed, very well, and Lady Mary, who was astonishingly frank and communicative upon all subjects, had been no less so upon the matter of her sister's unfortunate marriage.

In her reply to his note Lady Mary named an afternoon when she would be alone. She was as good as her word, and when MacMaster arrived he found the drawing room empty. Lady Mary entered shortly after he was announced. She was a tall woman, thin and stiffly jointed, and her body stood out under the folds of her gown with the rigor of cast iron. This rather metallic suggestion was further carried out in her heavily knuckled hands, her stiff gray hair, and her long, bold-featured face, which was saved from freakishness only by her alert eyes.

"Really," said Lady Mary, taking a seat beside him and giving him a sort of military inspection through her nose glasses, "really, I had begun to fear that I had lost you altogether. It's four years since I saw you at Nice, isn't it? I was in Paris last winter, but I heard nothing from you."

"I was in New York then."

"It occurred to me that you might be. And why are you in London?"

"Can you ask?" replied MacMaster gallantly.

Lady Mary smiled ironically. "But for what else, incidentally?"

"Well, incidentally, I came to see Treffinger's studio and his unfinished picture. Since I've been here, I've decided to stay the summer. I'm even thinking of attempting to do a biography of him."

"So that is what brought you to London?"

"Not exactly. I had really no intention of anything so serious when I came. It's his last picture, I fancy, that has rather thrust it upon me. The notion has settled down on me like a thing destined."

"You'll not be offended if I question the clemency of such a destiny," remarked Lady Mary dryly. "Isn't there rather a surplus of books on that subject already?"

"Such as they are. Oh, I've read them all"—here MacMaster faced Lady Mary triumphantly. "He has quite escaped your amiable critics," he added, smiling.

"I know well enough what you think, and I daresay we are not much on art," said Lady Mary with tolerant good humor. "We leave that to peoples who have no physique. Treffinger made a stir for a time, but it seems that we are not capable of a sustained appreciation of such extraordinary methods. In the end we go back to the pictures we find agreeable and unperplexing. He was regarded as an experiment, I fancy; and now it seems that he was rather an unsuccessful one. If you've come to us in a missionary spirit, we'll tolerate you politely, but we'll laugh in our sleeve, I warn you."

"That really doesn't daunt me, Lady Mary," declared

MacMaster blandly. "As I told you, I'm a man with a mission."

Lady Mary laughed her hoarse, baritone laugh. "Bravo! And you've come to me for inspiration for your panegyric?"

MacMaster smiled with some embarrassment. "Not altogether for that purpose. But I want to consult you, Lady Mary, about the advisability of troubling Lady Ellen Treffinger in the matter. It seems scarcely legitimate to go on without asking her to give some sort of grace to my proceedings, yet I feared the whole subject might be painful to her. I shall rely wholly upon your discretion."

"I think she would prefer to be consulted," replied Lady Mary judicially. "I can't understand how she endures to have the wretched affair continually raked up, but she does. She seems to feel a sort of moral responsibility. Ellen has always been singularly conscientious about this matter, insofar as her light goes,—which rather puzzles me, as hers is not exactly a magnanimous nature. She is certainly trying to do what she believes to be the right thing. I shall write to her, and you can see her when she returns from Italy."

"I want very much to meet her. She is, I hope, quite recovered in every way," queried MacMaster, hesitatingly.

"No, I can't say that she is. She has remained in much the same condition she sank to before his death. He trampled over pretty much whatever there was in her, I fancy. Women don't recover from wounds of that sort—at least, not women of Ellen's grain. They go on bleeding inwardly."

"You, at any rate, have not grown more reconciled," MacMaster ventured.

"Oh, I give him his dues. He was a colorist, I grant you; but that is a vague and unsatisfactory quality to marry to; Lady Ellen Treffinger found it so."

"But, my dear Lady Mary," expostulated MacMaster, "and just repress me if I'm becoming too personal—but it must, in the first place, have been a marriage of choice on her part as well as on his."

Lady Mary poised her glasses on her large forefinger and assumed an attitude suggestive of the clinical lecture room as she replied. "Ellen, my dear boy, is an essentially romantic person. She is quiet about it, but she runs deep. I never knew how deep until I came against her on the issue of that marriage. She was always discontented as a girl; she found things dull and prosaic, and the ardor of his courtship was agreeable to her. He met her during her first season in town. She is handsome, and there were plenty of other men, but I grant you your scowling brigand was the most picturesque of the lot. In his courtship, as in everything else, he was theatrical to the point of being ridiculous, but Ellen's sense of humor is not her strongest quality. He had the charm of celebrity, the air of a man who could storm his way through anything to get what he wanted. That sort of vehemence is particularly effective with women like Ellen, who can be warmed only by reflected heat, and she couldn't at all stand out against it. He convinced her of his necessity; and that done, all's done."

"I can't help thinking that, even on such a basis, the marriage should have turned out better," MacMaster remarked reflectively.

"The marriage," Lady Mary continued with a shrug, "was made on the basis of a mutual misunderstanding. Ellen, in the nature of the case, believed that she was doing something quite out of the ordinary in accepting him, and expected concessions which, apparently, it never occurred to him to make. After his marriage he relapsed into his old habits of incessant work, broken by violent and often brutal relaxations. He insulted her friends and foisted his own upon her—many of them well calculated to arouse aversion in any well-bred girl. He had Ghillini constantly at the house—a homeless vagabond, whose conversation was impossible. I don't say, mind you, that he had not grievances on his side. He had probably overrated the girl's possibilities, and he let her see that he was disappointed in her. Only a large and generous nature could have borne with him, and Ellen's is not that. She could not at all understand that odious strain of plebeian pride which plumes itself upon not having risen above its sources."

As MacMaster drove back to his hotel he reflected that Lady Mary Percy had probably had good cause for dissatisfaction with her brother-in-law. Treffinger was, indeed, the last man who should have married into the Percy family. The son of a small tobacconist, he had grown up a sign-painter's apprentice; idle, lawless, and practically letterless until he had drifted into the night classes of the Albert League, where Ghillini sometimes lectured. From the moment he came under the eye and influence of that erratic Italian, then a political exile, his life had swerved sharply from its old channel. This man had been at once incentive and guide, friend and master, to his pupil. He had taken the raw clay out of the London streets and molded it anew. Seemingly he had divined at once where the boy's possibilities lay, and had thrown aside every canon of orthodox instruction in the training of him. Under him Treffinger acquired his superficial, yet facile, knowledge of the classics; had steeped himself in the monkish Latin and medieval romances which later gave his work so naive and remote a quality. That was the beginning of the wattle fences, the cobble pave, the brown roof beams, the cunningly wrought fabrics that gave to his pictures such a richness of decorative effect.

As he had told Lady Mary Percy, MacMaster had found the imperative inspiration of his purpose in Treffinger's unfinished picture, the *Marriage of Phaedra*. He had always believed that the key to Treffinger's individuality lay in his singular education; in the *Roman de la Rose*, in Boccaccio, and Amadis, those works which had literally transcribed themselves upon the blank soul of the London street boy, and through which he had been born into the world of spiritual things. Treffinger had been a man who lived after his imagination; and his mind, his ideals and, as MacMaster believed, even his personal ethics, had to the last been colored by the trend of his early training. There was in him alike the freshness and spontaneity, the frank brutality and the religious mysticism, which lay well back of the fifteenth century. In the *Marriage of Phaedra* MacMaster found the ultimate expression of this spirit, the final word as to Treffinger's point of view.

As in all Treffinger's classical subjects, the conception was wholly medieval. This Phaedra, just turning from her husband and maidens to greet her husband's son, giving him her first fearsome glance from under her half-lifted veil, was no daughter of Minos. The daughter of *heathen-esse* and the early church she was; doomed to torturing visions and scourgings, and the wrangling of soul with flesh. The venerable Theseus might have been victorious Charlemagne, and Phaedra's maidens belonged rather in the train of Blanche of Castile than at the Cretan court. In the earlier studies Hippolytus had been done with a more pagan suggestion; but in each successive drawing the glorious figure had been deflowered of something of its serene unconsciousness, until, in the canvas under the skylight, he appeared a very Christian knight. This male figure, and the face of Phaedra, painted with such magical preservation of tone under the heavy shadow of the veil, were plainly Treffinger's highest achievements of craftsmanship. By what labor he had reached the seemingly inevitable composition of the picture—with its twenty figures, its plenitude of light and air, its restful distances seen through white porticoes—countless studies bore witness.

From James's attitude toward the picture MacMaster could well conjecture what the painter's had been. This picture was always uppermost in James's mind; its custodianship formed, in his eyes, his occupation. He was manifestly apprehensive when visitors—not many came nowadays—lingered near it. "It was the *Marriage* as killed 'im," he would often say, "and for the matter 'o that, it did like to 'av been the death of all of us."

By the end of his second week in London MacMaster had begun the notes for his study of Hugh Treffinger and his work. When his researches led him occasionally to visit the studios of Treffinger's friends and erstwhile disciples, he found their Treffinger manner fading as the ring of Treffinger's personality died out in them. One by one they were stealing back into the fold of national British art; the hand that had wound them up was still. MacMaster despaired of them and confined himself more and more exclusively to the studio, to such of Treffinger's letters as were available—they were for the most part singularly negative and colorless—and to his interrogation of Treffinger's man.

He could not himself have traced the successive steps

by which he was gradually admitted into James's confidence. Certainly most of his adroit strategies to that end failed humiliatingly, and whatever it was that built up an understanding between them must have been instinctive and intuitive on both sides. When at last James became anecdotal, personal, there was that in every word he let fall which put breath and blood into MacMaster's book. James had so long been steeped in that penetrating personality that he fairly exuded it. Many of his very phrases, mannerisms, and opinions were impressions that he had taken on like wet plaster in his daily contact with Treffinger. Inwardly he was lined with cast-off epitheliums, as outwardly he was clad in the painter's discarded coats. If the painter's letters were formal and perfunctory, if his expressions to his friends had been extravagant, contradictory, and often apparently insincere—still, MacMaster felt himself not entirely without authentic sources. It was James who possessed Treffinger's legend; it was with James that he had laid aside his pose. Only in his studio, alone, and face to face with his work, as it seemed, had the man invariably been himself. James had known him in the one attitude in which he was entirely honest; their relation had fallen well within the painter's only indubitable integrity. James's report of Treffinger was distorted by no hallucination of artistic insight, colored by no interpretation of his own. He merely held what he had heard and seen; his mind was a sort of camera obscura. His very limitations made him the more literal and minutely accurate.

One morning, when MacMaster was seated before the *Marriage of Phaedra*, James entered on his usual round of dusting.

"I've 'eard from Lydy Elling by the post, sir," he remarked, "an' she's give h'orders to 'ave the 'ouse put in readiness. I doubt she'll be 'ere by Thursday or Friday next."

"She spends most of her time abroad?" queried MacMaster; on the subject of Lady Treffinger James consistently maintained a very delicate reserve.

"Well, you could 'ardly say she does that, sir. She finds the 'ouse a bit dull, I daresay, so durin' the season she stops mostly with Lydy Mary Percy, at Grosvenor

Square. Lydy Mary's a h'only sister." After a few moments
he continued, speaking in jerks governed by the rigor of
his dusting: "H'only this morning I come upon this scarf-
pin," exhibiting a very striking instance of that article, "an'
I recalled as 'ow Sir 'Ugh give it me when 'e was acourting
of Lydy Elling. Blowed if I ever see a man go in for a
'oman like 'im! 'E was that gone, sir. 'E never went in on
anythink so 'ard before nor since, till 'e went in on the
Marriage there—though 'e mostly went in on things pretty
keen; 'ad the measles when 'e was thirty, strong as cholera, an' come close to dyin' of 'em. 'E wasn't strong for
Lydy Elling's set; they was a bit too stiff for 'im. A free an'
easy gentleman, 'e was; 'e liked 'is dinner with a few
friends an' them jolly, but 'e wasn't much on what you
might call big affairs. But once 'e went in for Lydy Elling
'e broke 'imself to new paces. He give away 'is rings an'
pins, an' the tylor's man an' the 'aberdasher's man was at
'is rooms continual. 'E got 'imself put up for a club in
Piccadilly; 'e starved 'imself thin, an' worrited 'imself white,
an' ironed 'imself out, an' drawed 'imself tight as a bow
string. It was a good job 'e come a winner, or I don't know
w'at'd 'a been to pay."

The next week, in consequence of an invitation from
Lady Ellen Treffinger, MacMaster went one afternoon to
take tea with her. He was shown into the garden that lay
between the residence and the studio, where the tea table
was set under a gnarled pear tree. Lady Ellen rose as he
approached—he was astonished to note how tall she was—
and greeted him graciously, saying that she already knew
him through her sister. MacMaster felt a certain satisfaction in her; in her reassuring poise and repose, in the
charming modulations of her voice and the indolent reserve of her full, almond eyes. He was even delighted to
find her face so inscrutable, though it chilled his own
warmth and made the open frankness he had wished to
permit himself impossible. It was a long face, narrow at
the chin, very delicately featured, yet steeled by an im-
passive mask of self-control. It was behind just such finely
cut, close-sealed faces, MacMaster reflected, that nature
sometimes hid astonishing secrets. But in spite of this
suggestion of hardness he felt that the unerring taste that

Treffinger had always shown in larger matters had not deserted him when he came to the choosing of a wife, and he admitted that he could not himself have selected a woman who looked more as Treffinger's wife should look.

While he was explaining the purpose of his frequent visits to the studio she heard him with courteous interest. "I have read, I think, everything that has been published on Sir Hugh Treffinger's work, and it seems to me that there is much left to be said," he concluded.

"I believe they are rather inadequate," she remarked vaguely. She hesitated a moment, absently fingering the ribbons of her gown, then continued, without raising her eyes; "I hope you will not think me too exacting if I ask to see the proofs of such chapters of your work as have to do with Sir Hugh's personal life. I have always asked that privilege."

MacMaster hastily assured her as to this, adding, "I mean to touch on only such facts in his personal life as have to do directly with his work—such as his monkish education under Ghillini."

"I see your meaning, I think," said Lady Ellen, looking at him with wide, uncomprehending eyes.

When MacMaster stopped at the studio on leaving the house he stood for some time before Treffinger's one portrait of himself; that brigand of a picture, with its full throat and square head; the short upper lip blackened by the close-clipped mustache, the wiry hair tossed down over the forehead, the strong white teeth set hard on a short pipestem. He could well understand what manifold tortures the mere grain of the man's strong red and brown flesh might have inflicted upon a woman like Lady Ellen. He could conjecture, too, Treffinger's impotent revolt against that very repose which had so dazzled him when it first defied his daring; and how once possessed of it, his first instinct had been to crush it, since he could not melt it.

Toward the close of the season Lady Ellen Treffinger left town. MacMaster's work was progressing rapidly, and he and James wore away the days in their peculiar relation, which by this time had much of friendliness. Excepting for the regular visits of a Jewish picture dealer, there were few intrusions upon their solitude. Occasionally a party of Americans rang at the little door in the garden wall, but usually they departed speedily for the Moorish hall and tinkling fountain of the great show studio of London, not far away.

This Jew, an Austrian by birth, who had a large business in Melbourne, Australia, was a man of considerable discrimination, and at once selected the *Marriage of Phaedra* as the object of his especial interest. When, upon his first visit, Lichtenstein had declared the picture one of the things done for time, MacMaster had rather warmed toward him and had talked to him very freely. Later, however, the man's repulsive personality and innate vulgarity so wore upon him that, the more genuine the Jew's appreciation, the more he resented it and the more base he somehow felt it to be. It annoyed him to see Lichtenstein walking up and down before the picture, shaking his head and blinking his watery eyes over his nose glasses, ejaculating: "Dot is a chem, a chem! It is wordt to gome den dousant miles for such a bainting, eh? To make Eurobe abbreciate such a work of ardt it is necessary to take it away while she is napping. She has never abbreciated until she has lost, but," knowingly, "she will buy back."

James had, from the first, felt such a distrust of the man that he would never leave him alone in the studio for a moment. When Lichtenstein insisted upon having Lady Ellen Treffinger's address James rose to the point of insolence. "It ayn't no use to give it, noway. Lydy Treffinger never has nothink to do with dealers." MacMaster quietly repented his rash confidences, fearing that he might indirectly cause Lady Ellen annoyance from this merciless speculator, and he recalled with chagrin that Lichtenstein had extorted from him, little by little, pretty much the entire plan of his book, and especially the place in it which the *Marriage of Phaedra* was to occupy.

By this time the first chapters of MacMaster's book were in the hands of his publisher, and his visits to the studio were necessarily less frequent. The greater part of his time was now employed with the engravers who were to reproduce such of Treffinger's pictures as he intended to use as illustrations.

He returned to his hotel late one evening after a long

and vexing day at the engravers to find James in his room, seated on his steamer trunk by the window, with the outline of a great square draped in sheets resting against his knee.

"Why, James, what's up?" he cried in astonishment, glancing inquiringly at the sheeted object.

"Ayn't you seen the pypers, sir?" jerked out the man.

"No, now I think of it, I haven't even looked at a paper. I've been at the engravers' plant all day. I haven't seen anything."

James drew a copy of the *Times* from his pocket and handed it to him, pointing with a tragic finger to a paragraph in the social column. It was merely the announcement of Lady Ellen Treffinger's engagement to Captain Alexander Gresham.

"Well, what of it, my man? That surely is her privilege."

James took the paper, turned to another page, and silently pointed to a paragraph in the art notes which stated that Lady Treffinger had presented to the X— gallery the entire collection of paintings and sketches now in her late husband's studio, with the exception of his unfinished picture, the *Marriage of Phaedra*, which she had sold for a large sum to an Australian dealer who had come to London purposely to secure some of Treffinger's paintings.

MacMaster pursed up his lips and sat down, his overcoat still on. "Well, James, this is something of a—something of a jolt, eh? It never occurred to me she'd really do it."

"Lord, you don't know 'er, sir," said James bitterly, still staring at the floor in an attitude of abandoned dejection.

MacMaster started up in a flash of enlightenment, "What on earth have you got there, James? It's not— surely it's not—"

"Yes, it is, sir," broke in the man excitedly. "It's the *Marriage* itself. It ayn't agoing to H'Australia, no'ow!"

"But man, what are you going to do with it? It's Lichtenstein's property now, as it seems."

"It ayn't, sir, that it ayn't. No, by Gawd, it ayn't!" shouted James, breaking into a choking fury. He controlled himself with an effort and added supplicatingly: "Oh, sir, you ayn't agoing to see it go to H'Australia, w'ere they send convic's?" He unpinned and flung aside the sheets as though to let *Phaedra* plead for herself.

MacMaster sat down again and looked sadly at the doomed masterpiece. The notion of James having carried it across London that night rather appealed to his fancy. There was certainly a flavor about such a highhanded proceeding. "However did you get it here?" he queried.

"I got a four-wheeler and come over direct, sir. Good job I 'appened to 'ave the chaynge about me."

"You came up High Street, up Piccadilly, through the Haymarket and Trafalgar Square, and into the Strand?" queried MacMaster with a relish.

"Yes, sir. Of course, sir," assented James with surprise.

MacMaster laughed delightedly. "It was a beautiful idea, James, but I'm afraid we can't carry it any further."

"I was thinkin' as 'ow it would be a rare chance to get you to take the *Marriage* over to Paris for a year or two, sir, until the thing blows over?" suggested James blandly.

"I'm afraid that's out of the question, James. I haven't the right stuff in me for a pirate, or even a vulgar smuggler, I'm afraid." MacMaster found it surprisingly difficult to say this, and he busied himself with the lamp as he said it. He heard James's hand fall heavily on the trunk top, and he discovered that he very much disliked sinking in the man's estimation.

"Well, sir," remarked James in a more formal tone, after a protracted silence; "then there's nothink for it but as 'ow I'll 'ave to make way with it myself."

"And how about your character, James? The evidence would be heavy against you, and even if Lady Treffinger didn't prosecute you'd be done for."

"Blow my character!—your pardon, sir," cried James, starting to his feet. "W'at do I want of a character? I'll chuck the 'ole thing, and damned lively, too. The shop's to be sold out, an' my place is gone any'ow. I'm agoing to enlist, or try the gold fields. I've lived too long with h'artists; I'd never give satisfaction in livery now. You know 'ow it is yourself, sir; there ayn't no life like it, no'ow."

For a moment MacMaster was almost equal to abetting James in his theft. He reflected that pictures had been whitewashed, or hidden in the crypts of churches, or under the floors of palaces from meaner motives, and to save them from a fate less ignominious. But presently, with a sigh, he shook his head.

"No, James, it won't do at all. It has been tried over and over again, ever since the world has been agoing and pictures amaking. It was tried in Florence and in Venice, but the pictures were always carried away in the end. You see, the difficulty is that, although Treffinger told you what was not to be done with the picture, he did not say definitely what was to be done with it. Do you think Lady Treffinger really understands that he did not want it to be sold?"

"Well, sir, it was like this, sir," said James, resuming his seat on the trunk and again resting the picture against his knee. "My memory is as clear as glass about it. After Sir 'Ugh got up from 'is first stroke, 'e took a fresh start at the *Marriage*. Before that 'e 'ad been working at it only at night for a while back; the *Legend* was the big picture then, an' was under the north light w'ere 'e worked of a morning. But one day 'e bid me take the *Legend* down an' put the *Marriage* in its place, an' 'e says, dashin' on 'is jacket, 'Jymes, this is a start for the finish, this time.'

"From that on 'e worked at the night picture in the mornin'—a thing contrary to 'is custom. The *Marriage* went wrong, and wrong—an' Sir 'Ugh agettin' seedier an' seedier every day. 'E tried models an' models, an' smudged an' pynted out on account of 'er face goin' wrong in the shadow. Sometimes 'e layed it on the colors, an' swore at me an' things in general. He got that discouraged about 'imself that on 'is low days 'e used to say to me: 'Jymes, remember one thing; if anythink 'appens to me, the *Marriage* is not to go out of 'ere unfinished. It's worth the lot of 'em, my boy, an' it's not agoing to go shabby for lack of pains.' 'E said things to that effect repeated.

"He was workin' at the picture the last day, before 'e went to 'is club. 'E kept the carriage waitin' near an hour while 'e put on a stroke an' then drawed back for to look at it, an' then put on another, careful like. After 'e 'ad 'is

gloves on, 'e come back an' took away the brushes I was
startin' to clean, an' put in another touch or two. 'It's
acomin', Jymes,' 'e says, 'by gad if it ayn't.' An' with that 'e
goes out. It was cruel sudden, w'at come after.

"That night I was lookin' to 'is clothes at the 'ouse
when they brought 'im 'ome. He was conscious, but w'en
I ran downstairs for to 'elp lift 'im up, I knowed 'e was a
finished man. After we got 'im into bed 'e kept lookin'
restless at me and then at Lydy Elling and ajerkin' of 'is
'and. Finally 'e quite raised it an' shot 'is thumb out
toward the wall. 'He wants water; ring, Jymes,' says Lydy
Elling, placid. But I knowed 'e was pointin' to the shop.

" 'Lydy Treffinger,' says I, bold, 'he's pointin' to the
studio. He means about the *Marriage;* 'e told me today as
'ow 'e never wanted it sold unfinished. Is that it, Sir
'Ugh?'

"He smiled an' nodded slight an' closed 'is eyes.
'Thank you, Jymes,' says Lydy Elling, placid. Then 'e
opened 'is eyes an' looked long and 'ard at Lydy Elling.

" 'Of course I'll try to do as you'd wish about the
picture, 'Ugh, if that's w'at's troublin' you,' she says quiet.
With that 'e closed 'is eyes and 'e never opened 'em. He
died unconscious at four that mornin'.

"You see, sir, Lydy Elling was always cruel 'ard on
the *Marriage*. From the first it went wrong, an' Sir 'Ugh
was out of temper pretty constant. She came into the
studio one day and looked at the picture an' asked 'im why
'e didn't throw it up an' quit aworriting 'imself. He answered sharp, an' with that she said as 'ow she didn't see
w'at there was to make such a row about, no'ow. She
spoke 'er mind about that picture, free; an' Sir 'Ugh swore
'ot an' let a 'andful of brushes fly at 'is study, an' Lydy
Elling picked up 'er skirts careful an' chill, an' drifted out
of the studio with 'er eyes calm and 'er chin 'igh. If there
was one thing Lydy Elling 'ad no comprehension of, it was
the usefulness of swearin'. So the *Marriage* was a sore
thing between 'em. She is uncommon calm, but uncommon bitter, is Lydy Elling. She's never come anear the
studio since that day she went out 'oldin' up of 'er skirts.
W'en 'er friends goes over she excuses 'erself along o' the

strain. Strain—Gawd!" James ground his wrath short in
his teeth.

"I'll tell you what I'll do, James, and it's our only
hope. I'll see Lady Ellen tomorrow. The *Times* says she
returned today. You take the picture back to its place, and
I'll do what I can for it. If anything is done to save it, it
must be done through Lady Ellen Treffinger herself; that
much is clear. I can't think that she fully understands the
situation. If she did, you know, she really couldn't have
any motive—" He stopped suddenly. Somehow, in the
dusky lamplight, her small, close-sealed face came ominously back to him. He rubbed his forehead and knitted
his brows thoughtfully. After a moment he shook his head
and went on: "I am positive that nothing can be gained by
highhanded methods, James. Captain Gresham is one of
the most popular men in London, and his friends would
tear up Treffinger's bones if he were annoyed by any
scandal of our making—and this scheme you propose would
inevitably result in scandal. Lady Ellen has, of course,
every legal right to sell the picture. Treffinger made considerable inroads upon her estate, and, as she is about to
marry a man without income, she doubtless feels that she
has a right to replenish her patrimony."

He found James amenable, though doggedly skepti-
cal. He went down into the street, called a carriage, and
saw James and his burden into it. Standing in the doorway, he watched the carriage roll away through the driz-
zling mist, weave in and out among the wet, black vehicles
and darting cab lights, until it was swallowed up in the
glare and confusion of the Strand. "It is rather a fine touch
of irony," he reflected, "that he, who is so out of it, should
be the one to really care. Poor Treffinger," he murmured
as, with a rather spiritless smile, he turned back into his
hotel. "Poor Treffinger; *sic transit gloria.*"

The next afternoon MacMaster kept his promise. When
he arrived at Lady Mary Percy's house he saw prepara-
tions for a function of some sort, but he went resolutely up
the steps, telling the footman that his business was urgent.
Lady Ellen came down alone, excusing her sister. She was
dressed for receiving, and MacMaster had never seen one

so beautiful. The color in her cheeks sent a softening glow over her small, delicately cut features.

MacMaster apologized for his intrusion and came unflinchingly to the object of his call. He had come, he said, not only to offer her his warmest congratulations, but to express his regret that a great work of art was to leave England.

Lady Treffinger looked at him in wide-eyed astonishment. Surely, she said, she had been careful to select the best of the pictures for the X— gallery, in accordance with Sir Hugh Treffinger's wishes.

"And did he—pardon me, Lady Treffinger, but in mercy set my mind at rest—did he or did he not express any definite wish concerning this one picture, which to me seems worth all the others, unfinished as it is?"

Lady Treffinger paled perceptibly, but it was not the pallor of confusion. When she spoke there was a sharp tremor in her smooth voice, the edge of a resentment that tore her like pain. "I think his man has some such impression, but I believe it to be utterly unfounded. I cannot find that he ever expressed any wish concerning the disposition of the picture to any of his friends. Unfortunately, Sir Hugh was not always discreet in his remarks to his servants."

"Captain Gresham, Lady Ellingham, and Miss Ellingham," announced a servant, appearing at the door.

There was a murmur in the hall, and MacMaster greeted the smiling Captain and his aunt as he bowed himself out.

To all intents and purposes the *Marriage of Phaedra* was already entombed in a vague continent in the Pacific, somewhere on the other side of the world.

A Wagner Matinee

I received one morning a letter, written in pale ink on glassy, blue-lined notepaper, and bearing the postmark of a little Nebraska village. This communication, worn and rubbed, looking as though it had been carried for some days in a coat pocket that was none too clean, was from my Uncle Howard and informed me that his wife had been left a small legacy by a bachelor relative who had recently died, and that it would be necessary for her to go to Boston to attend to the settling of the estate. He requested me to meet her at the station and render her whatever services might be necessary. On examining the date indicated as that of her arrival I found it no later than tomorrow. He had characteristically delayed writing until, had I been away from home for a day, I must have missed the good woman altogether.

The name of my Aunt Georgiana called up not alone her own figure, at once pathetic and grotesque, but opened before my feet a gulf of recollection so wide and deep that, as the letter dropped from my hand, I felt suddenly a stranger to all the present conditions of my existence, wholly ill at ease and out of place amid the familiar surroundings of my study. I became, in short, the gangling farm boy my aunt had known, scourged with chilblains and bashfulness, my hands cracked and sore from the corn husking. I felt the knuckles of my thumb tentatively, as though they were raw again. I sat again before her parlor organ, fumbling the scales with my stiff, red hands, while she, beside me, made canvas mittens for the huskers.

The next morning, after preparing my landlady somewhat, I set out for the station. When the train arrived I had some difficulty in finding my aunt. She was the last of the passengers to alight, and it was not until I got her into the carriage that she seemed really to recognize me. She had come all the way in a day coach; her linen duster had become black with soot, and her black bonnet gray with dust, during the journey. When we arrived at my boarding-house the landlady put her to bed at once and I did not see her again until the next morning.

Whatever shock Mrs. Springer experienced at my aunt's appearance she considerately concealed. As for myself, I saw my aunt's misshapen figure with that feeling of awe and respect with which we behold explorers who have left their ears and fingers north of Franz Josef Land, or their health somewhere along the Upper Congo. My Aunt Georgiana had been a music teacher at the Boston Conservatory, somewhere back in the latter sixties. One summer, while visiting in the little village among the Green Mountains where her ancestors had dwelt for generations, she had kindled the callow fancy of the most idle and shiftless of all the village lads, and had conceived for this Howard Carpenter one of those extravagant passions which a handsome country boy of twenty-one sometimes inspires in an angular, spectacled woman of thirty. When she returned to her duties in Boston, Howard followed her, and the upshot of this inexplicable infatuation was that she eloped with him, eluding the reproaches of her family and the criticisms of her friends by going with him to the Nebraska frontier. Carpenter, who, of course, had no money, had taken a homestead in Red Willow County, fifty miles from the railroad. There they had measured off their quarter section themselves by driving across the prairie in a wagon, to the wheel of which they had tied a red cotton handkerchief, and counting off its revolutions. They built a dugout in the red hillside, one of those cave dwellings whose inmates so often reverted to primitive conditions. Their water they got from the lagoons where the buffalo drank, and their slender stock of provisions was always at the mercy of bands of roving Indians. For thirty years my aunt had not been further than fifty miles from the homestead.

But Mrs. Springer knew nothing of all this, and must have been considerably shocked at what was left of my kinswoman. Beneath the soiled linen duster which, on her arrival, was the most conspicuous feature of her costume, she wore a black stuff dress, whose ornamentation showed that she had surrendered herself unquestioningly into the hands of a country dressmaker. My poor aunt's figure, however, would have presented astonishing difficulties to any dressmaker. Originally stooped, her shoulders were now almost bent together over her sunken chest. She wore no stays, and her gown, which trailed unevenly behind, rose in a sort of peak over her abdomen. She wore ill-fitting false teeth, and her skin was as yellow as a Mongolian's from constant exposure to a pitiless wind and to the alkaline water which hardens the most transparent cuticle into a sort of flexible leather.

I owed to this woman most of the good that ever came my way in my boyhood, and had a reverential affection for her. During the years when I was riding herd for my uncle, my aunt, after cooking the three meals—the first of which was ready at six o'clock in the morning—and putting the six children to bed, would often stand until midnight at her ironing board, with me at the kitchen table beside her, hearing me recite Latin declensions and conjugations, gently shaking me when my drowsy head sank down over a page of irregular verbs. It was to her, at her ironing or mending, that I read my first Shakespeare, and her old textbook on mythology was the first that ever came into my empty hands. She taught me my scales and exercises, too—on the little parlor organ, which her husband had bought her after fifteen years, during which she had not so much as seen any instrument, but an accordion that belonged to one of the Norwegian farmhands. She would sit beside me by the hour, darning and counting while I struggled with the "Joyous Farmer," but she seldom talked to me about music, and I understood why. She was a pious woman; she had the consolations of religion and, to her at least, her martyrdom was not wholly sordid. Once when I had been doggedly beating out some easy passages from an old score of *Euryanthe* I had found among her music books, she came up to me and, putting her hands over my eyes, gently drew my head back upon her shoulder, saying tremulously, "Don't love it so well,

Clark, or it may be taken from you. Oh, dear boy, pray that whatever your sacrifice may be, it be not that."

When my aunt appeared on the morning after her arrival she was still in a semisomnambulant state. She seemed not to realize that she was in the city where she had spent her youth, the place longed for hungrily half a lifetime. She had been so wretchedly train-sick throughout the journey that she had no recollection of anything but her discomfort, and, to all intents and purposes, there were but a few hours of nightmare between the farm in Red Willow County and my study on Newbury Street. I had planned a little pleasure for her that afternoon, to repay her for some of the glorious moments she had given me when we used to milk together in the straw-thatched cowshed and she, because I was more than usually tired, or because her husband had spoken sharply to me, would tell me of the splendid performance of the *Huguenots* she had seen in Paris, in her youth. At two o'clock the Symphony Orchestra was to give a Wagner program, and I intended to take my aunt; though, as I conversed with her I grew doubtful about her enjoyment of it. Indeed, for her own sake, I could only wish her taste for such things quite dead, and the long struggle mercifully ended at last. I suggested our visiting the Conservatory and the Common before lunch, but she seemed altogether too timid to wish to venture out. She questioned me absently about various changes in the city, but she was chiefly concerned that she had forgotten to leave instructions about feeding half-skimmed milk to a certain weakling calf, "old Maggie's calf, you know, Clark," she explained, evidently having forgotten how long I had been away. She was further troubled because she had neglected to tell her daughter about the freshly opened kit of mackerel in the cellar, which would spoil if it were not used directly.

I asked her whether she had ever heard any of the Wagnerian operas and found that she had not, though she was perfectly familiar with their respective situations, and had once possessed the piano score of *The Flying Dutchman*. I began to think it would have been best to get her back to Red Willow County without waking her, and regretted having suggested the concert.

From the time we entered the concert hall, however, she was a trifle less passive and inert, and for the first time seemed to perceive her surroundings. I had felt some trepidation lest she might become aware of the absurdities of her attire, or might experience some painful embarrassment at stepping suddenly into the world to which she had been dead for a quarter of a century. But, again, I found how superficially I had judged her. She sat looking about her with eyes as impersonal, almost as stony, as those with which the granite Rameses in a museum watches the froth and fret that ebbs and flows about his pedestal—separated from it by the lonely stretch of centuries. I have seen this same aloofness in old miners who drift into the Brown Hotel at Denver, their pockets full of bullion, their linen soiled, their haggard faces unshaven; standing in the thronged corridors as solitary as though they were still in a frozen camp on the Yukon, conscious that certain experiences have isolated them from their fellows by a gulf no haberdasher could bridge.

We sat at the extreme left of the first balcony, facing the arc of our own and the balcony above us, veritable hanging gardens, brilliant as tulip beds. The matinee audience was made up chiefly of women. One lost the contour of faces and figures—indeed, any effect of line whatever—and there was only the color of bodices past counting, the shimmer of fabrics soft and firm, silky and sheer: red, mauve, pink, blue, lilac, purple, ecru, rose, yellow, cream, and white, all the colors that an impressionist finds in a sunlit landscape, with here and there the dead shadow of a frock coat. My Aunt Georgiana regarded them as though they had been so many daubs of tube-paint on a palette.

When the musicians came out and took their places, she gave a little stir of anticipation and looked with quickening interest down over the rail at that invariable grouping, perhaps the first wholly familiar thing that had greeted her eye since she had left old Maggie and her weakling calf. I could feel how all those details sank into her soul, for I had not forgotten how they had sunk into mine when I came fresh from plowing forever and forever between green aisles of corn, where, as in a treadmill, one might walk from daybreak to dusk without perceiving a shadow

of change. The clean profiles of the musicians, the gloss of
their linen, the dull black of their coats, the beloved
shapes of the instruments, the patches of yellow light
thrown by the green-shaded lamps on the smooth, var-
nished bellies of the cellos and the bass viols in the rear,
the restless, wind-tossed forest of fiddle necks and bows—
I recalled how, in the first orchestra I had ever heard,
those long bow strokes seemed to draw the heart out of
me, as a conjurer's stick reels out yards of paper ribbon
from a hat.

The first number was the *Tannhauser* overture. When
the horns drew out the first strain of the Pilgrim's chorus
my Aunt Georgiana clutched my coat sleeve. Then it was I
first realized that for her this broke a silence of thirty
years; the inconceivable silence of the plains. With the
battle between the two motives, with the frenzy of the
Venusberg theme and its ripping of strings, there came to
me an overwhelming sense of the waste and wear we are
so powerless to combat; and I saw again the tall, naked
house on the prairie, black and grim as a wooden fortress;
the black pond where I had learned to swim, its margin
pitted with sun-dried cattle tracks; the rain-gullied clay
banks about the naked house, the four dwarf ash seedlings
where the dishcloths were always hung to dry before the
kitchen door. The world there was the flat world of the
ancients; to the east, a cornfield that stretched to daybreak; to the west, a corral that reached to sunset; between, the conquests of peace, dearer bought than those
of war.

The overture closed; my aunt released my coat sleeve,
but she said nothing. She sat staring at the orchestra
through a dullness of thirty years, through the films made
little by little by each of the three hundred and sixty-five
days in every one of them. What, I wondered, did she get
from it? She had been a good pianist in her day I knew,
and her musical education had been broader than that of
most music teachers of a quarter of a century ago. She had
often told me of Mozart's operas and Meyerbeer's, and I
could remember hearing her sing, years ago, certain melo-
dies of Verdi's. When I had fallen ill with a fever in her
house she used to sit by my cot in the evening—when the

cool, night wind blew in through the faded mosquito netting tacked over the window, and I lay watching a certain bright star that burned red above the cornfield—and sing "Home to our mountains, O, let us return!" in a way fit to break the heart of a Vermont boy near dead of homesickness already.

I watched her closely through the prelude to *Tristan and Isolde*, trying vainly to conjecture what that seething turmoil of strings and winds might mean to her, but she sat mutely staring at the violin bows that drove obliquely downward, like the pelting streaks of rain in a summer shower. Had this music any message for her? Had she enough left to at all comprehend this power which had kindled the world since she had left it? I was in a fever of curiosity, but Aunt Georgiana sat silent upon her peak in Darien. She preserved this utter immobility throughout the number from *The Flying Dutchman*, though her fingers worked mechanically upon her black dress, as though, of themselves, they were recalling the piano score they had once played. Poor old hands! They had been stretched and twisted into mere tentacles to hold and lift and knead with; the palms unduly swollen, the fingers bent and knotted—on one of them a thin, worn band that had once been a wedding ring. As I pressed and gently quieted one of those groping hands I remembered with quivering eyelids their services for me in other days.

Soon after the tenor began the "Prize Song," I heard a quick drawn breath and turned to my aunt. Her eyes were closed, but the tears were glistening on her cheeks, and I think, in a moment more, they were in my eyes as well. It never really died, then—the soul that can suffer so excruciatingly and so interminably; it withers to the outward eye only; like that strange moss which can lie on a dusty shelf half a century and yet, if placed in water, grows green again. She wept so throughout the development and elaboration of the melody.

During the intermission before the second half of the concert, I questioned my aunt and found that the "Prize Song" was not new to her. Some years before there had drifted to the farm in Red Willow County a young German, a tramp cowpuncher, who had sung the chorus at

Bayreuth, when he was a boy, along with the other peasant boys and girls. Of a Sunday morning he used to sit on his gingham-sheeted bed in the hands' bedroom which opened off the kitchen, cleaning the leather of his boots and saddle, singing the "Prize Song," while my aunt went about her work in the kitchen. She had hovered about him until she had prevailed upon him to join the country church, though his sole fitness for this step, insofar as I could gather, lay in his boyish face and his possession of this divine melody. Shortly afterward he had gone to town on the Fourth of July, been drunk for several days, lost his money at a faro table, ridden a saddled Texan steer on a bet, and disappeared with a fractured collarbone. All this my aunt told me huskily, wanderingly, as though she were talking in the weak lapses of illness.

"Well, we have come to better things than the old *Trovatore* at any rate, Aunt Georgie?" I queried, with a well-meant effort at jocularity.

Her lip quivered and she hastily put her handkerchief up to her mouth. From behind it she murmured, "And you have been hearing this ever since you left me, Clark?" Her question was the gentlest and saddest of reproaches.

The second half of the program consisted of four numbers from the *Ring,* and closed with Siegfried's funeral march. My aunt wept quietly, but almost continuously, as a shallow vessel overflows in a rainstorm. From time to time her dim eyes looked up at the lights which studded the ceiling, burning softly under their dull glass globes; doubtless they were stars in truth to her. I was still perplexed as to what measure of musical comprehension was left to her, she who had heard nothing but the singing of gospel hymns at Methodist services in the square frame schoolhouse on Section Thirteen for so many years. I was wholly unable to gauge how much of it had been dissolved in soapsuds, or worked into bread, or milked into the bottom of a pail.

The deluge of sound poured on and on; I never knew what she found in the shining current of it; I never knew how far it bore her, or past what happy islands. From the trembling of her face I could well believe that before the last numbers she had been carried out where the myriad graves are, into the gray, nameless burying grounds of the sea; or into some world of death vaster yet, where, from the beginning of the world, hope has lain down with hope and dream with dream and, renouncing, slept.

The concert was over; the people filed out of the hall chattering and laughing, glad to relax and find the living level again, but my kinswoman made no effort to rise. The harpist slipped its green felt cover over his instrument; the flute players shook the water from their mouthpieces; the men of the orchestra went out one by one, leaving the stage to the chairs and music stands, empty as a winter cornfield.

I spoke to my aunt. She burst into tears and sobbed pleadingly. "I don't want to go, Clark, I don't want to go!"

I understood. For her, just outside the door of the concert hall, lay the black pond with the cattle-tracked bluffs; the tall, unpainted house, with weather-curled boards; naked as a tower, the crook-backed ash seedlings where the dishcloths hung to dry; the gaunt, molting turkeys picking up refuse about the kitchen door.

Paul's Case

A Study in Temperament

It was Paul's afternoon to appear before the faculty of the Pittsburgh High School to account for his various misdemeanors. He had been suspended a week ago, and his father had called at the Principal's office and confessed his perplexity about his son. Paul entered the faculty room suave and smiling. His clothes were a trifle outgrown, and the tan velvet on the collar of his open overcoat was frayed and worn; but for all that there was something of the dandy about him, and he wore an opal pin in his neatly knotted black four-in-hand, and a red carnation in his buttonhole. This latter adornment the faculty somehow felt was not properly significant of the contrite spirit befitting a boy under the ban of suspension.

Paul was tall for his age and very thin, with high, cramped shoulders and a narrow chest. His eyes were remarkable for a certain hysterical brilliancy, and he continually used them in a conscious, theatrical sort of way, peculiarly offensive in a boy. The pupils were abnormally large, as though he were addicted to belladonna, but there was a glassy glitter about them which that drug does not produce.

When questioned by the Principal as to why he was there Paul stated, politely enough, that he wanted to come back to school. This was a lie, but Paul was quite accustomed to lying; found it, indeed, indispensable for overcoming friction. His teachers were asked to state their respective charges against him, which they did with such a rancor and aggrievedness as evinced that this was not a usual case. Disorder and impertinence were among the offenses named, yet each of his instructors felt that it was scarcely possible to put into words the real cause of the trouble, which lay in a sort of hysterically defiant manner of the boy's; in the contempt which they all knew he felt for them, and which he seemingly made not the least effort to conceal. Once, when he had been making a synopsis of a paragraph at the blackboard, his English teacher had stepped to his side and attempted to guide his hand. Paul had started back with a shudder and thrust his hands violently behind him. The astonished woman could scarcely have been more hurt and embarrassed had he struck at her. The insult was so involuntary and definitely personal as to be unforgettable. In one way and another he had made all his teachers, men and women alike, conscious of the same feeling of physical aversion. In one class he habitually sat with his hand shading his eyes; in another he always looked out of the window during the recitation; in another he made a running commentary on the lecture, with humorous intention.

His teachers felt this afternoon that his whole attitude was symbolized by his shrug and his flippantly red carnation flower, and they fell upon him without mercy, his English teacher leading the pack. He stood through it smiling, his pale lips parted over his white teeth. (His lips were continually twitching, and he had a habit of raising his eyebrows that was contemptuous and irritating to the last degree.) Older boys than Paul had broken down and shed tears under that baptism of fire, but his set smile did not once desert him, and his only sign of discomfort was the nervous trembling of the fingers that toyed with the buttons of his overcoat, and an occasional jerking of the other hand that held his hat. Paul was always smiling, always glancing about him, seeming to feel that people might be watching him and trying to detect something. This conscious expression, since it was as far as possible from boyish mirthfulness, was usually attributed to insolence or "smartness."

As the inquisition proceeded one of his instructors repeated an impertinent remark of the boy's, and the Principal asked him whether he thought that a courteous speech to have made a woman. Paul shrugged his shoulders slightly and his eyebrows twitched.

"I don't know," he replied. "I didn't mean to be polite or impolite, either. I guess it's a sort of way I have of saying things regardless."

The Principal, who was a sympathetic man, asked him whether he didn't think that a way it would be well to get rid of. Paul grinned and said he guessed so. When he was told that he could go he bowed gracefully and went out. His bow was but a repetition of the scandalous red carnation.

His teachers were in despair, and his drawing master voiced the feeling of them all when he declared there was something about the boy which none of them understood. He added: "I don't really believe that smile of his comes altogether from insolence; there's something sort of haunted about it. The boy is not strong, for one thing. I happen to know that he was born in Colorado, only a few months before his mother died out there of a long illness. There is something wrong about the fellow."

The drawing master had come to realize that, in looking at Paul, one saw only his white teeth and the forced animation of his eyes. One warm afternoon the boy had gone to sleep at his drawing board, and his master had noted with amazement what a white, blue-veined face it was; drawn and wrinkled like an old man's about the eyes, the lips twitching even in his sleep, and stiff with a nervous tension that drew them back from his teeth.

His teachers left the building dissatisfied and unhappy; humiliated to have felt so vindictive toward a mere boy, to have uttered this feeling in cutting terms, and to have set each other on, as it were, in the gruesome game of intemperate reproach. Some of them remembered having seen a miserable street cat set at bay by a ring of tormentors.

As for Paul, he ran down the hill whistling the "Soldiers' Chorus" from *Faust*, looking wildly behind him now and then to see whether some of his teachers were not there to writhe under his lightheartedness. As it was now late in the afternoon and Paul was on duty that evening as usher at Carnegie Hall, he decided that he would not go

home to supper. When he reached the concert hall the
doors were not yet open and, as it was chilly outside, he
decided to go up into the picture gallery—always deserted
at this hour—where there were some of Raffelli's gay
studies of Paris streets and an airy blue Venetian scene or
two that always exhilarated him. He was delighted to find
no one in the gallery but the old guard, who sat in one
corner, a newspaper on his knee, a black patch over one
eye and the other closed. Paul possessed himself of the
place and walked confidently up and down, whistling under his breath. After a while he sat down before a blue
Rico and lost himself. When he bethought him to look at
his watch, it was after seven o'clock, and he rose with a
start and ran downstairs, making a face at Augustus, peering out from the cast room, and an evil gesture at the
Venus de Milo as he passed her on the stairway.

When Paul reached the ushers' dressing room half a
dozen boys were there already, and he began excitedly to
tumble into his uniform. It was one of the few that at all
approached fitting, and Paul thought it very becoming—
though he knew that the tight, straight coat accentuated
his narrow chest, about which he was exceedingly sensitive. He was always considerably excited while he dressed,
twanging all over to the tuning of the strings and the
preliminary flourishes of the horns in the music room; but
tonight he seemed quite beside himself, and he teased
and plagued the boys until, telling him that he was crazy,
they put him down on the floor and sat on him.

Somewhat calmed by his suppression, Paul dashed
out to the front of the house to seat the early comers. He
was a model usher; gracious and smiling he ran up and
down the aisles; nothing was too much trouble for him; he
carried messages and brought programs as though it were
his greatest pleasure in life, and all the people in his
section thought him a charming boy, feeling that he remembered and admired them. As the house filled, he
grew more and more vivacious and animated, and the
color came to his cheeks and lips. It was very much as
though this were a great reception and Paul were the host.
Just as the musicians came out to take their places, his
English teacher arrived with checks for the seats which a

prominent manufacturer had taken for the season. She
betrayed some embarrassment when she handed Paul the
tickets, and a hauteur which subsequently made her feel
very foolish. Paul was startled for a moment, and had the
feeling of wanting to put her out; what business had she
here among all these fine people and gay colors? He
looked her over and decided that she was not appropri-
ately dressed and must be a fool to sit downstairs in such
togs. The tickets had probably been sent her out of kindness, he reflected as he put down a seat for her, and she
had about as much right to sit there as he had.

When the symphony began Paul sank into one of the
rear seats with a long sigh of relief, and lost himself as he
had done before the Rico. It was not that symphonies, as
such, meant anything in particular to Paul, but the first
sigh of the instruments seemed to free some hilarious and
potent spirit within him; something that struggled there
like the genie in the bottle found by the Arab fisherman.
He felt a sudden zest of life; the lights danced before his
eyes and the concert hall blazed into unimaginable splendor. When the soprano soloist came on Paul forgot even
the nastiness of his teacher's being there and gave himself
up to the peculiar stimulus such personages always had for
him. The soloist chanced to be a German woman, by no
means in her first youth, and the mother of many children; but she wore an elaborate gown and a tiara, and
above all she had that indefinable air of achievement, that
world-shine upon her, which, in Paul's eyes, made her a
veritable queen of Romance.

After a concert was over Paul was always irritable and
wretched until he got to sleep, and tonight he was even
more than usually restless. He had the feeling of not being
able to let down, of its being impossible to give up this
delicious excitement which was the only thing that could
be called living at all. During the last number he withdrew and, after hastily changing his clothes in the dressing
room, slipped out to the side door where the soprano's
carriage stood. Here he began pacing rapidly up and down
the walk, waiting to see her come out.

Over yonder, the Schenley, in its vacant stretch,

loomed big and square through the fine rain, the windows of its twelve stories glowing like those of a lighted cardboard house under a Christmas tree. All the actors and singers of the better class stayed there when they were in the city, and a number of the big manufacturers of the place lived there in the winter. Paul had often hung about the hotel, watching the people go in and out, longing to enter and leave schoolmasters and dull care behind him forever.

At last the singer came out, accompanied by the conductor, who helped her into her carriage and closed the door with a cordial *auf wiedersehen* which set Paul to wondering whether she were not an old sweetheart of his. Paul followed the carriage over to the hotel, walking so rapidly as not to be far from the entrance when the singer alighted, and disappeared behind the swinging glass doors that were opened by a Negro in a tall hat and a long coat. In the moment that the door was ajar it seemed to Paul that he, too, entered. He seemed to feel himself go after her up the steps, into the warm, lighted building, into an exotic, tropical world of shiny, glistening surfaces and basking ease. He reflected upon the mysterious dishes that were brought into the dining room, the green bottles in buckets of ice, as he had seen them in the supper party pictures of the *Sunday World* supplement. A quick gust of wind brought the rain down with sudden vehemence, and Paul was startled to find that he was still outside in the slush of the gravel driveway; that his boots were letting in the water and his scanty overcoat was clinging wet about him; that the lights in front of the concert hall were out and that the rain was driving in sheets between him and the orange glow of the windows above him. There it was, what he wanted—tangibly before him, like the fairy world of a Christmas pantomime—but mocking spirits stood guard at the doors, and, as the rain beat in his face, Paul wondered whether he were destined always to shiver in the black night outside, looking up at it.

He turned and walked reluctantly toward the car tracks. The end had to come sometime; his father in his nightclothes at the top of the stairs, explanations that did not explain, hastily improvised fictions that were forever tripping him up, his upstairs room and its horrible yellow wallpaper, the creaking bureau with the greasy plush collar-box, and over his painted wooden bed the pictures of George Washington and John Calvin, and the framed motto, "Feed my Lambs," which had been worked in red worsted by his mother.

Half an hour later Paul alighted from his car and went slowly down one of the side streets off the main thoroughfare. It was a highly respectable street, where all the houses were exactly alike, and where businessmen of moderate means begot and reared large families of children, all of whom went to Sabbath school and learned the shorter catechism, and were interested in arithmetic; all of whom were as exactly alike as their homes, and of a piece with the monotony in which they lived. Paul never went up Cordelia Street without a shudder of loathing. His home was next to the house of the Cumberland minister. He approached it tonight with the nerveless sense of defeat, the hopeless feeling of sinking back forever into ugliness and commonness that he had always had when he came home. The moment he turned into Cordelia Street he felt the waters close above his head. After each of these orgies of living he experienced all the physical depression which follows a debauch; the loathing of respectable beds, of common food, of a house penetrated by kitchen odors; a shuddering repulsion for the flavorless, colorless mass of everyday existence; a morbid desire for cool things and soft lights and fresh flowers.

The nearer he approached the house, the more absolutely unequal Paul felt to the sight of it all: his ugly sleeping chamber; the cold bathroom with the grimy zinc tub, the cracked mirror, the dripping spiggots; his father, at the top of the stairs, his hairy legs sticking out from his nightshirt, his feet thrust into carpet slippers. He was so much later than usual that there would certainly be inquiries and reproaches. Paul stopped short before the door. He felt that he could not be accosted by his father tonight; that he could not toss again on that miserable bed. He would not go in. He would tell his father that he had no carfare and it was raining so hard he had gone home with one of the boys and stayed all night.

Meanwhile, he was wet and cold. He went around to the back of the house and tried one of the basement windows, found it open, raised it cautiously, and scrambled down the cellar wall to the floor. There he stood, holding his breath, terrified by the noise he had made, but the floor above him was silent, and there was no creak on the stairs. He found a soapbox, and carried it over to the soft ring of light that streamed from the furnace door, and sat down. He was horribly afraid of rats, so he did not try to sleep, but sat looking distrustfully at the dark, still terrified lest he might have awakened his father. In such reactions, after one of the experiences which made days and nights out of the dreary blanks of the calendar, when his senses were deadened, Paul's head was always singularly clear. Suppose his father had heard him getting in at the window and had come down and shot him for a burglar? Then, again, suppose his father had come down, pistol in hand, and he had cried out in time to save himself, and his father had been horrified to think how nearly he had killed him? Then, again, suppose a day should come when his father would remember that night, and wish there had been no warning cry to stay his hand? With this last supposition Paul entertained himself until daybreak.

The following Sunday was fine; the sodden November chill was broken by the last flash of autumnal summer. In the morning Paul had to go to church and Sabbath school, as always. On seasonable Sunday afternoons the burghers of Cordelia Street always sat out on their front stoops and talked to their neighbors on the next stoop, or called to those across the street in neighborly fashion. The men usually sat on gay cushions placed upon the steps that led down to the sidewalk, while the women, in their Sunday "waists," sat in rockers on the cramped porches, pretending to be greatly at their ease. The children played in the streets; there were so many of them that the place resembled the recreation grounds of a kindergarten. The men on the steps—all in their shirt sleeves, their vests unbuttoned—sat with their legs well apart, their stomachs comfortably protruding, and talked of the prices of things, or told anecdotes of the sagacity of their various chiefs and overlords. They occasionally looked over the multitude of squabbling children, listened affectionately to their high-pitched, nasal voices, smiling to see their own proclivities reproduced in their offspring, and interspersed their legends of the iron kings with remarks about their sons' progress at school, their grades in arithmetic, and the amounts they had saved in their toy banks.

On this last Sunday of November Paul sat all the afternoon on the lowest step of his stoop, staring into the street, while his sisters, in their rockers, were talking to the minister's daughters next door about how many shirt-waists they had made in the last week, and how many waffles someone had eaten at the last church supper. When the weather was warm, and his father was in a particularly jovial frame of mind, the girls made lemonade, which was always brought out in a red-glass pitcher, ornamented with forget-me-nots in blue enamel. This the girls thought very fine, and the neighbors always joked about the suspicious color of the pitcher.

Today Paul's father sat on the top step, talking to a young man who shifted a restless baby from knee to knee. He happened to be the young man who was daily held up to Paul as a model, and after whom it was his father's dearest hope that he would pattern. This young man was of a ruddy complexion, with a compressed, red mouth, and faded, nearsighted eyes, over which he wore thick spectacles, with gold bows that curved about his ears. He was clerk to one of the magnates of a great steel corporation, and was looked upon in Cordelia Street as a young man with a future. There was a story that, some five years ago—he was now barely twenty-six—he had been a trifle dissipated, but in order to curb his appetites and save the loss of time and strength that a sowing of wild oats might have entailed, he had taken his chief's advice, oft reiterated to his employees, and at twenty-one had married the first woman whom he could persuade to share his fortunes. She happened to be an angular schoolmistress, much older than he, who also wore thick glasses, and who had now borne him four children, all nearsighted, like herself.

The young man was relating how his chief, now cruising in the Mediterranean, kept in touch with all the details of the business, arranging his office hours on his yacht just as though he were at home, and "knocking off work enough to keep two stenographers busy." His father told, in turn, the plan his corporation was considering, of putting in an electric railway plant in Cairo. Paul snapped his teeth; he had an awful apprehension that they might spoil it all before he got there. Yet he rather liked to hear these legends of the iron kings that were told and retold on Sundays and holidays; these stories of palaces in Venice, yachts on the Mediterranean, and high play at Monte Carlo appealed to his fancy, and he was interested in the triumphs of these cash boys who had become famous, though he had no mind for the cash-boy stage.

After supper was over and he had helped to dry the dishes, Paul nervously asked his father whether he could go to George's to get some help in his geometry, and still more nervously asked for carfare. This latter request he had to repeat, as his father, on principle, did not like to hear requests for money, whether much or little. He asked Paul whether he could not go to some boy who lived nearer, and told him that he ought not to leave his schoolwork until Sunday; but he gave him the dime. He was not a poor man, but he had a worthy ambition to come up in the world. His only reason for allowing Paul to usher was that he thought a boy ought to be earning a little.

Paul bounded upstairs, scrubbed the greasy odor of the dishwater from his hands with the ill-smelling soap he hated, and then shook over his fingers a few drops of violet water from the bottle he kept hidden in his drawer. He left the house with his geometry conspicuously under his arm, and the moment he got out of Cordelia Street and boarded a downtown car, he shook off the lethargy of two deadening days and began to live again.

The leading juvenile of the permanent stock company which played at one of the downtown theaters was an acquaintance of Paul's, and the boy had been invited to drop in at the Sunday-night rehearsals whenever he could. For more than a year Paul had spent every available moment loitering about Charley Edwards's dressing room. He had won a place among Edwards's following not only because the young actor, who could not afford to employ a dresser, often found him useful, but because he recognized in Paul something akin to what churchmen term "vocation."

It was at the theater and at Carnegie Hall that Paul really lived; the rest was but a sleep and a forgetting. This was Paul's fairy tale, and it had for him all the allurement of a secret love. The moment he inhaled the gassy, painty, dusty odor behind the scenes, he breathed like a prisoner set free, and felt within him the possibility of doing or saying splendid, brilliant, poetic things. The moment the cracked orchestra beat out the overture from *Martha,* or jerked at the serenade from *Rigoletto,* all stupid and ugly things slid from him, and his senses were deliciously, yet delicately fired.

Perhaps it was because, in Paul's world, the natural nearly always wore the guise of ugliness, that a certain element of artificiality seemed to him necessary in beauty. Perhaps it was because his experience of life elsewhere was so full of Sabbath-school picnics, petty economies, wholesome advice as to how to succeed in life, and the inescapable odors of cooking, that he found this existence so alluring, these smartly clad men and women so attractive, that he was so moved by these starry apple orchards that bloomed perennially under the limelight.

It would be diffcult to put it strongly enough how convincingly the stage entrance of that theater was for Paul the actual portal of Romance. Certainly none of the company ever suspected it, least of all Charley Edwards. It was very like the old stories that used to float about London of fabulously rich Jews, who had subterranean halls there, with palms, and fountains, and soft lamps and richly appareled women who never saw the disenchanting light of London day. So, in the midst of that smoke-palled city, enamored of figures and grimy toil, Paul had his secret temple, his wishing carpet, his bit of blue-and-white Mediterranean shore bathed in perpetual sunshine.

Several of Paul's teachers had a theory that his imagination had been perverted by garish fiction, but the truth was that he scarcely ever read at all. The books at home were not such as would either tempt or corrupt a youthful mind, and as for reading the novels that some of his friends urged upon him—well, he got what he wanted much more quickly from music; any sort of music, from an orchestra to a barrel organ. He needed only the spark, the indescribable thrill that made his imagination master of his senses, and he could make plots and pictures enough of his own. It was equally true that he was not stagestruck— not, at any rate, in the usual acceptation of that expression. He had no desire to become an actor, any more than he had to become a musician. He felt no necessity to do any of these things; what he wanted was to see, to be in the atmosphere, float on the wave of it, to be carried out, blue league after blue league, away from everything.

After a night behind the scenes Paul found the schoolroom more than ever repulsive; the bare floors and naked walls; the prosy men who never wore frock coats, or violets in their buttonholes; the women with their dull gowns, shrill voices, and pitiful seriousness about prepositions that govern the dative. He could not bear to have the other pupils think, for a moment, that he took these people seriously; he must convey to them that he considered it all trivial, and was there only by way of a jest, anyway. He had autographed pictures of all the members of the stock company which he showed his classmates, telling them the most incredible stories of his familiarity with these people, of his acquaintance with the soloists who came to Carnegie Hall, his suppers with them and the flowers he sent them. When these stories lost their effect, and his audience grew listless, he became desperate and would bid all the boys good-by, announcing that he was going to travel for a while; going to Naples, to Venice, to Egypt. Then, next Monday, he would slip back, conscious and nervously smiling; his sister was ill, and he should have to defer his voyage until spring.

Matters went steadily worse with Paul at school. In the itch to let his instructors know how heartily he despised them and their homilies, and how thoroughly he was appreciated elsewhere, he mentioned once or twice that he had no time to fool with theorems; adding—with a twitch of the eyebrows and a touch of that nervous bravado which so perplexed them—that he was helping the people down at the stock company; they were old friends of his.

The upshot of the matter was that the Principal went to Paul's father, and Paul was taken out of school and put to work. The manager at Carnegie Hall was told to get another usher in his stead; the doorkeeper at the theater was warned not to admit him to the house; and Charley Edwards remorsefully promised the boy's father not to see him again.

The members of the stock company were vastly amused when some of Paul's stories reached them—especially the women. They were hardworking women, most of them supporting indigent husbands or brothers, and they laughed rather bitterly at having stirred the boy to such fervid and florid inventions. They agreed with the faculty and with his father that Paul's was a bad case.

The eastbound train was plowing through a January snowstorm; the dull dawn was beginning to show gray when the engine whistled a mile out of Newark. Paul started up from the seat where he had lain curled in uneasy slumber, rubbed the breath-misted window glass with his hand, and peered out. The snow was whirling in curling eddies above the white bottom lands, and the drifts lay already deep in the fields and along the fences, while here and there the long dead grass and dried weed stalks protruded black above it. Lights shone from the scattered houses, and a gang of laborers who stood beside the track waved their lanterns.

Paul had slept very little, and he felt grimy and uncomfortable. He had made the all-night journey in a day coach, partly because he was ashamed, dressed as he was, to go into a Pullman, and partly because he was afraid of being seen there by some Pittsburgh business-man, who might have noticed him in Denny & Carson's office. When the whistle awoke him, he clutched quickly at his breast pocket, glancing about him with an uncertain smile. But the little, clay-bespattered Italians were still sleeping, the slatternly women across the aisle were in open-mouthed oblivion, and even the crumby, crying babies were for the nonce stilled. Paul settled back to struggle with his impatience as best he could.

When he arrived at the Jersey City station he hurried

through his breakfast, manifestly ill at ease and keeping a sharp eye about him. After he reached the Twenty-third Street station, he consulted a cabman and had himself driven to a men's-furnishings establishment that was just opening for the day. He spent upward of two hours there, buying with endless reconsidering and great care. His new street suit he put on in the fitting room; the frock coat and dress clothes he had bundled into the cab with his linen. Then he drove to a hatter's and a shoe house. His next errand was at Tiffany's, where he selected his silver and a new scarf pin. He would not wait to have his silver marked, he said. Lastly, he stopped at a trunk shop on Broadway and had his purchases packed into various traveling bags.

It was a little after one o'clock when he drove up to the Waldorf, and after settling with the cabman, went into the office. He registered from Washington; said his mother and father had been abroad, and that he had come down to await the arrival of their steamer. He told his story plausibly and had no trouble, since he volunteered to pay for them in advance, in engaging his rooms; a sleeping room, sitting room, and bath.

Not once, but a hundred times, Paul had planned this entry into New York. He had gone over every detail of it with Charley Edwards, and in his scrapbook at home there were pages of description about New York hotels, cut from the Sunday papers. When he was shown to his sitting room on the eighth floor he saw at a glance that everything was as it should be; there was but one detail in his mental picture that the place did not realize, so he rang for the bellboy and sent him down for flowers. He moved about nervously until the boy returned, putting away his new linen and fingering it delightedly as he did so. When the flowers came he put them hastily into water, and then tumbled into a hot bath. Presently he came out of his white bathroom, resplendent in his new silk underwear, and playing with the tassels of his red robe. The snow was whirling so fiercely outside his windows that he could scarcely see across the street, but within the air was deliciously soft and fragrant. He put the violets and jonquils on the taboret beside the couch, and threw himself down, with a long sigh, covering himself with a Roman blanket. He was thoroughly tired; he had been in such haste, he had stood up to such a strain, covered so much ground in the last twenty-four hours, that he wanted to think how it had all come about. Lulled by the sound of the wind, the warm air, and the cool fragrance of the flowers, he sank into deep, drowsy retrospection.

It had been wonderfully simple; when they had shut him out of the theater and concert hall, when they had taken away his bone, the whole thing was virtually determined. The rest was a mere matter of opportunity. The only thing that at all surprised him was his own courage— for he realized well enough that he had always been tormented by fear, a sort of apprehensive dread that, of late years, as the meshes of the lies he had told closed about him, had been pulling the muscles of his body tighter and tighter. Until now he could not remember the time when he had not been dreading something. Even when he was a little boy it was always there—behind him, or before, or on either side. There had always been the shadowed corner, the dark place into which he dared not look, but from which something seemed always to be watching him—and Paul had done things that were not pretty to watch, he knew.

But now he had a curious sense of relief, as though he had at last thrown down the gauntlet to the thing in the corner.

Yet it was but a day since he had been sulking in the traces; but yesterday afternoon that he had been sent to the bank with Denny & Carson's deposit, as usual—but this time he was instructed to leave the book to be balanced. There was above two thousand dollars in checks, and nearly a thousand in the bank notes which he had taken from the book and quietly transferred to his pocket. At the bank he had made out a new deposit slip. His nerves had been steady enough to permit of his returning to the office, where he had finished his work and asked for a full day's holiday tomorrow, Saturday, giving a perfectly reasonable pretext. The bankbook, he knew, would not be returned before Monday or Tuesday, and his father would be out of town for the next week. From the time he slipped the bank notes into his pocket until he boarded the night train for New York, he had not known a moment's hesitation. It was not the first time Paul had steered through treacherous waters.

How astonishingly easy it had all been; here he was, the thing done; and this time there would be no awakening, no figure at the top of the stairs. He watched the snowflakes whirling by his window until he fell asleep.

When he awoke, it was three o'clock in the afternoon. He bounded up with a start; half of one of his precious days gone already! He spent more than an hour in dressing, watching every stage of his toilet carefully in the mirror. Everything was quite perfect; he was exactly the kind of boy he had always wanted to be.

When he went downstairs Paul took a carriage and drove up Fifth Avenue toward the Park. The snow had somewhat abated; carriages and tradesmen's wagons were hurrying soundlessly to and fro in the winter twilight; boys in woolen mufflers were shoveling off the doorsteps; the avenue stages made fine spots of color against the white street. Here and there on the corners were stands, with whole flower gardens blooming under glass cases, against the sides of which the snowflakes stuck and melted; violets, roses, carnations, lilies of the valley—somehow vastly more lovely and alluring that they blossomed thus unnaturally in the snow. The Park itself was a wonderful stage winterpiece.

When he returned, the pause of the twilight had ceased and the tune of the streets had changed. The snow was falling faster, lights streamed from the hotels that reared their dozen stories fearlessly up into the storm, defying the raging Atlantic winds. A long, black stream of carriages poured down the avenue, intersected here and there by other streams, tending horizontally. There were a score of cabs about the entrance of his hotel, and his driver had to wait. Boys in livery were running in and out of the awning stretched across the sidewalk, up and down the red velvet carpet laid from the door to the street. Above, about, within it all was the rumble and roar, the hurry and toss of thousands of human beings as hot for pleasure as himself, and on every side of him towered the glaring affirmation of the omnipotence of wealth.

The boy set his teeth and drew his shoulders together in a spasm of realization; the plot of all dramas, the text of all romances, the nerve-stuff of all sensations was whirling about him like the snowflakes. He burnt like a faggot in a tempest.

When Paul went down to dinner the music of the orchestra came floating up the elevator shaft to greet him. His head whirled as he stepped into the thronged corridor, and he sank back into one of the chairs against the wall to get his breath. The lights, the chatter, the perfumes, the bewildering medley of color—he had, for a moment, the feeling of not being able to stand it. But only for a moment; these were his own people, he told himself. He went slowly about the corridors, through the writing rooms, smoking rooms, reception rooms, as though he were exploring the chambers of an enchanted palace, built and peopled for him alone.

When he reached the dining room he sat down at a table near a window. The flowers, the white linen, the many-colored wineglasses, the gay toilettes of the women, the low popping of corks, the undulating repetitions of the *Blue Danube* from the orchestra, all flooded Paul's dream with bewildering radiance. When the roseate tinge of his champagne was added—that cold, precious, bubbling stuff that creamed and foamed in his glass—Paul wondered that there were honest men in the world at all. This was what all the world was fighting for, he reflected; this was what all the struggle was about. He doubted the reality of his past. Had he ever known a place called Cordelia Street, a place where fagged-looking businessmen got on the early car; mere rivets in a machine they seemed to Paul,—sickening men, with combings of children's hair always hanging to their coats, and the smell of cooking in their clothes. Cordelia Street—Ah, that belonged to another time and country; had he not always been thus, had he not sat here night after night, from as far back as he could remember, looking pensively over just such shimmering textures and slowly twirling the stem of a glass like this one between his thumb and middle finger? He rather thought he had.

He was not in the least abashed or lonely. He had no especial desire to meet or to know any of these people; all he demanded was the right to look on and conjecture, to watch the pageant. The mere stage properties were all he contended for. Nor was he lonely later in the evening, in his lodge at the Metropolitan. He was now entirely rid of his nervous misgivings, of his forced aggressiveness, of the imperative desire to show himself different from his surroundings. He felt now that his surroundings explained him. Nobody questioned the purple; he had only to wear it passively. He had only to glance down at his attire to reassure himself that here it would be impossible for anyone to humiliate him.

He found it hard to leave his beautiful sitting room to go to bed that night, and sat long watching the raging storm from his turret window. When he went to sleep it was with the lights turned on in his bedroom; partly because of his old timidity, and partly so that, if he should wake in the night, there would be no wretched moment of doubt, no horrible suspicion of yellow wallpaper, or of Washington and Calvin above his bed.

Sunday morning the city was practically snowbound. Paul breakfasted late, and in the afternoon he fell in with a wild San Francisco boy, a freshman at Yale, who said he had run down for a "little flyer" over Sunday. The young man offered to show Paul the night side of the town, and the two boys went out together after dinner, not returning to the hotel until seven o'clock the next morning. They had started out in the confiding warmth of a champagne friendship, but their parting in the elevator was singularly cool. The freshman pulled himself together to make his train, and Paul went to bed. He awoke at two o'clock in the afternoon, very thirsty and dizzy, and rang for ice-water, coffee, and the Pittsburgh papers.

On the part of the hotel management, Paul excited no suspicion. There was this to be said for him, that he wore his spoils with dignity and in no way made himself conspicuous. Even under the glow of his wine he was never boisterous, though he found the stuff like a magician's wand for wonder-building. His chief greediness lay in his ears and eyes, and his excesses were not offensive ones. His dearest pleasures were the gray winter twilights in his sitting room; his quiet enjoyment of his flowers, his clothes, his wide divan, his cigarette, and his sense of power. He could not remember a time when he had felt so at peace with himself. The mere release from the necessity of petty lying, lying every day and every day, restored his self-respect. He had never lied for pleasure, even at school; but to be noticed and admired, to assert his difference from other Cordelia Street boys; and he felt a good deal more manly, more honest, even, now that he had no need for boastful pretensions, now that he could, as his actor friends used to say, "dress the part." It was characteristic that remorse did not occur to him. His golden days went by without a shadow, and he made each as perfect as he could.

On the eighth day after his arrival in New York he found the whole affair exploited in the Pittsburgh papers, exploited with a wealth of detail which indicated that local news of a sensational nature was at a low ebb. The firm of Denny & Carson announced that the boy's father had refunded the full amount of the theft and that they had no intention of prosecuting. The Cumberland minister had been interviewed, and expressed his hope of yet reclaiming the motherless lad, and his Sabbath-school teacher declared that she would spare no effort to that end. The rumor had reached Pittsburgh that the boy had been seen in a New York hotel, and his father had gone East to find him and bring him home.

Paul had just come in to dress for dinner; he sank into a chair, weak to the knees, and clasped his head in his hands. It was to be worse than jail, even; the tepid waters of Cordelia Street were to close over him finally and forever. The gray monotony stretched before him in hopeless, unrelieved years; Sabbath school, Young People's Meeting, the yellow-papered room, the damp dishtowels; it all rushed back upon him with a sickening vividness. He had the old feeling that the orchestra had suddenly stopped, the sinking sensation that the play was over. The sweat broke out on his face, and he sprang to his feet, looked about him with his white, conscious smile, and winked at himself in the mirror. With something of the old childish belief in miracles with which he had so often gone to class, all his lessons unlearned, Paul dressed and dashed whistling down the corridor to the elevator.

He had no sooner entered the dining room and caught the measure of the music than his remembrance was lightened by his old elastic power of claiming the moment, mounting with it, and finding it all-sufficient. The glare and glitter about him, the mere scenic accessories had again, and for the last time, their old potency. He would show himself that he was game, he would finish the thing splendidly. He doubted, more than ever, the existence of Cordelia Street, and for the first time he drank his wine recklessly. Was he not, after all, one of those fortunate beings born to the purple, was he not still himself and in his own place? He drummed a nervous accompaniment to the Pagliacci music and looked about him, telling himself over and over that it had paid.

He reflected drowsily, to the swell of the music and the chill sweetness of his wine, that he might have done it more wisely. He might have caught an outbound steamer and been well out of their clutches before now. But the other side of the world had seemed too far away and too uncertain then; he could not have waited for it; his need had been too sharp. If he had to choose over again, he would do the same thing tomorrow. He looked affectionately about the dining room, now gilded with a soft mist. Ah, it had paid indeed!

Paul was awakened next morning by a painful throbbing in his head and feet. He had thrown himself across the bed without undressing, and had slept with his shoes on. His limbs and hands were lead heavy, and his tongue and throat were parched and burnt. There came upon him one of those fateful attacks of clearheadedness that never occurred except when he was physically exhausted and his nerves hung loose. He lay still, closed his eyes, and let the tide of things wash over him.

His father was in New York; "stopping at some joint or other," he told himself. The memory of successive summers on the front stoop fell upon him like a weight of black water. He had not a hundred dollars left; and he knew now, more than ever, that money was everything, the wall that stood between all he loathed and all he wanted. The thing was winding itself up; he had thought of that on his first glorious day in New York, and had even provided a way to snap the thread. It lay on his dressing table now; he had got it out last night when he came blindly up from dinner, but the shiny metal hurt his eyes, and he disliked the looks of it.

He rose and moved about with a painful effort, succumbing now and again to attacks of nausea. It was the old depression exaggerated; all the world had become Cordelia Street. Yet somehow he was not afraid of anything, was absolutely calm; perhaps because he had looked into the dark corner at last and knew. It was bad enough, what he saw there, but somehow not so bad as his long fear of it had been. He saw everything clearly now. He had a feeling that he had made the best of it, that he had lived the sort of life he was meant to live, and for half an hour he sat staring at the revolver. But he told himself that was not the way, so he went downstairs and took a cab to the ferry.

When Paul arrived in Newark he got off the train and took another cab, directing the driver to follow the Pennsylvania tracks out of the town. The snow lay heavy on the roadways and had drifted deep in the open fields. Only here and there the dead grass or dried weed stalks projected, singularly black, above it. Once well into the country, Paul dismissed the carriage and walked, floundering along the tracks, his mind a medley of irrelevant things. He seemed to hold in his brain an actual picture of everything he had seen that morning. He remembered every feature of both his drivers, of the toothless old woman from whom he had bought the red flowers in his coat, the agent from whom he had got his ticket, and all of his fellow passengers on the ferry. His mind, unable to cope with vital matters near at hand, worked feverishly and deftly at sorting and grouping these images. They made for him a part of the ugliness of the world, of the ache in his head, and the bitter burning on his tongue. He stooped and put a handful of snow into his mouth as he walked, but that, too, seemed hot. When he reached a little hillside, where the tracks ran through a cut some twenty feet below him, he stopped and sat down.

The carnations in his coat were drooping with the cold, he noticed, their red glory all over. It occurred to him that all the flowers he had seen in the glass cases that first night must have gone the same way, long before this. It was only one splendid breath they had, in spite of their brave mockery at the winter outside the glass; and it was a losing game in the end, it seemed, this revolt against the homilies by which the world is run. Paul took one of the blossoms carefully from his coat and scooped a little hole in the snow, where he covered it up. Then he dozed awhile, from his weak condition, seemingly insensible to the cold.

The sound of an approaching train awoke him, and he started to his feet, remembering only his resolution, and afraid lest he should be too late. He stood watching the approaching locomotive, his teeth chattering, his lips drawn away from them in a frightened smile; once or twice he glanced nervously sidewise, as though he were being watched. When the right moment came, he jumped. As he fell, the folly of his haste occurred to him with merciless clearness, the vastness of what he had left undone. There flashed through his brain, clearer than ever before, the blue of Adriatic water, the yellow of Algerian sands.

He felt something strike his chest, and that his body was being thrown swiftly through the air, on and on, immeasurably far and fast, while his limbs were gently relaxed. Then, because the picture-making mechanism was crushed, the disturbing visions flashed into black, and Paul dropped back into the immense design of things.

Bantam Classics bring you the world's greatest literature—books that have stood the test of time. These beautifully designed books will be proud additions to your bookshelf. You'll want all these time-tested classics for your own reading pleasure.

Titles by the Brontës:

☐ 21140   JANE ERYE Charlotte Brontë $2.25
☐ 21258   WUTHERING HEIGHTS Emily Brontë $2.50

Titles by Charles Dickens:

☐ 21123   THE PICKWICK PAPERS $4.95
☐ 21223   BLEAK HOUSE $4.95
☐ 21265   NICHOLAS NICKLEBY $4.95
☐ 21342   GREAT EXPECTATIONS $2.95
☐ 21176   A TALE OF TWO CITIES $2.50
☐ 21016   HARD TIMES $2.95
☐ 21102   OLIVER TWIST $2.50
☐ 21244   A CHRISTMAS CAROL & OTHER $1.95
          VICTORIAN TALES

Titles by Henry James:

☐ 21127   PORTRAIT OF A LADY $3.95
☐ 21059   THE TURN OF THE SCREW $1.95

Look for them at your bookstore or use this page to order:

Bantam Classics bring you the world's greatest literature—books that have stood the test of time—at specially
low prices. These beautifully designed books will be proud
additions to your bookshelf. You'll want all these time-
tested classics for your own reading pleasure.

Titles by Mark Twain:

☐	21079	**ADVENTURES OF HUCKLEBERRY FINN**	$1.95
☐	21128	**ADVENTURES OF TOM SAWYER**	$1.95
☐	21195	**COMPLETE SHORT STORIES**	$4.95
☐	21143	**A CONNECTICUT YANKEE IN KING ARTHUR'S COURT**	$2.95
☐	21349	**LIFE ON THE MISSISSIPPI**	$2.50
☐	21256	**THE PRINCE AND THE PAUPER**	$2.25
☐	21158	**PUDD'NHEAD WILSON**	$2.25

Other Great Classics:

☐	21274	**BILLY BUDD** Herman Melville	$2.95
☐	21311	**MOBY DICK** Herman Melville	$2.25
☐	21233	**THE CALL OF THE WILD & WHITE FANG** Jack London	$2.50
☐	21011	**THE RED BADGE OF COURAGE** Stephen Crane	$1.75
☐	21350	**THE COUNT OF MONTE CRISTO** Alexander Dumas	$4.95

Bantam Books, Dept. CL2, 414 East Golf Road, Des Plaines, IL 60016

Please send me the items I have checked above. I am enclosing $_____
(please add $2.00 to cover postage and handling). Send check or money
order, no cash or C.O.D.s please.

Mr/Ms _____

Address _____

City/State_____ Zip_____

CL2–9/90

Please allow four to six weeks for delivery.
Prices and availability subject to change without notice.